Mrs. Bennet's Advice to Young Ladies

A Mother's View of Pride & Prejudice

Victoria Grossack

Copyright © 2021 Victoria Grossack
All rights reserved.
ISBN: 979-8748761642

Cover based on Portrait of Marie Gabrielle de Gramont, Duchesse de Caderousse, by the painter Elisabeth Louise Vigée

To Patricia Walton, another Young Lady,
and a dear friend since our days in college.

CONTENTS

Beginnings	1
Chapter 1	5
Chapter 2	12
Chapter 3	20
Chapter 4	24
Chapter 5	30
Chapter 6	35
Chapter 7	40
Chapter 8	43
Chapter 9	48
Chapter 10	50
Chapter 11	53
Chapter 12	60
Chapter 13	63
Chapter 14	66
Chapter 15	69
Chapter 16	72
Chapter 17	76
Chapter 18	79
Chapter 19	82

Chapter 20	88
Chapter 21	93
Chapter 22	98
Chapter 23	102
Chapter 24	105
Chapter 25	108
Chapter 26	114
Chapter 27	119
Chapter 28	124
Chapter 29	129
Chapter 30	134
Chapter 31	138
Chapter 32	142
Chapter 33	146
Chapter 34	150
Chapter 35	156
Chapter 36	160
Chapter 37	163
Endings	168
Collection of Mrs, Bennet's Advice	170
Author's Note	173

BEGINNINGS

I was reclined on the sofa, my computer on my lap, when Mrs. Bennet came to me again. Over the years, Mrs. Bennet has come to me often, telling me she wanted me to write a book with her. I had used various excuses to put her off, but she is a most insistent character, and she finally happened upon me at a moment when my health was good and I had some time.

"I am glad to hear it," she said, and then, without waiting for my response, continued. "You will do the writing," she said, "but I will give you the ideas."

"What ideas?" I asked, for when she had called on me before, I had been at a loss as to what she wanted.

"I want someone to tell my story. Miss Jane Austen wrote too much about my daughters, and not enough about me."

I told her I was not prepared to criticize Jane Austen, whose works I highly esteemed.

"Yes, she was very talented, and we are all grateful to her. I do not speak ill of her. Still, Miss Jane Austen did not give me enough credit. Nothing would have happened in *Pride & Prejudice* if it were not for me!"

As the mother of the young ladies who starred in the novel, I supposed her argument was reasonable.

"You misunderstand me," said Mrs. Bennet. "Of course, being the mother of five daughters, bearing them and raising them, is no small matter! We all owe our mothers a great deal; we owe them our very lives. However, I speak of the particular events of *Pride & Prejudice*. The story is really mine. What does Miss Jane Austen write at the end of her very first chapter?"

I opened a copy of *Pride & Prejudice*, and in the first chapter I read, in a passage about Mrs. Bennet:

> *The business of her life was to get her daughters married; its solace was visiting and news.*

Mrs. Bennet was triumphant. "It was not the business of my daughters to get themselves married, although I did all I could to impress the importance of that on them. No, it was *my* business to get them married. And I succeeded!"

Contemplating the words, I hesitated, not wanting to give offense, but not wanting her declaration to go uncontested. "Yes, two of your daughters

1

married well, but many would argue the happy unions of Mrs. Bingley and Mrs. Darcy are not completely to *your* credit. Some – many – would say those daughters did well, not *because* of you, but *despite* you."

"Rubbish!" said Mrs. Bennet. "People say many things, but does that make them true? And that is why I want to set the record straight."

"Jane Austen recorded events incorrectly?"

"Miss Jane Austen was young when she wrote our story. Besides, she never was a mother. She could not feel what a mother feels."

My opinion had always been that Austen had done a remarkable job of creating a range of diverse characters, and empathizing from their points of view, but I did not argue Mrs. Bennet's assertions. Instead, I introduced another issue. "What about Lydia – Mrs. Wickham? From the end, it's clear her marriage was not especially happy."

Mrs. Bennet sighed. "If Wickham only had a better income! But not everyone can be the first-born son on an estate with an income of 10,000 £. As to Lydia's happiness with her husband, you must be aware that few marriages are ideal. Besides, it's not as if happiness and marriage come with a book telling you what you should do."

I disagreed. Perhaps in her time few such books had existed, but in the centuries since her creator had penned her into being, many books on these topics had appeared, not to mention magazine articles, blogs, podcasts and more.

Nevertheless, Mrs. Bennet insisted. "I want to give advice to young ladies. As a mother of five daughters, I am an expert. That is another reason to write my story."

Again, I objected. She had been created more than two centuries ago, and since then the world had changed drastically. Young ladies – or rather, young women as they were now usually called – had different problems and desires.

"Do they not still want to marry and to have children?" Mrs. Bennet asked.

"Yes, or at least, some women do, but women can do so much more." I explained that these days, women worked; women were journalists, scientists, doctors and astronauts (that required explanation); women were even in positions of power. The United Kingdom had had more than one female Prime Minister. Even my country, the United States, had elected a woman to its second highest office.

"Have young ladies changed so much? Do they not want money? Do they not want to dance, to dress well, to eat well, to have servants, to ride in fine carriages? Do they not want to fall in love and go to parties?"

I supposed some did, although people did not ride in carriages anymore, but drove vehicles called automobiles. Only a few had live-in servants, not unless they were wealthy or were infirm and required constant assistance.

Instead, most people did their own chores, with the assistance of labor-saving devices. Machines washed clothes and dishes; vacuum cleaners, some completely automated, sucked dirt and dust off the floor. If you craved a particular type of food, you could order it and have it delivered to your front door.

I had other objections. First, I did not care for her focus on just one gender. "Why only address ladies?"

Mrs. Bennet said she really only had experience bringing up females, but she had no objection to males reading and following her advice. "Mr. Bennet, even though he does not give me credit, often takes my advice," she said. She also had opinions on smaller matters and was happy to share them.

Then I explained that these days there were no longer exactly two genders – in fact, there had never been, but now it was recognized as a continuum. I was not proud of my attempt to explain the matter, but to my surprise, Mrs. Bennet nodded sagaciously.

"Of course," said Mrs. Bennet.

"You are aware of people like that?"

She was. "Mr. Bennet and I dine with four-and-twenty families; do you not think we know of people of every sort? Many, of course, keep their natures hidden. I have often wondered about Mrs. Collins. Others, like one of my sister's servants – a slim older fellow called Chamberlayne – will dress in women's clothing if they can." She reminded me of a passage in *Pride & Prejudice* that described the man's donning female attire.

"My advice may be read by anyone, male, female, or other," she concluded. "I do not know what words you use."

I nodded, then raised a finger, for I had another objection to her project. She wanted to dispense advice not just to ladies, but to *young* ladies. "Why do you wish to exclude those who are older?"

"How old are you?" asked Mrs. Bennet.

Demurring, I declined to answer precisely, but confessed I was older than most of the characters in the pages of *Pride & Prejudice*.

"But more than two hundred years have passed since those pages were written," said Mrs. Bennet, "adding to my age. I am more than two hundred, perhaps even two hundred and fifty! To *me*, you are a Young Lady. And even if you believe I am no older than you, does not a fresh perspective on a problem help?"

I agreed her perspective was probably different from mine.

"I know you have ambitions you have not achieved," continued Mrs. Bennet. "I know you are not completely satisfied. You could be happier than you are."

"My life is very good," I countered. "I cannot complain."

"That is your problem! You don't complain. If you won't complain, how can you expect things to improve?"

We were both silent a moment, but silence was not a condition Mrs. Bennet could tolerate long. "Now, my dear Young Lady, I also want you to tell *my* story."

"What do you mean?"

"My story," she repeated. "My youth in Meryton with my sister and my brother; Colonel Miller's regiment; my engagement and marriage with Mr. Bennet."

I *was* curious about Mr. and Mrs. Bennet; they seemed such an unlikely pair.

"And the events in Miss Jane Austen's text – but from my point of view."

I was intrigued. "Very well," I said, but before we could start, we had some details to settle. "What is your first name? It's never mentioned in the pages of *Pride & Prejudice*. I always assumed that your eldest daughter was named for you and so that it has to be Jane. However, most fan fiction uses Fanny, which is more convenient."

"Why is Fanny more convenient?" asked Mrs. Bennet. "Jane has fewer letters."

"Because the point of names in stories is to make the characters easy to tell apart; readers become confused when several characters in a book have the same name," I explained. *"Pride & Prejudice* already has a Jane."

Mrs. Bennet said the readers in my era must be unintelligent, if they could not distinguish a Sir William Lucas from a Mr. William Collins. "You do not choose names in order to honor people? To show a connection to family?"

"Sure, but this is art, not life. May I call you Fanny?"

Mrs. Bennet, happy to have a biographer, said that was acceptable. We agreed on several other first names: Mr. Bennet was John; Lady Lucas was Isabel; and Mrs. Phillips would be Agnes and her husband Thomas. Mrs. Bennet's brother's name we already knew; his name was Mr. Edward Gardiner.

"Thanks," I said, writing down the information.

"Do not thank me yet, Young Lady," said Mrs. Bennet. "We have a long way to go."

CHAPTER 1

Mr. Gardiner was the leading attorney in Meryton, with a large, handsome apartment next to his office in the market town. He and his wife had three children who survived to adulthood. Agnes was the oldest; Frances, usually called Fanny, followed; Edward finished the trio of young Gardiners.

As the market town and the surrounding areas were not heavily populated, Fanny Gardiner knew nearly everyone, at least by sight, including Mr. John Bennet. In Fanny's youth, he was Mr. John Bennet, because he had a father, Mr. James Bennet, and an older brother, Mr. Walter Bennet. As the second son, with an estate that was entailed, Mr. John Bennet's inheritance was expected to be small; he never planned to be the master at Longbourn. Mr. John Bennet wanted to do something completely different with his life: to take notes on the world around him, like several famous naturalists of the day, and perhaps publish them if he discovered something worth sharing. The only problem was he preferred reading about the discoveries to the tedious business of going about making them himself.

The brothers were not close; their expectations were too different. Mr. Walter Bennet enjoyed every aspect of farming, while Mr. John Bennet preferred reading about farming in the Longbourn library. Still, both young men respected and obeyed their father, who insisted his sons understand the work, and so Mr. John Bennet, in addition to acquiring the usual education of a gentleman, learned everything that was needed to run the estate.

The tasks around Longbourn included ploughing fields, harvesting crops, and even milking cows – not that any gentleman would be expected to engage in all of these chores on a regular basis, but Mr. James Bennet insisted that his sons should have a true appreciation of the practice as well as the theory. To Mr. John Bennet's annoyance, after milking the Longbourn cows, he came down with cowpox. The disease left an unsightly scar on his arm and exposed him to teasing by his older brother, Mr. Walter Bennet, who had managed to avoid the disease when he had been compelled to learn milking.

"You have no scars at all," retorted Mr. John Bennet. "What sort of hero does that make you?"

Mr. Walter Bennet did not read much, but he liked romances in which adventurous heroes saved the day. "As this part of England has no dragons that need slaying, it just means I am not clumsy."

Hertfordshire had no dragons, only country full of forest and fields. Its air was considered healthy compared to the air of London, but sometimes visitors brought bad air with them. A few years after Mr. John Bennet mastered cow-milking, Mr. James Bennet welcomed the visit of an old friend who arrived with his wife and small child. The child was feverish, and illness spread through the Longbourn estate. It was the smallpox, a disease that broke out often in London but less frequently in the country. The child died; the old friend's wife died; even Mr. James Bennet and Mr. Walter Bennet fell ill. Sickness struck some of the servants as well, and the whole neighborhood avoided Longbourn House.

A few at Longbourn, including Mr. John Bennet, remained healthy; the second son found himself in charge of both running the estate and caring for the sick. "Why are you not ill?" gasped Walter, as John wiped his older brother's feverish brow.

There was resentment in Walter's question, but also curiosity. "I do not know," said Mr. John Bennet.

That evening Walter died, and during the night, their father, leaving Mr. John Bennet alone in the world.

The local vicar said it was God's will, which was considered true for everything, but Mr. John Bennet could not understand why God would want to make *him* master of Longbourn House. He wondered if there were another, more satisfactory explanation.

"You may learn it in time," said the clergyman, who did not appreciate the probing nature of the young man's questions and had long since come up with a standard method of deflecting them. The vicar changed the subject, reminding the new master that Longbourn House had always contributed significantly to his living.

After about a month there were no new smallpox cases on the estate or in the neighborhood. Some had died, some would be scarred for life, and one unlucky soul was blind. In the meantime, Mr. John Bennet – now Mr. Bennet – was in charge at Longbourn, and others began to risk crossing its threshold.

The Gardiner girls, like all the locals, were aware of the illnesses and deaths at Longbourn. Their mother even arranged for food to be taken to Longbourn during the illness, in case the servants were too ill to prepare anything, while their father, as the town's leading attorney, advised the new heir on legal items pertaining to his new position. The Gardiner girls heard about these things, as did everyone in the area, but Fanny and Agnes were not interested because something far more thrilling had occurred.

The War Office had quartered a regiment of the militia in Meryton!

Meryton had always been so quiet, so rural, so dull, but suddenly it was enlivened with men dressed in scarlet. Mr. Gardiner made a point of inviting over officers, partly for business, partly for pleasure, and also because he had two eligible daughters. Agnes and Fanny and even Edward enjoyed the afternoons and evenings with new company, instead of the neighbors they had known all their lives.

Edward asked about the uniforms. "Does the bright red not make you easier targets when fighting enemies?"

Lieutenant Hodges, to whom the question was posed, said the brilliance of the uniform had both advantages and disadvantages. You always knew a fellow officer and brother, which was useful, both in peace and in battle. Of course, in enemy territory, the visibility could be a problem. This had been an especially true in the conflict with America, where the colonialists had disregarded the rules of war.

Lieutenant Higbee added, "It also saves deciding what to wear every morning."

"Oh! I would not like having only one gown to choose from," said Agnes.

"I think the red coat is very becoming," said Fanny. "And as Meryton has no colonialists, the soldiers should be safe."

Lieutenant Higbee was handsome, amusing, and an excellent dancer, lively but smooth. Fanny had never met such an attractive man; she thought he felt the same for her and she hoped he would propose. Agnes, who had previously encouraged the attentions of Mr. Thomas Phillips, a clerk of their father's, was also interested in the charming Higbee.

The Miss Gardiners were enthusiastic about the officers, but their parents were cautious. "Be careful, girls," warned Mr. Gardiner. "We do not know the backgrounds of these men. Nor their incomes!"

"And I could not bear it if you were to move away," said Mrs. Gardiner, who was suffering maternal pangs as Edward had just departed for London to continue his studies. "The regiment will not stay in Meryton forever, and if you marry an officer, you would be forced to leave."

The girls were torn. They had a strong attachment to Meryton, where they had so many friends and family and were the two leading beauties, but they did long for more amusement and adventure.

Mostly, however, the Miss Gardiners enjoyed the addition to local society. Netherfield's owner gave a ball, and so did the Gouldings, and Fanny Gardiner had never known such gay times. She was light on her feet, and her dances with Lieutenant Higbee were the most rapturous experiences she had ever known.

After a dance at Pulvis Lodge, Fanny let her partner kiss her behind a curtain.

"Miss Gardiner – Fanny – you are exquisite," said Lieutenant Higbee.

For once in her life, she could say nothing.

"I cannot bear for us to be separated," said Higbee.

"Why should we be?" asked Fanny, her heart pounding hard. She expected him to make a declaration then and there.

Instead, he pulled her close, and she was not sure what to do – draw closer or pull back? – when they were interrupted by Lieutenant Hodges.

MRS. BENNET'S ADVICE TO YOUNG LADIES

Fanny had never liked Hodges as much as Higbee, and at that moment she hated him. Her face flushing, she took a step back.

"Higbee, Colonel Miller wants to speak with you," said Hodges.

Higbee protested, but Hodges insisted, so Higbee departed, leaving Fanny confused. She was angry with Hodges; she was certain that Higbee had been about to propose, but if he loved her and could not bear to be separated from her, he would be back as soon as he could. "Why does the colonel want to speak with Higbee?" she inquired.

"I don't know," said Hodges, looking down at her with piercing dark eyes. "I should warn you, Miss Gardiner, Higbee already has a lady in his life."

Fanny began to dislike Hodges even more. "What sort of lady? A mother? A sister? An aunt? Or – do you mean he has given his heart to someone else?"

"I don't know who owns his heart, Miss Frances, but I know who claims his hand. In Cornwall there is a Mrs. Higbee – his wife."

Fanny was shocked. "Why has he never spoken of her?"

"Again, I don't know." Hodges bowed and departed.

Fanny was both humiliated and confused. Higbee, married? How could that be? She was not sure what she should do – confront Higbee? Or run away? She stood by the curtain, looking around the room, but so stunned she could not focus on anything or anyone, at least not until her sister joined her.

"We must go," said Agnes. "At once."

"Yes," said Fanny, not protesting as she usually did at the end of a dance, but for once, glad to leave. The sisters, escorted by their parents, returned to their apartment in Meryton.

Fanny tossed and turned that night, her mind full of what had happened – Higbee's passionate kiss – followed by Hodges's claim that Higbee was married. Was it true? Or was Hodges telling lies about Higbee for some reason?

Her sighs woke her sister. "What is it?" Agnes demanded.

Fanny did not confess to kissing Higbee, but she told Agnes how Hodges had claimed Higbee was married. "Could that be true?"

Agnes, who had been annoyed that Higbee had preferred her younger sister to her, was not displeased by the possibility. "Father warned us that we do not know these men."

"Tomorrow I will find out," resolved Fanny, and she wondered which officer she should speak to, which one she could trust. Perhaps Colonel Miller himself?

Her worries kept her awake for so long that once she fell asleep, she slept late, missing breakfast. Only later did she have the strength to rise from her bed, dress, and go out into the market town to discover the marital status of Lieutenant Higbee.

The day was cold and windy. As Fanny walked up the street, she saw no familiar officers – in fact, she saw no officers at all. Perhaps they were conducting exercises? Finally, she went into an inn frequented by the regiment, with a large room in which meals and ale were often served. Yet the large room also contained no officers; only a few customers sat at various tables.

"Miss Frances Gardiner, can I help you?" asked the proprietor.

Fanny asked why no officers were in the establishment.

"Have you not heard? The regiment has gone!" said the proprietor.

"I am surprised *you* are asking this question, Miss Fanny," said a customer. "Don't *you* know where all the officers are at every moment?"

Fanny ignored the customer's teasing and persisted. "Gone? Where? Why?" she asked. Had they left for Cornwall, so that Higbee could reunite with his wife? But reuniting Lieutenant Higbee with Mrs. Higbee would not require the departure of the entire regiment.

The explanation was simple; some skirmish required the presence of the army, and so the militia had been summoned.

"Will they return?" she asked, but no one could answer that question, as no one knew how long the skirmish would last.

"The affair could be bloody," said the owner of the inn. "Some of the officers might be killed."

Fanny gasped at the idea of the men she had so recently danced with dying at the end of a French musket or bayonet.

Young Mr. Lucas, married to Fanny's friend Isabel, was also in the tavern. He opined the reassignment of the militia was just for show, to keep the French from thinking they should invade England, and that none of the fine soldiers they knew would be in danger.

Fanny wondered if she could write to the War Office, but she did not know the address. "I suppose it must be hard for the wives of these officers, not to know if their husbands are in danger."

"Yes, Miss Frances, although it is hard for us to consider losing our friends, how much more difficult it must be for wives to be facing the possible loss of their husbands," said Mr. Lucas.

"Which of the officers are married?" asked Fanny.

The proprietor and the patrons in the tavern answered her question as best they could. They did not mention Lieutenant Higbee, so Fanny asked directly.

"Oh! You are right, Miss Frances, Lieutenant Higbee is married," said Mr. Lucas.

The tavern owner frowned. "I heard Higbee was not married."

"Why would Higbee claim he is married when he is not?" asked Mr. Lucas.

No one could explain this deception, but they could imagine the reverse – a man claiming to be free when he was encumbered.

Fanny left the tavern, walked home, went to her room and wept.

Mrs. Bennet's Advice

I switched on the water heater for my morning oatmeal, and then chopped up an apple to add to it. Mrs. Bennet was beside me.

"I was always curious about you and Colonel Miller's regiment," I said. "So, when the regiment left Meryton, you did not shed tears for all the officers, but for one particular lieutenant."

"Yes. Lieutenant Higbee," said Mrs. Bennet.

"But he was married," I said as I poured hot water into the bowl.

"Yes. That was such a disappointment, such a great disappointment! I sometimes wonder if he kissed me because he was unhappy in his marriage."

Stirring my oatmeal so it would thicken, and then adding cinnamon and honey, I agreed many marriages were not successful. I was divorced myself, something that caused Mrs. Bennet concern. I assured her that, at least in my country, divorce was not the scandal it had been two centuries ago. In fact, I had married again, and my second marriage had lasted twice as long as my first and was still going strong. "But this is not my story," I said, moving the bowl to the table. "Lieutenant Higbee's marriage may not have been happy, but that could be because he was a terrible man who preyed on young ladies like yourself."

Mrs. Bennet sighed. "You may be right. I was tempted to make a dreadful mistake, but at that time, I was young and inexperienced. And I believed he was single, when he was not. I should have put more effort into learning the truth about him."

"Ah. Gossip," I said, and put a spoonful of oatmeal into my mouth. Mrs. Bennet, whose solace in life was 'visiting and news,' had to enjoy gossip.

Mrs. Bennet drew herself up straight. "What *you* call gossip, *I* call showing interest in people. It is how you make sure no one takes advantage of you. It is how you discover if a friend or relative needs assistance."

"What if the information you hear is false?" I asked. This was a serious problem in my own day, when nearly half my country's population were convinced that the other half were mistaken or deliberately lying. "Falsehoods spread so quickly, often far more quickly than truth."

"Oh! You make an excellent point. So many people are taken in! And, what is worse, so many people want to be taken in! The falsehoods, however, are often extremely amusing. I suppose they are designed that way. But here is my advice to you: seek out the truth, Young Lady, even when it is not to your liking."

As I continued eating my breakfast, I considered times in my past when I had refused to recognize the truths I did not like. For example, I had remained in several relationships for far too long. There was also a job I never should have taken. I wondered what truth I was ignoring now, because I did not like the alternative? Several areas of my life deserved closer inspection.

"These are questions you should ask yourself," said Mrs. Bennet.

I wiped my mouth with a napkin and promised I would do so, but then reminded her this was supposed to be her story and not mine. "Aren't you going to tell me how you and Mr. Bennet met?"

"I do not recall our first meeting," said Mrs. Bennet. "We always knew each other by sight. Now, Mr. John Bennet, a farmer, did not place the same importance on making friends and acquaintances as did my father, an attorney – or the local men of business, such as Mr. Lucas. Still, Mr. Bennet was clever and was aware of everyone in the area. Besides, although I am known, through that book, as a matron and a mother and the mistress of Longbourn, once I was a young lady myself. I was even considered very pretty."

I told her I thought she must have been a great beauty.

She smiled at the compliment. "I cannot tell you when Mr. Bennet and I first met; it must have been when I was only a child. But I will tell you how our courtship began."

CHAPTER 2

For two days, Fanny shed tears. Was Lieutenant Higbee married or not? She hoped Mr. Lucas had somehow heard incorrectly, and the handsome officer was as free as his behavior had indicated. Her friend's husband, however, was one of Meryton's most reliable sources, and so his information was most likely true.

Fanny also hoped to receive some sort of communication from Lieutenant Higbee. Unless they were engaged, a male corresponding with a female was frowned upon, but if Higbee were bold enough to kiss her, he ought to be bold enough to send her a letter. Besides, that particular restriction had never made sense to Fanny. She could understand why chaperones were needed for young men and young women when they were together in person – when they could do things reserved for married couples – but why forbid correspondence? One could not embrace through paper.

Every day she watched whenever the post was delivered, but nothing came for her. Perhaps Lieutenant Higbee was married, as Mr. Lucas had said, and he had only kissed her in a moment of weakness. Or perhaps he was single but was indifferent. At any rate, she never heard from him again.

Fanny and her sister discussed why so few officers had chosen local ladies for wives. Only a private and a milkmaid had married; the rest of the local young ladies remained single. True, the regiment had been called away quite suddenly, but prior to its departure, it had been in Meryton long enough for attachments to form.

"What are we doing wrong?" Fanny asked, who was mystified on how any young lady caught a husband.

"Perhaps we are not rich enough," said Agnes.

Each Miss Gardiner could expect a dowry of several thousand pounds. The amounts did not make them heiresses, but the sums were considered liberal for the area.

Mrs. Gardiner, aware of the unhappiness in her daughters, was kind but firm. The handsome young men were gone; they were unlikely to return. Fanny's spirits would not improve until she stopped hiding in her bedroom and started seeing her friends again. To make this happen, Mrs. Gardiner sent Fanny to go to the drapery and see what sort of new material had arrived.

"Make yourself presentable," Mrs. Gardiner ordered her younger daughter. "Put that new ribbon in your hair."

With the regiment departed, no officer in a red coat would notice her ribbon, but Mrs. Gardiner insisted. Fanny put the ribbon in her hair and went out through the door of her parents' apartment, where she encountered Mr. John Bennet, coming out of the door that led to her father's offices.

Mr. John Bennet, or rather, Mr. Bennet since the deaths of his father and his older brother, was in many ways the opposite of Miss Frances Gardiner. Mr. John Bennet was tall, spare, and fair, and although he was only in his twenties, he already wore spectacles to read, of which he did a great deal. Miss Frances Gardiner was shorter, rounder, and darker, with rich dark curls.

Miss Frances Gardiner's spirits, in their subdued state, made her easier for the young man to approach. And Mr. Bennet, now that the red coats were departed, was more noticeable to Fanny.

"Miss Frances," said Mr. Bennet.

"Mr. John Bennet – I mean, Mr. Bennet," said Fanny Gardiner, amending her address. They happened to be heading in the same direction; he was going to Clarke's Library, while her object was the Lucas Drapery across the street from it. "How are you?"

"Well enough. And you?"

She said she was also well, and then remarked it was a pleasant day for a stroll. She would prefer dancing, of course, but no one was obliging enough to arrange an assembly now the militia had departed from Meryton.

Mr. Bennet told her he was not especially fond of dancing.

Fanny found this attitude incomprehensible. "How can anyone not be fond of dancing? Do you object to the exercise? Or do you dislike music?"

"As Longbourn's fields always require attention, I do not want for exercise," said Mr. Bennet. "I grant you, the music can be pleasant, although it could be listened to just as well, or perhaps even better, sitting quietly in a chair instead of prancing up and down a room."

"A dance also gives you the opportunity to speak with agreeable people," added Fanny.

"Too many people," opined Mr. Bennet. "One cannot have a serious conversation at a dance."

"Must all conversations be serious? Do you not wish for amusement? Do you not ever become lonely?"

"I prefer my books."

"Show me what you find worth reading," demanded Fanny, and instead of waiting for him to hand her the books he was returning to the library, she took them from him. One was a volume by James Boswell; the other was about plants and farming.

Mr. Bennet did not object to Fanny's impertinence; instead, he defended each choice. "The volume on farming needs no explanation. As I am now master at Longbourn, I wish to learn about the newest techniques. And the book by Boswell supplies me with more wit than I can expect to find in Meryton."

"Perhaps you have not found wit in Meryton because you have failed to look for it," said Fanny, returning his books to him. "And would not speaking with other local farmers be the best way to learn about local farming?"

To these questions, Mr. Bennet made no answer. This was because he was truly considering her words, her point of view, but Fanny took his silence as a sign that he found her ideas unworthy. As she had no interest in Mr. Bennet, his lack of response did not offend her.

They had reached the library. Miss Frances Gardiner bade Mr. Bennet farewell, and continued across the street to the Lucas Drapery, leaving him alone to enter the library.

Fanny, with her sparkling dark eyes, and yes, the ribbon in her hair, was then a very pretty girl. That explained some of Mr. Bennet's notice of her, but he was also intrigued by her frank manner of speech. She was right; he *was* lonely at Longbourn, and after the liveliness of Miss Frances Gardiner, the dim and dusty library was unsatisfying. As he returned the books and picked up the volumes reserved for him, they seemed a poor substitute for conversation with real people.

Fanny, however, was unaware of the interest she had sparked in Mr. John Bennet. At that moment, her heart still ached for Lieutenant Higbee. Besides, even though Mr. Bennet's situation had changed, she still thought of him as Mr. John Bennet, a younger son with uncertain prospects, instead of *the* Mr. Bennet, a gentleman with an estate worth 2000£ per year.

Fanny went into the drapers, first doing the inspection commanded by her mother – a pretty muslin was available, and with the regiment gone, they could negotiate a better price – and then calling on her friend, young Mrs. Lucas, who was not yet Lady Lucas. The women played with the Lucas's young children, four-year-old Charlotte and her two little brothers.

Mrs. Lucas told her that her husband was aware of the gloom that had fallen on Meryton since the withdrawal of the militia, which he confirmed was not expected to return for several years. Mr. Lucas was arranging a series of amusements for the town, including an assembly, and had already determined a date.

"Who could care for dancing now?" asked Fanny, who thought an assembly without red coats would be dull. She was also, despite herself, influenced by Mr. Bennet's disinterest in the activity.

Mrs. Lucas, however, told her young friend she had to attend. "Mr. Lucas depends on you," she said. "You, Fanny, are required at the assembly or it will be a complete failure."

"There will not be enough partners," Fanny objected.

"Perhaps, but *you* will not be sitting down," said Mrs. Lucas.

The flattery and the prediction, as well as the fact that Fanny loved to dance, persuaded her to make the effort. Her expectations and her spirits might be low, but she would do what she could to assist young Mr. Lucas. Besides, she knew herself well enough to realize that sitting at home while others danced would distress her even more. Still, she expressed her reservations to her parents, who were also attending the event.

"An event often turns out different than expected," said Mr. Gardiner.

To Fanny's surprise, when they entered the assembly room, Mr. Bennet was also in it. He told her that he had decided to take her advice and to exchange solitude for company, at least for an evening. Without the competition of Colonel Miller's officers, the gentleman appeared taller and handsomer than he had before. Furthermore, instead of taking a seat by the wall so that he could listen to the music, he asked her for the honor of the first two dances. They spent much of the evening together, either dancing, listening to the music, or shouting observations over the noise of the crowd.

"Did the evening please you?" Fanny asked him as the crowd pressed to the exit.

"It was not disagreeable," said Mr. Bennet, and he delivered her to her parents.

As soon as the Gardiners were in the privacy of their own home, they discussed the evening. "Mr. Bennet took plenty of notice of you, Fanny," observed Mrs. Gardiner.

"He is not a red coat," said Agnes.

"The red coats are gone," said Mr. Gardiner. "Mr. Bennet, although he reads too much, is here."

"What sort of business has he been to see you about?" inquired Mrs. Gardiner. Fanny might still be too inexperienced to realize the importance of understanding a young man's situation, but her mother was not.

"Only a dispute with a cousin," said Mr. Gardiner. "I know of nothing that would sully young Mr. Bennet's character or diminish his estate."

"I suppose Fanny could do worse," said Agnes, who had not yet altered the impression of Mr. John Bennet she had had since childhood.

"Mr. Bennet is a gentleman. I believe Fanny could not do better," said Mr. Gardiner. Then he added, "This is no reflection on you, Fanny, but a reflection of our status and where we live."

"If Mr. Bennet spends his hours reading," observed Mrs. Gardiner, "that may be because he lives alone. And most husbands have far more serious flaws."

"My dear!" exclaimed Mr. Gardiner.

"Not you, my love," said Mrs. Gardiner.

"Mr. Bennet does need company," said Fanny.

After that Fanny, with the assistance of her mother and the encouragement of her father and her sister, put effort into catching young Mr. Bennet. Fanny borrowed a volume by Boswell from the library and actually perused several of its pages. Mr. Bennet was invited to take tea with them, and when he discovered the book – which had been placed where he was meant to discover it – he read aloud his favorite passage to them. It was not as entertaining, to be sure, as dancing the evening away with an officer in a red coat, but nevertheless it was pleasant.

Fanny, after having a friend explain the rudiments to her, asked Mr. Bennet questions about farming and actually listened to his answers. Farming was not as exciting as muskets and bayonets, but the nation needed to eat. Mr. Bennet and Fanny met, too, at the Lucases, where Fanny displayed her maternal tendencies by singing to the small children. Mr. and Mrs. Lucas did what they could to encourage the young couple.

"Mr. Bennet is very clever," Mrs. Lucas said to Fanny one morning. "Mr. Lucas believes, if he would only take the trouble, Mr. Bennet could be the best farmer in the area."

"And even if he does not, he is agreeable enough," said Mr. Lucas.

"If you marry him, you will move across the river," said Mrs. Lucas, as Mr. Bennet's estate was not in Meryton proper but in the hamlet of Longbourn. "I will miss you."

"Miss Frances will only be about a mile away," said Mr. Lucas. "And I hope for us to follow someday ourselves. Several houses on that side of the river could be improved to accommodate a growing family. We could call our new home William's Villa – or Lucas Lodge."

Mr. Bennet realized he needed a wife to manage the domestic side of Longbourn House, so that he would no longer have to discuss meals and laundry with the housekeeper. He had a fine income – or so it seemed at the time – and he wanted someone to help him spend the money. Besides, Mr. Bennet was, as Fanny had noted, lonely, and it was tiresome to have to keep leaving his comfortable home in search of company whenever he wanted a conversation with someone who was not a servant. It would be much easier, he thought, to have the company installed in his home. Finally, a wife was necessary for producing a son to help him to cut off the entail from the cousin with whom he was at war.

Miss Frances Gardiner was a very pretty girl; she would keep him sociable; she spurred him on in the ways he thought he needed to be spurred. And so, about two months later, Mr. Bennet proposed.

The offer of marriage was made at Longbourn House. Mr. Bennet had, in a burst of effort, actually invited the Gardiners over for dinner, an occasion which astonished the servants, who had to set about polishing additional pieces of silver. Mr. Bennet and Fanny were seated at one end of the living-room, ostensibly looking at items in his cabinet of curiosities – he had some odd shells and some strange feathers – and Fanny duly admired them but privately thought the display at Lucas drapery was more interesting.

"What a charming prospect," said Fanny with more enthusiasm, for they were near a window that looked out on the Longbourn shrubbery.

"I am glad it pleases you, Miss Frances," said Mr. Bennet, "for I am hoping you will often look out this window."

"Oh!" said Fanny, who was quick in social matters, even if she knew nothing about shells. "Do you mean—?" and she stopped. Although she was sure what he meant, he had to ask the question himself.

"Yes," said Mr. Bennet. "I am asking you to make me the happiest of men and to do me the honor of becoming my wife."

His words, besides conveying the message Fanny wanted to hear, impressed her. That would have pleased Mr. Bennet, who, before arranging this day, had studied his late brother's romances in order to determine what was appropriate. Most of the conditions he rejected as absurd, but he did at least find some language he deemed suitable for a proposal of marriage.

Fanny accepted – and Mr. Bennet's smile elevated him to handsome in her eyes, and she felt an excited fluttering inside her – on the condition her parents approved. As her parents were only half a room away, the approval was quickly sought for and given.

The Gardiners were delighted to have a daughter so well settled, and at such an easy distance. Mr. Bennet refurbished his carriage and within two months, Miss Frances Gardiner became Mrs. Bennet.

The marriage, however, was not always easy. Each of them had engaged in small deceptions to win the other. Mr. Bennet – partly because he believed she had a point – had attempted to be more sociable than he naturally was. But now with a wife at Longbourn, who could talk for all her waking hours, Mr. Bennet rediscovered something that he had known before: for him, at least, there was the possibility of too much company. And Mrs. Bennet, although she allowed her husband to read to her in the evenings, never picked up a book on her own. Nevertheless, they were married, for better or for worse, in sickness and in health, and despite some disappointments, they managed.

Mrs. Bennet's Advice

I was rinsing dishes and stacking them in the dishwasher. "I'm sorry your marriage has been so difficult," I said to Mrs. Bennet, who hovered near me.

Mrs. Bennet appreciated sympathy, but my attitude bordered on pity, and that she did not like. "Why do you believe my marriage with Mr. Bennet is not satisfactory?"

After closing the dishwasher, I showed her several passages from the text. "This is from chapter 1."

MRS. BENNET'S ADVICE TO YOUNG LADIES

Mr. Bennet was so odd a mixture of quick parts, sarcastic humour, reserve, and caprice, that the experience of three-and-twenty years had been insufficient to make his wife understand his character. Her mind was less difficult to develop. She was a woman of mean understanding, little information, and uncertain temper.

Mrs. Bennet flushed with anger.
"And this," I added, "is from later in the text, chapter 42."

Elizabeth, however, had never been blind to the impropriety of her father's behaviour as a husband. She had always seen it with pain; but respecting his abilities, and grateful for his affectionate treatment of herself, she endeavoured to forget what she could not overlook, and to banish from her thoughts that continual breach of conjugal obligation and decorum which, in exposing his wife to the contempt of her own children, was so highly reprehensible. But she had never felt so strongly as now the disadvantages which must attend the children of so unsuitable a marriage, nor ever been so fully aware of the evils arising from so ill-judged a direction of talents; talents, which, rightly used, might at least have preserved the respectability of his daughters, even if incapable of enlarging the mind of his wife.

Mrs. Bennet folded her arms and snorted. She was aware of those passages; they had upset her greatly when she first encountered them, but she had not studied them in ages, for what purpose did they serve but to make her angry with Miss Jane Austen? "It was cruel of her to describe me this way, for she was my creator, and without me, she would have had no story at all. Mean understanding, really!"

I put down the text, then gathered cups and glasses and carried them into the kitchen. "Jane Austen was not kind to Mr. Bennet, either."

Mrs. Bennet rubbed her nose and continued. "No, she was not. Miss Jane Austen wished to make Lizzy appear superior by degrading her parents. The technique works; a young lady with only moderate beauty appears prettiest when seated next to someone who is plain. However, despite Miss Austen's unkind words, my marriage with Mr. Bennet is, in my opinion, a success."

"How so?"

"Our characters are very different. Mr. Bennet likes his books and his quiet. He is not enterprising, like my brother Gardiner or my brother-in-law Phillips. These are things I find frustrating, but these are precisely the reasons he needs me. *I* have prevented Mr. Bennet from being lonely. *I* have given him children; *I* have kept him connected to the world. Without *me*, Mr. Bennet might know what is happening in the Royal Society of London, or even in the Americas, but he would be ignorant of anything going on with his neighbors in Meryton."

Then, after some reflection, she added: "*Perhaps* another woman in

Great Britain might have suited Mr. Bennet better – some lady in Northamptonshire or Derbyshire. But Mr. John Bennet would never have taken the trouble to find her and to woo her!"

I examined a bowl from which I had eaten spaghetti and decided it needed to soak. I filled the bowl with warm water and put it in the sink. There was no room for the bowl in the dishwasher anyway.

"You are probably correct," I said.

"A good marriage works with the strengths *and* the defects of both partners."

"I suppose," I said.

"My question to you, Young Lady, is about *your* marriage. Is it a success?"

I did not wish to discuss my marriage. I tried to ignore her as I rummaged under the sink for a box with dishwasher pellets.

"You told me you're divorced, so you have one failed marriage behind you."

"True." I pulled out a box, realized it was empty, and groped under the sink for another.

"Do you take advantage of your husband's strengths – and his weaknesses?"

I considered a moment, and realized that I did. The last time he had lost his temper, I had redirected his anger into moving the furniture. He had worked off his bad mood, and we had finally positioned a new rug properly.

"Does he take advantage of your strengths and weaknesses?" inquired Mrs. Bennet.

Her question was disconcerting. I did not know if my husband was manipulating me or not. I also did not like to contemplate my own defects.

I put the pellet into the dishwasher and started it. "Let's get back to your story," I said.

CHAPTER 3

Mr. and Mrs. Bennet had been married several years; they had four daughters. Jane and Lizzy were little girls; Mary was taking her first unsteady steps, and Kitty was a newborn infant in her mother's arms. Mrs. Bennet exulted in Jane's golden beauty, while Mr. Bennet was delighted with three-year-old Lizzy's obvious intelligence, but they were disappointed that Kitty was not a boy.

During the month after the birth, Mrs. Bennet kept mostly to her rooms, but not to her bed. It was March, but a soggy, chilly March, when remaining indoors had much to recommend it. Jane and Elizabeth also stayed inside with their mother, Mary and their new sister. Jane adored spring flowers, especially violets, but she disliked the cold and wet. Elizabeth, however, would have gone outside had her parents permitted it, as she did not mind mud, but even her indulgent father refused permission.

"No, it is raining too hard," said her father, closing the door after opening it to take in the post.

"I am not afraid of the rain."

"You may go out and play when the weather changes."

"When will the weather change, Papa?"

"I do not know, but in England one thing is true: the weather always changes, so you will be able to run outside soon. Let us go up to your mother; you can stay with her." Carrying a letter with one hand, he held out his other to her.

Mr. Bennet and Lizzy climbed the stairs together and entered Mrs. Bennet's rooms, where she was with Jane and Mary and the newborn Kitty. "One of your daughters was trying to escape," reported Mr. Bennet.

"Oh! Mr. Bennet, come in and talk to me. Is there any news? After a fortnight of rain with a new infant, I am desperate for conversation."

"A letter has arrived," said Mr. Bennet.

"That sounds promising."

He opened the missive and glanced at it. "It is from my cousin, Mr. Collins."

"No! That odious man."

"Would you rather I not read it to you? It is not long."

She signaled he should go ahead, and Mr. Bennet read:

Dear Mr. Bennet,

I understand you and Mrs. Bennet have brought another girl into the world. I suppose congratulations are expected, and of course I wish her the best. Good wishes are necessary these days.

William, my son, thrives, and shows great devotion to his letters and to the prayer-

book. For such a young lad, he has an excellent vocabulary, and will one day enjoy the library at Longbourn House.

Yours, etc.

Charles Collins

"He is triumphing over us," said Mrs. Bennet. "Because I have produced another daughter. We need a son."

"A son would cut off the entail," agreed Mr. Bennet. "If something should happen to me, your comfort would be assured."

Mrs. Bennet, who believed the fact that she had produced another daughter rather than a son was her fault, promised to try again.

"I do not like to put you to so much trouble, Mrs. Bennet," said Mr. Bennet.

"I am still young, and we have fewer children than the Lucases," said Mrs. Bennet. At that time Mr. and Mrs. Lucas had seven children, and Mrs. Lucas was expecting again. "Besides, I cannot bear the thought of your precious books being polluted by a Collins." The Longbourn library was the one area in which Mr. Bennet, after a last stand, ruled supreme – Mrs. Bennet having campaigned successfully to usurp control of the rest of the house. Mrs. Bennet believed, not without some reason, her husband preferred his books to the rest of his family, and naturally felt resentment towards the volumes in question. Still, on this occasion she was moved to defend her husband's collection, and, while rocking the infant, continued with vehemence. Little William Collins would never enjoy the Longbourn library. How could that evil cousin suggest it? Why, she would take the books and throw them to the pigs before she would allow any Collins to touch them!

"Mrs. Bennet, much as I appreciate your enthusiasm, if such a thing should happen, I hope you will treat the books better. If this young William is as clever as his father says, his reading my books should not be discouraged. And if he is not clever, then this William will probably ignore them, and they can wait for other hands to turn their pages. Please, my love, if I do not survive you, do not give them to the pigs. We should not assume young William is as unworthy as his father."

"Impossible!" pronounced Mrs. Bennet. She had never met either Collins, but she hated them all as a matter of principle.

"Mamma, please do not put Papa's books in the pigsty. I want to read them when I am older," petitioned Elizabeth.

"See, one of our daughters is interested in my library."

Jane said she also wished to read, and was rewarded with praise from Mr. Bennet.

"The girls are still too young for your books," said Mrs. Bennet. "When they grow older, they may like them less than they expect. However, to protect your library, the best security is to have a son, and then none of this will matter."

"First, my dear, you must recover," said Mr. Bennet.

Mrs. Bennet's Advice

I went out to the mailbox. Mrs. Bennet was fascinated by the fact that letters were waiting for me in it.

"Why does this surprise you?" I asked, because I always thought mail would be expected in a mailbox.

"In my day, the recipient had to pay to receive the letter."

I explained that in my day, the sender usually paid to send the mail.

Mrs. Bennet found the arrangement peculiar. "First, the deliverer, if already paid, may not feel a need to complete the delivery. Second, it is you, Young Lady, who are receiving something of value. You should be paying."

"You are assuming the post is of value," I said, and then showed what had arrived: a bank statement and two pieces of advertising. The mail from the bank was covered by fees, and the advertisers wanted my attention. I assured her there were occasions, such as deliveries of packages, when I paid in advance.

After we were done with the mail, I changed the subject. "The entail. It is the plot point that makes your life difficult."

"Oh! The entail is so vile."

I told her I agreed, and that in most societies these days, daughters were not disinherited.

"Then you are a lucky woman, to live when you do. At that point in my life I was doing everything I could to end the entail, but I kept producing daughters."

I agreed that, at that period of her life, she had done everything she could to stop it.

"I was always aware what threatened us – a problem my daughters did not adequately acknowledge later. You cannot take steps to improve your life until you understand what is troubling you. What troubles you most, Young Lady? Your marriage, as we were discussing earlier?"

"My marriage is fine," I assured her. "We get along reasonably well – when we're together."

Mrs. Bennet wanted to know why we were not together, and I explained the current situation in the world. A disease had struck the entire planet, and my husband and I expected to be stuck in different places for months. We communicated every day, and eventually we would get back together, but for the moment, travel was restricted. "The pandemic is what troubles me most," I said.

"Oh, dear!" cried Mrs. Bennet. She asked about my own health, in part out of concern for me, but also because she wanted me to stay alive in order to complete her project. "Can anything be done?"

I explained that in my day, diseases were understood, and doctors knew what precautions were necessary to prevent the illness from spreading. Isolation, mostly – which was one reason I had time for her – for months on end, interacting with only a few people in person, and doing my shopping carefully and infrequently. Most shops required people to wear masks, which were unpleasant but effective.

"Masks?" Mrs. Bennet asked, intrigued, and she said how she had always wanted to be invited to a masquerade ball, probably one in London, as elegant as could be. She could wear a crown! Or a train! And so many jewels. After discussing possibilities, she returned to our original topic. "I do not, however, understand how this works! How can disguising yourself prevent you from becoming ill?"

Before I could answer, Mrs. Bennet continued. "Oh! Are the masks meant to frighten away the disease? I have heard of such things, but is that not a heathen approach? Full of superstition? Or do such practices actually work? Mr. Bennet has told me they do not, but what a wonder that would be, to learn that he has been wrong all along!"

I laughed, and explained about cloth masks that covered the nose and the mouth, so that the illness could not spread from one person to the next.

"Bad air," said Mrs. Bennet, nodding sagaciously. "Our apothecary has warned against it."

I told her the pandemic had lasted more than a year, and people were tired of the solitude and the face coverings. Even I was fatigued by the whole business.

"Can nothing else be done?"

Yes, I told her. Vaccinations had recently been developed, and they were expected to prevent the disease in more than 90% of the recipients. Yet many people were reluctant to take them.

"Vaccinations," Mrs. Bennet said. Mrs. Bennet thought she had heard the word, or something similar, something relating to cows. Some Latin word, which she did not know, but which Mr. Bennet had been especially enthusiastic about for a while, something he had used to protect those at Longbourn.

I put away the mail and invited her to tell me.

CHAPTER 4

A commotion at the front door alerted them to the fact that someone had arrived. Mrs. Bennet's mother, who had gotten a lift to Longbourn in the carriage of a neighbor, was soon admitted into Mrs. Bennet's rooms. Mr. Bennet remained as he welcomed the addition of another adult and perhaps some different news, as information was scant due to the incessant rains.

After Mrs. Gardiner admired her newest granddaughter, she produced a letter from Mrs. Bennet's brother. Mr. Edward Gardiner had started a business in London. Mrs. Gardiner read aloud from it, describing her son's fine dinners and his courtship of a pretty, intelligent young woman.

"How I long to go to London," cried Mrs. Bennet, who had only visited twice. "Theatres! Shops!"

"Impossible, Fanny! You have four little girls!"

"Oh, Mamma, if one is determined, one can do anything," said Mrs. Bennet. "If one hires enough servants, one can certainly make such a journey. And I am desperate for a bit of fun."

"The weather in London is probably as unpleasant as it is here," said Mr. Bennet. "Only there one would be in the cramped rooms of an inn – incurring much more expense for an inferior situation."

"I do not advise visiting London just now," said Mrs. Gardiner. "Nor would your brother."

"Why, what does Edward say?" asked Mrs. Bennet.

"The red plague has returned. Your brother writes it has led to the deaths of several small children in his neighborhood."

Their grandmother's words caught the attention of the little girls. "What is the red plague, Mamma?" Jane inquired.

"Mr. Bennet can explain better than I," said Mrs. Bennet to her oldest daughter. "His father and his brother died from it years before you were born."

"That is true, the red plague does not always stay in London," agreed Mrs. Gardiner.

This alarmed the little girls even more. Jane was too frightened to ask for further information, but Lizzy insisted on her father telling them whatever he could.

Mr. Bennet explained that the disease made people very hot, a condition that was called a fever. The invalids would be sick for weeks, and then they would either recover – or they would die. But sometimes the red plague left people scarred or even blind. The red plague was also called the smallpox.

While Lizzy closed her eyes in an attempt to see what it would be like to be blind, Jane asked, as there was a small pox, if there were also a large pox.

"There are many kinds of poxes, some making you very sick, and others making you only a little sick," explained Mr. Bennet, and then he fell silent, gazing fixedly at an old scar on the back of his hand.

"We pray none of you will be stricken and die, but if you are, it would be God's will," said Mrs. Gardiner.

"Mother! Do not speak that way before my children!" said Mrs. Bennet, horrified. Her maternal feelings were so strong that she was ready to defend her daughters against anyone, including her mother and God.

"Fanny, everyone dies," said Mrs. Gardiner. "Is that not true, Mr. Bennet?"

But Mr. Bennet, who had continued to stare at his own hand, did not respond to his wife's mother. Instead, he put his teacup down on a little table, rose from his chair and left the room without explanation.

"How peculiar," remarked Mrs. Gardiner "Is he unwell? Given you have no sons, it would be good to make sure he is healthy, Fanny."

Elizabeth went to the hall, listened, and then returned to make a report. "Papa has gone into his library."

Mrs. Gardiner frowned. "That child is too clever for her own good."

"Lizzy only answered your question, Grandmamma," said Jane.

Jane, usually so placid, rarely spoke up, but she always defended Lizzy, whom she viewed as her own special playmate, against anyone. Mrs. Bennet was pleased to see her daughters form such a tight bond; she hoped Jane and Lizzy would be as close as she was with Agnes, who had become Mrs. Phillips.

They heard the front door open and close, and hoped for another visitor – Mrs. Bennet longed for more company – but no one was announced. Lizzy climbed on a chair and looked out a window and reported that Papa had gone outside, despite the fact that rain was still falling.

"Really? Is he heading to Meryton?" Mrs. Bennet asked, while Mrs. Gardiner prepared to be offended. If her son-in-law intended to go to Meryton, he ought to wait and accompany her. She was hoping to be taken back home in the Bennets' carriage.

Lizzy reported that Mr. Bennet was walking in a different direction, towards a field where they had several cows. "He has gone out in the rain!" she exclaimed and complained that Papa had not allowed *her* to go outside in this weather.

"I suppose something on the farm requires his urgent attention," Mrs. Bennet said to her mother.

At this notion, Mrs. Gardiner felt less slighted. Mr. Bennet was peculiar; he had always been peculiar, but many husbands behaved far worse than her son-in-law. She changed the subject. "I think your brother may marry," said Mrs. Gardiner, "and in that case his wife may report on the latest fashions. I am glad to see you and the baby are well, but next time, dear, you really ought to produce a boy."

"Is there any way to make that happen?" cried Mrs. Bennet.

The ladies had a lengthy, detailed discussion, full of things Mrs. Bennet ought to do and to eat, and after arranging for the horses to be brought back from the farm, Mrs. Gardiner left in her daughter's carriage.

After his mother-in-law's departure, Mr. Bennet returned to the rooms of his lady, a small bowl in his hand. "Mrs. Bennet, I am concerned about the smallpox. Our daughters may be in especial danger."

"Why? London is so far away! I know your father and brother died from it, but what can we do besides avoid bad air?"

"I believe there *is* something we can do."

Now, Mrs. Bennet was generally for doing something far more than doing nothing, while doing nothing was Mr. Bennet's natural inclination. The fact that he had an idea he wanted to try was unusual; Mrs. Bennet was intrigued.

Mr. Bennet spoke about an experiment done by a fellow named Jenner who lived in Gloucestershire. How having the cowpox now could prevent them all from getting the smallpox later.

"Cowpox! Like a common milkmaid?"

"Yes. Milkmaids never get the smallpox, my dear. And I had the cowpox myself, but my father and my brother did not. When the smallpox came to Longbourn, I did not even fall ill."

Mrs. Bennet did not want any of them to become ill with the smallpox and suffer and die, or even worse, become blind or hideously scarred to live a long, miserable life. "What must we do?"

Mr. Bennet showed her his bowl. He had managed to find a cow with cowpox – she had hideous pustules on her udders – and scraped them and gathered the scrapings in a bowl. He said he wanted to infect his family by making a small cut with a knife on each of them and then rubbing the cowpox scrapings on the cut.

"But you already had the cowpox, Mr. Bennet, did you not?"

"I probably cannot become ill again, but we need to set a good example so that Jane and Lizzy are not frightened."

Mrs. Bennet looked at the scar on her husband's hand, and although she did not want her daughters to fall ill, nor did she want their natural beauty to be diminished. After some discussion, Mr. and Mrs. Bennet arrived at a solution: performing the operation where one could not see, settling on a spot just above one of the knees. Mr. Bennet began with his wife, then Mrs. Bennet performed the same surgery on him. The girls, naturally, cried when their father took his knife to their little legs, but they trusted him and allowed him to do it. Mary screamed and the parents decided Kitty was too young.

"We will do this when Kitty is older," said Mr. Bennet, taking the bowl and his knife to see if he could persuade the servants at Longbourn to try the same remedy.

Shortly afterwards, as predicted, the pustules formed – they were ugly, horrifying to Jane but objects of interest to Lizzy – and Mrs. Bennet prayed that Jane would lose none of her looks. Smallpox, Mr. Bennet reminded her, would be far, far worse, and he promised his daughters they would not suffer long.

Eventually the pustules passed, and although each daughter had a small scar above her knee, the blemishes faded, becoming little worse than a few freckles. A husband would have to search hard with the brightness of a dozen candles to find those imperfections, and who lit a dozen candles in the bedroom?

Mr. Bennet, as the master of Longbourn, was able to tell everyone living on it to undergo this procedure. He recommended the operation to others in the neighborhood, but most had little confidence in a distant physician or even in the experiences of Mr. Bennet himself. Besides, they preferred to think of the smallpox as being at a distance. London was so far away; their own air was so good; surely, the red plague would not reach them!

But Mr. Bennet was right, and the smallpox did come to Meryton, and Mrs. Bennet admired her husband for his cleverness. No one at Longbourn fell ill, but the Lucases buried a daughter and a son, while their eldest child, Charlotte, was covered with the evil pustules. "I am more worried for her than for my other children, who now with their maker," wept Mrs. Lucas. "She will be marred for life."

Charlotte survived, but she was scarred – not terribly, not as badly as some, but from then on, she would be considered plain. Mrs. Long's nieces lost both their parents, while the girls survived. The mayor of Meryton died, too, and Mr. Lucas decided to campaign for that office, pledging to do what he could to make Meryton healthy and whole – not just the businesses, but the people, too. Mayor Lucas worked with Mr. Bennet, who was happy to transfer his knowledge to local apothecaries and to resume his natural state of indolence.

As Mrs. Bennet had lost none of her daughters, the memory of the red plague faded. In fact, the pox that had marred so many local faces ensured that the Bennet girls would reign as local beauties when they were older, although she preferred to think of them as naturally beautiful instead.

Mr. and Mrs. Bennet tried their luck again, and Mrs. Bennet followed her mother's advice and consumed many foods that were supposed to guarantee that her child would be a boy. Instead, Mrs. Bennet brought into the world her fifth daughter; they christened her Lydia.

Mrs. Bennet's Advice

As we paused our project to enjoy some virtual cake, I asked Mrs.

Bennet what lesson I was supposed to learn from the previous chapter.

Mrs. Bennet blinked her eyes. "Oh! Is it not obvious? If you can do something to avoid getting the red plague, the smallpox, or whatever sickness prevails in your time, then do it! As nothing happened to us – none of our daughters died from the smallpox – the occasion is not so strong in my memory. Mr. Bennet's actions seem trivial, and I am still not sure if the cowpox prevented us getting the smallpox; perhaps it was just good luck, or as my mother would say, God's will. Still, two Lucas children died – and Charlotte was scarred for life."

I explained that getting cowpox did protect people from smallpox. Scientists had discovered how this all worked, and in consequence had been able to extinguish smallpox from the entire planet. I launched into an explanation of germ theory – due to the current pandemic, it was on my mind – and how many diseases were caused by tiny creatures too small to be seen by the naked eye, too small, even to have been seen by most microscopes available in her time.

I realized I had reached the limit of Mrs. Bennet's interest in this matter, so I introduced another topic. "Were you disappointed that Lydia was another girl?"

"How could I be disappointed? Lydia was so much fun, so lively, so ready for anything!"

"But didn't you want a son?"

"Perhaps, before she was born, I thought a son would be more convenient. But I adored her the moment she was put in my arms. She looked at me as if she knew me," said Mrs. Bennet.

I would not quarrel with Mrs. Bennet's maternal feelings.

"Besides, when Lydia was born, I was still young. I thought I would bear more children, and that the son would appear eventually."

"Yes, that's in the text," I said, and opened my copy of *Pride & Prejudice*. In chapter 50 I found the words:

Five daughters successively entered the world, but yet the son was to come; and Mrs. Bennet, for many years after Lydia's birth, had been certain that he would.

"That is true," said Mrs. Bennet. "I blamed myself. Mrs. Lucas had more children, both boys and girls, but I only produced girls, and after Lydia, I was never with child again. As I could not protect my daughters by giving them a brother, or persuade Mr. Bennet to cut off the entail, I resolved to protect them by finding them husbands."

"But producing only daughters was not your fault." I then told her about another age-old mystery that scientists had resolved: that a woman might carry and bear a child, but the man's contribution, although his participation was brief, determined a child's sex.

"Nonsense!" retorted Mrs. Bennet, and then, with interest, added: "How can that be?"

I explained about Y-chromosomes and X-chromosomes, and Mrs. Bennet did her best to attend, but after a few minutes she declared it was beyond her comprehension. Moreover, this talk of natural philosophy – I explained we now called it science, or more precisely, molecular biology – made her head ache. "It is worse than mathematics."

"I like mathematics," I protested.

"You would," said Mrs. Bennet, but her tone was not unkind. "Still, I am convinced that even if *I* do not understand this matter, *you* understand it. But the main thing is that Mr. Bennet, and not I, was responsible for the fact that I produced only daughters. For the past two centuries, I thought it was my fault!"

"True, that is the main point."

She went on for a bit about what she might say to Mr. Bennet the next time he emerged from his library, and I had to emphasize to her that a man – certainly, no man back in his time – could do much about the sex of a child he fathered either, no more than he could have changed the color of his eyes.

She agreed not to reproach him, but she was not yet ready to leave the topic. "I must say, it all seems so unfair."

"What, exactly? That you, and so many women for so many thousands of years, were blamed for producing daughters instead of sons?"

"Oh, that! Yes, indeed! But I mean it is unfair that men should determine whether a child is male or female when women do all the work."

I agreed it was unfair, but we could not change biology, or at least not that biology, at least not yet, and even if we could, I was not sure we should. Besides, these days, the outlook for young ladies was far superior to what it had been in the past. The situation was not perfect, and in some parts of the globe conditions were still wretched, but compared to what our sex had been subjected to, the age was golden.

I then reminded Mrs. Bennet she was a character in a novel. "Therefore, it is not really your fault – or even Mr. Bennet's – that you only had daughters. Jane Austen created you; *she* decided that you should only have daughters."

This observation put color into Mrs. Bennet's cheeks and made her eyes sparkle. She sat up straight and leaned towards me. "True, very true! If I had had a son, Miss Jane Austen would have had no story!"

I believed Jane Austen, with her magnificent talent, would have managed, but I did not want to argue with my guest. "Let's resume your biography," I said.

CHAPTER 5

Mrs. Bennet followed her mother's advice and watched Mr. Bennet's health carefully, as her situation and the welfare of her children depended on his survival. Fortunately, his habits were moderate: he exercised by supervising the work in Longbourn's fields, and he did not eat or drink too much. He did not become stout the way so many men did when they aged. Mr. Bennet had the appearance of a man who would live more than his three score and ten, but life was always uncertain; death could strike at any moment.

The years passed. Mrs. Bennet's brother married; the elder Gardiners died; Mr. Phillips took over from his father-in-law and became the leading attorney of Meryton. The Bennet girls grew without any brother to cut off the entail; their prospects remained insecure.

As there was no son, Mrs. Bennet's business was to get her daughters married, but to whom? She knew all the eligible and even marginally eligible gentlemen in the area, but none would do, or at least she saw none she would settle for, not while her daughters were so lovely and lively, with a reputation for beauty that spread throughout the county. She wanted the best husbands for her girls: men who were rich, handsome and agreeable, but gentlemen uniting these qualities were in short supply. Mr. Robinson was a widower, but even older than Mr. Bennet, and his temper was not the best. The Gouldings had several sons, but they were all too young for Mrs. Bennet's daughters. The eldest Lucas boy was pleasant, and Mrs. Bennet was fond of Sir William and Lady Lucas, but despite the smallpox, they had so many children! Sir William's property was not entailed, so he would be giving portions to all his children.

Mr. Phillips had a few clerks, and perhaps one would rise sufficiently in the business to be worthy of one of the Bennet daughters, but that could only supply one.

Mrs. Bennet journeyed occasionally with her two eldest daughters to London, and left Jane and Elizabeth in the care of Mrs. Bennet's brother and sister – Mr. and Mrs. Gardiner – with the hopes that their uncle and aunt would introduce them to eligible men. Jane's golden beauty was especially promising, and when she was fifteen, she inspired a gentleman to poetry. *No candle can compete with Miss Bennet's sweet soft glow.* Beautiful words, treasured more by Mrs. Bennet than by Miss Bennet, but the poet never made his inspiration an offer. Mrs. Bennet consoled herself with the fact that Jane was only fifteen at the time, but the poem was, surely, a good omen.

Nevertheless, the years kept passing, without any offers. Mr. and Mrs. Gardiner, with several small children themselves, were too busy to dedicate themselves to chaperoning their nieces to places where they could meet eligible men, so Mrs. Bennet usually kept her daughters with her in Hertfordshire.

Then Mrs. Bennet learned, from her friend Mrs. Long, that Netherfield Hall had been let at last. The Netherfield estate was only three miles away from Longbourn: an easy distance by carriage or horse, and even a reasonable walk for servants carrying messages or goods. Alas, its owner was a dissolute spendthrift who had moved to Brighton in order to be by the sea, with heirs at a distance who from reputation appeared no more worthy than the owner. But the tenant, a Mr. Bingley, was a potential piece of good luck. A single man with an income of four, maybe five thousand, a year!

Mrs. Bennet informed her husband immediately. Really, without her, Mr. Bennet would know nothing about the neighborhood; his head would only be full of the writings of ancient authors such as Cicero or that physician in the North, Jenner, who at least had proved useful. "What a fine thing for our girls!" she exclaimed.

"How so? How can it affect them?" asked Mr. Bennet.

"My dear Mr. Bennet," she replied, "how can you be so tiresome? You must know that I am thinking of his marrying one of them."

Her husband teased her with some nonsense about her being as handsome as her daughters – words Mrs. Bennet appreciated; at least Mr. Bennet did not reproach her for becoming older, as some men complained to their wives – and pretended not to understand her.

Mrs. Bennet believed her husband cared for her and his daughters as much as he could. However, he was not a man of passion or energy, and getting Mr. Bennet to do anything was always a project for Mrs. Bennet, as she campaigned against his natural indolence. How could he neglect such a potentially useful acquaintance? And with such foolish arguments?

She made these statements to him, and then later, because she was still so vexed by the subject, to Mrs. Long.

"Mr. Bennet must know the arguments are foolish," said Mrs. Long, and promised Mrs. Bennet that she would send Mr. Long to wait on Mr. Bingley. If Mrs. Bennet could not persuade Mr. Bennet to make the call, Mrs. Long would be able to introduce the Bennet daughters to the new tenant of Netherfield.

Mrs. Bennet did not trust Mrs. Long; her friend had two nieces of marriageable age, and even if her intentions were as honorable as she pretended, Mrs. Long was going to London for a few days and could not make the hoped-for introduction before the next assembly – and where better to fall in love but at a dance? Even Mrs. Bennet, when she was still Miss Frances Gardiner, had become attracted to Mr. Bennet at a dance.

Still, Mrs. Long's words reminded Mrs. Bennet that Mr. Bennet was *not* a foolish man. Of *course*, Mr. Bennet *would* call on Mr. Bingley. Mr. Bennet was sly about it, pretending to go out into the farms to look at some field, but actually ordering the carriage to be brought down the driveway and then setting off for Netherfield. A discreet inquiry, sent by Hill, assured Mrs. Bennet of this fact. Well, one of Mr. Bennet's pleasures in life was teasing his wife – which tried her poor nerves – but many other husbands' vices were worse.

So, even though Mrs. Bennet was aware Mr. Bennet had gone to Netherfield in the morning, in the evening she said, after Mr. Bennet mentioned Mr. Bingley, "We are not in a way to know *what* Mr. Bingley likes, since we are not to visit."

The mistress of Longbourn made her tone resentful, something that was easy to do, because she was genuinely irritated by his deception and because he had not yet told her how the visit had gone. Perhaps Mr. Bingley had not been at home and so there was no acquaintance. Mrs. Bennet was disingenuous, not letting him know that she knew, and forcing him to introduce the topic again.

"Let us return to Mr. Bingley," said Mr. Bennet.

"I am sick of Mr. Bingley!" cried Mrs. Bennet.

"I am sorry to hear *that*; but why did not you tell me that before? If I had known as much this morning, I certainly would not have called on him. It is very unlucky; but as I have actually paid the visit, we cannot escape the acquaintance now."

The girls were genuinely astonished. Mrs. Bennet was not, but she knew what her husband's vanity required, and she pretended to be as taken aback as the rest. Then she praised him, because she was aware of how much he disliked making a call on a stranger. "How good it was in you, my dear Mr. Bennet! But I knew I should persuade you at last. I was sure you loved your girls too well to neglect such an acquaintance. Well, how pleased I am! and it is such a good joke, too, that you should have gone this morning and never said a word about it till now."

Mr. Bennet, having delivered his news, soon retreated to his library, leaving Mrs. Bennet and her daughters to speculate on when they might meet the neighborhood's new gentleman.

Mrs. Bennet's Advice

I was dubious. "You *knew* Mr. Bennet went to Netherfield?"

Mrs. Bennet joined me as I removed items from the mantelpiece. "Of course, I knew! Mr. Bennet is not personally vain; he has never bothered to acquire a large wardrobe, and he has a favorite coat that he always wears on formal calls. Now, he did not wear the coat at breakfast, because he wished to deceive me, but he took it to his library and donned it later. I know because I went into his dressing room and saw that it was missing; I then went to his library, where I found the coat that he had been wearing at breakfast."

"You are certain? None of these details are mentioned in *Pride & Prejudice*. In fact, your words contradict Jane Austen's text."

"Miss Jane Austen! Miss Jane Austen never married, and so she may have not known how aware husbands and wives are of each other's movements."

As I wiped down the mantelpiece, I thought of another of Austen's books, *Persuasion*, when she wrote about how well husbands and wives understood each other. However, that novel had been written considerably after *Pride & Prejudice*; it was possible that Austen had gained in understanding on this matter in the intervening years.

Mrs. Bennet persisted. "Watching Mr. Bennet leave the house, after he had said he did not want to be disturbed that morning in his library – something he did not need to emphasize, as we rarely intruded on him in his library – I was certain he was going to call on Mr. Bingley. Why else would he use such secrecy?"

I objected to her assertion. "You behaved as if you did not know that Mr. Bennet had gone to Netherfield. You were even cross about it, and cross with others, scolding Kitty for coughing and getting on your nerves."

Mrs. Bennet said that it had not been difficult to do, partly because she was cross with him, but also because she knew he loved to triumph in the idea that he had fooled her. "I even praised him for making such a good joke."

I was silent as I dusted the various items – photographs, candleholders, a weather station – and return them to the mantelpiece.

"You doubt me, do you not?"

I admitted I did, and not just because it contradicted the text. "You don't seem to have a personality that keeps silent about anything," I explained. "And, because of that, you don't seem capable of deception."

"Oh! That is what you think?" asked Mrs. Bennet, and her tone was defiant. She assured me she was capable of both holding her tongue and deceiving others, and later she would give me an example from the text I esteemed so highly. "You will see!"

I wondered if she might be right, and if loud behavior could be more deceptive than silence.

"We have already talked about marriages," said Mrs. Bennet, "but it is such an important part of life, I think it deserves more. Do you not depend on your husband to take care of matters for you that you cannot? Do you not make it as agreeable as you can for him to take care of these matters?"

I considered her question. I disliked most aspects of automobiles, and so I praised my husband inordinately when he took care of things like the tires. He enjoyed the admiration very much. Of course, my admiration was genuine, because I was grateful to have him take care of the car.

"Yes, admiration, vanity, pride!" Mrs. Bennet exclaimed. "Mr. Bennet takes great pride in the idea that he is cleverer than me, and indeed, in some things he is, such as when he protected us from the smallpox. However, Mr. Bennet is less clever than I am about our neighbors and not nearly as well informed."

I thought she made a good point. Male vanity existed – as did female vanity. One could appeal to both.

"We have to rely on husbands, or partners, or whatever you call them in your day, to do the things we cannot," said Mrs. Bennet. "I would have visited Mr. Bingley if it were allowed; but in my era, I had to make Mr. Bennet do it. He fulfilled his paternal duty by making the call, and after that, events proceeded."

"What is your advice?" I asked, as I returned the last object to the mantelpiece.

Her dark eyes twinkled. "Oh! It is this, Young Lady: When you require others to do something for you, make it as pleasant as possible for them. Now, on with the story."

CHAPTER 6

The Meryton assemblies were always held on the night of the full moon, so its beams could give the tired dancers and their coachmen light by which to make their way home. As Mr. Bingley was expected to make an appearance at the next assembly, the full moon was anticipated with greater than the usual enthusiasm.

Mrs. Bennet made sure her daughters were elegantly dressed and accompanied them to the assembly. With so many Miss Bennets and no young Mr. Bennets, wherever they went, the ladies usually outnumbered the gentlemen. On the other hand, as their beauty could not be denied, the Miss Bennets were invited everywhere.

The only Miss Bennet not deemed beautiful was poor Mary. She would have preferred to remain at home, but Mrs. Bennet would never permit it. Husbands, Mrs. Bennet pointed out, were not to be found in Mary's books! "You just need to make an effort, Mary, and who knows what might happen?" Mary, aware she would never win this argument, was resigned to coming.

Mrs. Bennet shepherded her daughters into the large room, and they quickly spread throughout the crowd. Jane and Elizabeth went to speak to Charlotte Lucas; Mary secured a seat by the wall; and Kitty and Lydia soon found partners. Mrs. Bennet circulated around the room, gathering the latest news from Lady Lucas and Mrs. Long.

The entrance of the party from Netherfield occurred shortly after the arrival of the Bennets. Mr. Bingley was recognized by Mrs. Bennet, but the other four, two elegantly dressed ladies and two fine looking gentlemen, needed explanation. The Lucases – Sir William Lucas was such a treasure, the fount of information Mr. Bennet refused to be – supplied the information Mrs. Bennet required. The two ladies were the sisters of Mr. Bingley. The older sister was married to one of the gentlemen, a Mr. Hurst; the younger sister was unmarried. Of most interest to everyone in the assembly room was the other gentleman, a Mr. Darcy. Mr. Darcy was single, tall, and soon declared twice as handsome as Mr. Bingley, a natural consequence of his income being twice as large.

"Ten thousand a year!" exclaimed Mrs. Bennet, as Sir William Lucas went to welcome the new arrivals. Would that not be fine for one of her girls?

Two new single gentlemen in the area! Meryton, which had been so barren, so lacking in opportunities, was now a bounty of riches. But how to catch them?

Mrs. Bennet did not waste a moment. She summoned Jane and Elizabeth – Kitty and Lydia already had partners, and Mrs. Bennet did not want to remove Mary from her comfortable chair – and positioned them so they would be noticed by the two gentlemen.

Mr. Bingley first led Charlotte Lucas to the floor, a result of his having been greeted by Sir William Lucas. Really, Mr. Bennet, by declining to socialize put them often at a disadvantage! On the other hand, Mrs. Bennet rather liked managing these occasions herself. Besides, Miss Lucas, although her dear friend's daughter, was plain; the smallpox scars had faded, but Charlotte lacked the radiant skin of the Miss Bennets.

The strategic placement of her daughters had the desired effect. Mr. Bingley noticed both Jane and Elizabeth, and he asked for Miss Bennet's hand for the very next dance.

Mrs. Bennet remained with Elizabeth, stationed so they had an excellent view of the rest of the Netherfield party. Mr. Hurst escorted Mrs. Hurst to the floor; Lady Lucas conversed with Miss Bingley, but Mr. Darcy stood, tall and silent, apart from everyone, even rebuffing the cordial overtures of Sir William, who eventually went to speak with others who appreciated his conversation more. Mr. Darcy, despite his great income, did not like to dance.

After Mr. Bingley finished his set with Jane, he went to his friend. Mrs. Bennet, seated with Elizabeth, overheard their conversation. "Come, Darcy," said the gentleman from Netherfield, "I must have you dance. I hate to see you standing about by yourself in this stupid manner. You had much better dance."

Mrs. Bennet was in complete agreement with Mr. Bingley. What was the point in going to a dance and not dancing? She supposed that *some* might have reasons: for example, she, as a mother, attended in order to put her daughters forward, and another might have a bad ankle and simply want to listen to the music and to speak to friends. But a single man, healthy and whole?

Mr. Darcy, the handsome man with 10,000£ per annum, responded to his friend. "I certainly shall not. You know how I detest it, unless I am particularly acquainted with my partner. At such an assembly as this it would be insupportable. Your sisters are engaged, and there is not another woman in the room whom it would not be a punishment to me to stand up with."

Mrs. Bennet was indignant at Mr. Darcy's set-down: *an assembly such as this!* How could anyone, no matter their income, be so rude?

Mr. Bingley, bless him, made the objections Mrs. Bennet could not say aloud. "I would not be so fastidious as you are," cried the young man, "for a kingdom! Upon my honor, I never met with so many pleasant girls in my life as I have this evening; and there are several of them, you see, uncommonly pretty."

Yes, thought Mrs. Bennet, Mr. Bingley was as agreeable as could be! How glad she was that *he* had leased Netherfield! And what was wrong with his friend?

"*You* are dancing with the only handsome girl in the room," said Mr. Darcy.

Mrs. Bennet watched both Bingley and Darcy glance towards Jane. Jane *was* blooming that evening, and Mrs. Bennet's heart swelled with pride in her eldest daughter. How glad she was she had insisted on purchasing that blue dress, over Mr. Bennet's objections. Her heart yielded a little even in Mr. Darcy's direction at this notice of Jane. Of course, Jane was the prettiest young lady in Meryton!

"Oh! She is the most beautiful creature I ever beheld!" said Mr. Bingley, words that Mrs. Bennet treasured even more than Mr. Darcy's words, even more than the lines that poet had written on Jane's behalf years before. Mrs. Bennet smiled at Elizabeth, who had also heard the compliments, and who was always delighted when Jane was praised.

Mr. Bingley continued, and his words were such that they attracted even more interest from Mrs. Bennet and Miss Elizabeth Bennet. "But there is one of her sisters sitting down just behind you, who is very pretty, and I dare say, very agreeable. Do let me ask my partner to introduce you."

Mrs. Bennet was ready to forgive Mr. Darcy anything if he asked Elizabeth to dance with him. His opinion of the assembly could be excused by the high probability that he was accustomed to the most richly appointed rooms in England.

"Which do you mean?" asked Mr. Darcy. He followed Mr. Bingley's gesture and looked at Elizabeth. Mrs. Bennet was glad that Elizabeth returned the gaze.

Mr. Darcy, instead of telling Mr. Bingley to arrange the introduction to Mrs. Bennet's second daughter, spoke other words to his friend: "She is tolerable, but not handsome enough to tempt *me*; I am in no humor at present to give consequence to young ladies who are slighted by other men. You had better return to your partner and enjoy her smiles, for you are wasting your time with me."

Mrs. Bennet was furious, and even Elizabeth opened her eyes wide with shock at the insult. "Excuse me, Mamma," she said in a clear voice, "I wish to go to another part of the room."

"Of course, my dear," said Mrs. Bennet, at that moment prepared to support her daughter with whatever she needed.

Elizabeth, however, proved the resilience of her character. Instead of reddening from embarrassment or wilting with shame, she rose, walked deliberately past Mr. Darcy to Charlotte Lucas, and soon the two were laughing together. Mrs. Bennet watched as Mr. Darcy's gaze followed

Elizabeth; did he realize his rude words had been overheard? She hoped so; he ought to be heartily ashamed of himself! But Mrs. Bennet was certain Mr. Darcy was incapable of shame!

Angry though she was, with five daughters to supervise, Mrs. Bennet could not spend her time scowling at Mr. Darcy, and the rest of the evening gave her much pleasure. Lydia and Kitty always had partners, brightening the room; Jane was invited to the floor a second time by Mr. Bingley, who afterwards danced with Elizabeth, compensating a little for his friend's dreadful insult. Mary was gratified by overhearing herself described to Miss Bingley as the most accomplished young lady in the neighborhood.

As for Mr. Darcy, he only danced twice – once with Miss Bingley and once with Mrs. Hurst – and his general disdain made him unpopular throughout the room. He stood there in a stupid manner, giving no pleasure to anyone, but taking none, either.

At the usual time, the assembly ended. Mrs. Bennet and her daughters crammed into the carriage, which then carried them home.

Mrs. Bennet's Advice

Fetching a cup of coffee and returning to the sofa, I told Mrs. Bennet I enjoyed experiencing the assembly from her point of view. I was not sure, however, what I was supposed to learn from it.

"My dear Young Lady, there is so much! Do you not see? Jane's blue dress helped her catch Mr. Bingley's attention. Which brings me to something I have been meaning to discuss with you: you should take more care with your appearance. Now, I understand fashion has changed over time – you are wearing long breeches, as if you were a man, but ladies seem to do many things these days that were once reserved for only the male sex."

I interrupted to say, "Pants. In my part of the world, they're called pants, and they're both practical and comfortable."

"I will not quarrel with current fashion. But your outfit is dirty and your hair—"

I protested that I was meeting with her in the morning, before I had the chance to shower or dress. "Besides, many say that looks don't matter."

"Looks don't matter? Unless the natures of men and women have changed completely over the last two centuries, that is complete nonsense! Bingley never would have noticed Jane if she were not so pretty. But Jane is settled; *you* are the problem. You will feel better about yourself if you make an effort, and others will show you more respect. When was the last time you did your hair properly? And when was the last time you bought yourself anything new?"

I explained we were in the middle of a pandemic, so getting my hair done by a professional had been out of the question for months and shopping was also difficult. Still, a glance at a mirror proved she had a point. And I remembered how an ad on the internet for brightly colored shirts had caught my attention.

"My dear Young Lady, if you can afford something new, get it; if you cannot, do better with what you have. My advice to you is this: Take care with your appearance. Perhaps looks *should* not matter, but they do. Now, shall we continue?"

"After I dress," I told her.

CHAPTER 7

When Mrs. Bennet and her daughters returned to Longbourn House, they were greeted by Mr. Bennet. Mr. Bennet had several reasons for staying up on this occasion. First, he greatly enjoyed the quiet evening, as he was able to read in the comfortable warmth of the drawing-room, instead of being forced to hide in the chill of his library; second, he was genuinely curious how the ladies in his family would react to the dance in Meryton. He rather expected them to be disappointed, mostly because he did not see how any event, so greatly anticipated, could live up to their hopes.

Mrs. Bennet, however, was satisfied with the assembly, and reported on the agreeableness of Mr. Bingley, Mr. Bingley's choice in partners, and tried to tell Mr. Bennet about the elegant fashion she had observed on Mr. Bingley's sisters. Mr. Bennet protested, and Mrs. Bennet ended up describing Mr. Darcy's shocking rudeness.

Mr. Bennet, as he had not been in attendance, and because he refused to discuss certain topics, could not satisfy Mrs. Bennet's need to examine the evening. Even though she was watchful, Mrs. Bennet could not know everything. A thorough review required other female observers; fortunately, on the following day, the Lucases walked over from Lucas Lodge for a mostly feminine chat.

Mrs. Bennet wanted every detail available on the newcomers, especially the single men. She opened the subject by addressing Miss Lucas. "*You* began the evening well, Charlotte. *You* were Mr. Bingley's first choice."

"Yes, but he seemed to like his second better," replied Charlotte, smiling.

The words were music to Mrs. Bennet's ears. "Oh! you mean Jane, I suppose, because he danced with her twice. To be sure that *did* seem as if he admired her — indeed I rather believe he *did* — I heard something about it — but I hardly know what — something about Mr. Robinson?"

Charlotte obliged by recounting what she had heard. "Perhaps you mean what I overheard between him and Mr. Robinson; did not I mention it to you? Mr. Robinson's asking him how he liked our Meryton assemblies, and whether he did not think there were a great many pretty women in the room, and *which* he thought the prettiest? and his answering immediately to the last question: 'Oh! the eldest Miss Bennet, beyond a doubt; there cannot be two opinions on that point.'"

"Upon my word! Well, that is very decided indeed — that does seem as if — but, however, it may all come to nothing, you know." Mrs. Bennet was trying hard to be reasonable; Mr. Bingley and Jane had only met for the first time the evening before. Still, she had not heard anything so pleasant in years, not perhaps since Mr. Bennet had proposed. Also, Mr. Bingley's income was more than twice as large as Mr. Bennet's and Mr. Bingley's estate was not entailed, as far as Mrs. Bennet knew. If Mrs. Bennet could catch Mr. Bingley for Jane, the future of Jane and her sisters would be secure.

The conversation then moved to the neighborhood's other new single gentleman, Mr. Darcy. He was a much less pleasant topic. "*My* overhearings were more to the purpose than *yours*, Eliza," said Charlotte. "Mr. Darcy is not so well worth listening to as his friend, is he? — poor Eliza! — to be only just *tolerable*."

Mrs. Bennet defended and supported her second daughter. "I beg you would not put it into Lizzy's head to be vexed by his ill-treatment, for he is *such* a disagreeable man, that it would be quite a misfortune to be liked by him. Mrs. Long told me last night that he sat close to her for half-an-hour without once opening his lips."

"Are you quite sure, ma'am? — is not there a little mistake?" asked Jane. She added she had seen Mr. Darcy speaking with Mrs. Long.

"Aye — because she asked him at last how he liked Netherfield, and he could not help answering her; but she said he seemed quite angry at being spoke to."

Jane, dear, sweet Jane, was ready to excuse anyone, even Mr. Darcy. "Miss Bingley told me," she said, "that he never speaks much, unless among his intimate acquaintances. With *them* he is remarkably agreeable."

Mrs. Bennet had trouble believing it; Mr. Darcy had refused to dance with Elizabeth and had declined to speak with Mrs. Long. Was that being agreeable?

"I do not mind his not talking to Mrs. Long," said Charlotte, "but I wish he had danced with Eliza."

"Another time, Lizzy," said Mrs. Bennet, "I would not dance with *him*, if I were you."

"I believe, ma'am, I may safely promise you *never* to dance with him," said Elizabeth.

And Mrs. Bennet knew, that even though Elizabeth had been brave the previous evening, Mr. Darcy's words had injured her deeply. Her maternal heart swelled with indignation on behalf of her daughter, and her anger towards Mr. Darcy increased. For several minutes Mrs. Bennet lost the thread of the conversation, only half-attending as Mary moralized about pride.

"If I were as rich as Mr. Darcy," cried a young Lucas, who came with his sisters, "I should not care how proud I was. I would keep a pack of foxhounds and drink a bottle of wine a day."

Mrs. Bennet, still angry with Mr. Darcy on her daughter's behalf, vented her feelings on the young Lucas. "Then you would drink a great deal more than you ought," she said, "and if I were to see you at it, I should take away your bottle directly."

Mrs. Bennet's Advice

We were in my office. "Your appearance is much improved," remarked Mrs. Bennet.

"Thanks," I said. I was dressed, my hair washed and pinned up, and I had put on make-up, even though no other human being was likely to see me that day.

"Looking good takes practice," she told me. "It is better to practice when others cannot see you. Did you order those new clothes?"

I told her I had not yet gotten around to it.

"They will not come until you order them," she said.

She was correct, so together we ordered me a new, brightly colored blouse. She tried to get me to order more than one, but as I was not sure how well it would fit, I refused to increase my order.

"Now, of course, you need to be able to wear it," she said. "What about arranging for a visit from your local apothecary?"

For a moment I did not understand her, then I realized what she meant. I told her I had an appointment for my first vaccination the next day.

Mrs. Bennet praised me, and then I said I wanted to return to the last scene. I remarked on how she had spoken of Mr. Darcy.

"Oh!" cried Mrs. Bennet, coloring at the recollection. "Not handsome enough to tempt him! After all this time, those words still anger me."

"We know Mr. Darcy eventually changes his mind."

"But why is he so rude in the first place? There is no excuse! Although Lizzy tried to laugh it off, his words wounded her deeply. And that is my lesson for you. You should make an effort to understand how those who are dear to you are feeling. You should be ready to defend them, especially when they will not defend themselves."

I contemplated this piece of advice. Mrs. Bennet was no impartial observer – and her bias could lead to mistakes of judgment – but I was in awe of her fierce love for her children.

"Let's continue," I said.

MRS. BENNET'S ADVICE TO YOUNG LADIES

CHAPTER 8

After the introductions at the assembly room, Mrs. Bennet pried the horses from the farm, where they were usually wanted, and had them harnessed to the carriage, so she and her daughters could call at Netherfield. Because the others were shy, at first Mrs. Bennet did much of the talking, but later she could let the others take over. With pleasure she saw how Jane was favored by Miss Bingley and Mrs. Hurst, but best of all were Mr. Bingley's attentions to her eldest daughter.

Netherfield, however, was not the only source of potential suitors. When Kitty and Lydia returned from calling on their aunt and uncle Phillips in Meryton, they reported the War Office was sending a regiment to the area, and that its headquarters would be Meryton.

"That is good news, indeed!" exclaimed Mrs. Bennet, thinking of all the single men who would be moving to the area. She was already counting on Jane becoming mistress of Netherfield, but her four other daughters also required husbands. She resolved to check the backgrounds of the officers, and she hoped no conflicts would force the regiment to depart suddenly.

"My uncle Phillips reports this will be good for the local businesses," reported Kitty.

"And my aunt Phillips says they will stay at least through the winter," said Lydia.

Mrs. Bennet's mind raced through possibilities: balls, dinners, cards and games, all leading to intimate chats before fireplaces, with proposals taking place while she sat in a chair at a distance, listening discreetly while she pretended not to hear the laughter, the jokes, and the passionate declarations of love. The young man would then turn to her – no, he would first go to Mr. Bennet, to ask for permission – and then Mrs. Bennet decided that, as long as this event was taking place solely in her imagination, she would arrange every detail to her liking. The young man, so handsome in a red coat – with a striking similarity to Lieutenant Higbee from her youth, only a little taller, and with better teeth – would turn first to *her* and ask for her permission. "Mrs. Bennet, my devotion to your daughter cannot be repressed! I thank you with all my heart for raising such an illustrious jewel! I must beg you for your blessing on my union with" – and then Mrs. Bennet's reveries had a little problem, because she was undecided which daughter, exactly, she should give the most important role in this flight of fancy. Lydia was usually her favorite, but Lydia was only fifteen, and if Lydia married an officer, she might leave Meryton forever!

Kitty's voice brought Mrs. Bennet back to reality. "As there are no hostilities at present, my uncle hopes the regiment's stay will be uninterrupted."

Mrs. Bennet, remembering the disappointment she had experienced when Colonel Miller and his soldiers were called away, said she was glad to hear it. "Ah, my dear girls! What an agreeable winter we will have! There is nothing like a handsome young man in uniform."

Mr. Bennet, who had entered the room in order to fetch a cup of tea, overheard her remark. "My dear, would you prefer to be with an army man?"

"What? No, Mr. Bennet, I am content as your wife and the mistress of Longbourn. I adore Hertfordshire and the country" – and although the statement was not a lie, it was not the complete truth, for Mrs. Bennet preferred the bustle of London – "and I would not give up all this for the world! However, the neighborhood does not contain many estates with eligible young men. Now the War Office is sending a regiment!"

"I hope you do not expect me to visit them," said Mr. Bennet. Their increase in social engagements, arranged by Mrs. Bennet so that Mr. Bingley and Jane might meet frequently, was exhausting for the master of Longbourn.

"Ah, Mr. Bennet, if you only would! But no matter; my brother Phillips will manage most of that for us. Your peace will be disturbed as little as possible; you can continue thinking great thoughts in your library."

"I am glad to hear it," said Mr. Bennet, and he returned to that room with his tea.

The regiment arrived, under the command of a Colonel Forster, and the streets in Meryton were brightened by soldiers in scarlet coats. Mrs. Bennet, with designs on Mr. Bingley for Jane, told her eldest daughter to remain at home, but she encouraged her four younger daughters to become acquainted with officers. Elizabeth, who loved exercise, walked occasionally to Meryton; Mary, who preferred to study, usually stayed at Longbourn. Lydia and Kitty, however, were entranced by the officers and called on their aunt Phillips nearly every day.

"I think Colonel Forster has a secret love, Mamma," Lydia announced one morning at breakfast.

"Why do you say that?" asked Mrs. Bennet.

"He had a letter from some woman in his pocket. It was definitely the hand of a woman."

"Could it be from a sister? Or even his mother?" asked Mrs. Bennet.

"No, Mamma, because his mother died two years ago, and he only has a brother."

"Colonel Forster has a brother? Is he married? Is there any chance Mr. Forster might visit?"

"Captain Forster is married and is in the navy," reported Kitty. "He is away at sea."

"I thought the letter might be from his brother's wife, so I asked if the letter was from Mrs. Forster," said Lydia. "And Colonel Forster blushed and said, 'Not yet'."

Mrs. Bennet thought it was a pity that Colonel Forster had the inclination for matrimony but already had someone else in mind.

"We teased him to tell us her name," said Kitty, "but he refused."

"Even when we tried to buy his confession with cake," added Lydia.

And the two youngest Bennet girls burst into laughter.

Mr. Bennet, who had been helping himself to broiled mackerel from the sideboard, carried his plate back to the head of the table. "From all that I can collect by your manner of talking, you must be two of the silliest girls in the country," he remarked. "I have suspected it some time, but I am now convinced."

Mrs. Bennet defended her daughters against everyone, including their father. "I am astonished, my dear," she said, "that you should be so ready to think your own children silly. If I wished to think slightingly of anybody's children, it should not be of my own, however."

"If my children are silly, I must hope to be always sensible of it."

"Yes — but as it happens, they are all of them very clever." Mrs. Bennet beamed at her girls; Mary smiled and sat up straighter, while Elizabeth winked at Jane.

Mr. Bennet did not let the argument go. "This is the only point, I flatter myself, on which we do not agree. I had hoped that our sentiments coincided in every particular, but I must so far differ from you as to think our two youngest daughters uncommonly foolish."

Mrs. Bennet reproached her husband, but she attempted to do it with tact. "My dear Mr. Bennet, you must not expect such girls to have the sense of their father and mother. When they get to our age, I dare say they will not think about officers any more than we do. I remember the time when I liked a red coat myself very well — and, indeed, so I do still at my heart; and if a smart young colonel, with five or six thousand a year, should want one of my girls I shall not say nay to him; and I thought Colonel Forster looked very becoming the other night at Sir William's in his regimentals."

Mrs. Bennet was satisfied that she had won the argument with her husband, or at least that she had talked enough to stop him from continuing to slight their children.

She glanced out the window; clouds were forming; the weather would not permit any excursions to Meryton that day.

Mrs. Bennet's Advice

I was in my bedroom, sorting through the clothes I had worn during the last two days, my movements somewhat slow. I had had my first vaccination the day before and my left arm ached.

MRS. BENNET'S ADVICE TO YOUNG LADIES

As I was still contemplating the last scene, Mrs. Bennet was with me. "You praised your daughters when their father would not."

"Yes! I *always* did that. I thought it was important, but as it happens, it was what I truly felt and believed. Do you not agree that a mother must always praise her children?"

I hesitated to offer an opinion. I was not a mother, at least not in the sense of having raised children since their births. I was the second wife to my second husband, a widower whose children had been young adults when I met them. I loved them dearly, but I was not sure my experience was sufficient to tell mothers what to do.

I sniffed a shirt and decided it was not ready for the hamper.

"At least you admit your limits," said Mrs. Bennet, who hovered nearby as I hung the shirt in my closet.

I shook out a pair of jeans, and then folded them as neatly as I could. "I believe parents should support their children. But if a kid has a real problem that needs attention, I don't think parents should ignore it."

"Of course not, my dear Young Lady! If a child is doing something wrong, you should correct that child. You cannot think I give my daughters free rein."

I gathered my socks and carried them to the hamper. True, Mrs. Bennet *did* occasionally criticize her daughters. She had actual disputes with Elizabeth; in fact, later in the story Mrs. Bennet would be quite angry with her. Mrs. Bennet also reproached Kitty for coughing. I might disagree with Mrs. Bennet's judgment – for example, I suspected poor Kitty had allergies, and could not control her coughs – but Mrs. Bennet did not leave her girls completely unchecked.

"I expect it's difficult, even for parents, always to know what's best," I said. "If it were easy, all children would grow into successful, well-adjusted adults."

"True," said Mrs. Bennet. "When you remember that, you can see that my girls have done very well. And one reason they have done so well is because I did my best to make sure their spirits were not oppressed by set-downs from their father – or anyone else."

I returned to the bedroom, straightening the covers and fluffing the pillows. I had never been a mother to small children, but as someone who had had authority over many employees, I had learned to be careful with criticism. My words had more power than I expected, and if uttered carelessly, could hurt far more than I intended.

"Exactly so! Why do so many people in authority not understand that?"

Some people wanted to be cruel, I thought, but that was another matter. I picked up a sock I had dropped. "Mr. Bennet obviously does not think you always make the right choices with your daughters."

"Are two parents ever in complete agreement?" retorted Mrs. Bennet.

"Besides, if Mr. Bennet wants more influence, no one is stopping him."

I shook my head as I dropped the stray sock into the hamper. Mrs. Bennet was stopping him, and she was formidable.

Mrs. Bennet was rather pleased at the idea that she intimidated Mr. Bennet.

"What is the lesson I should take from the scene above?" I asked, as I returned to my little office to continue our project.

Mrs. Bennet said, "Raising children is complicated, but praise yours when you can."

I wrote that down, and then turned back to the story. I warned her I might be a little slow as I would be typing one handed. "Where were we?"

"Still at breakfast," she said.

CHAPTER 9

Mrs. Bennet was listening to Lydia's chatter about the regiment, enjoying the animation of her youngest daughter while recalling her dances, in her own youth, with Lieutenants Higbee and Hodges. Despite her memories, she attended to the details of the current set of officers, always with the goal of discovering if any of them could be turned into husbands for her daughters.

Then, even better, the Longbourn footman entered with a note that he handed ceremoniously to Miss Bennet.

"Who sent it, Sam?" inquired Mrs. Bennet.

"It comes from Netherfield, mum," answered Sam. "Delivered by a servant; he waits for an answer."

Netherfield! Mrs. Bennet's eyes sparkled as she imagined its being a proposal from Mr. Bingley. But that was a result of her reverie about the officers, and prudently she asked, "Well, Jane, who is it from? What is it about? What does he say? Well, Jane, make haste and tell us; make haste, my love!"

"It is from Miss Bingley," said Jane, and then read it aloud.

"My dear friend, if you are not so compassionate as to dine today with Louisa and me, we shall be in danger of hating each other for the rest of our lives, for a whole day's *tête-à-tête* between two women can never end without a quarrel. Come as soon as you can on receipt of this. My brother and the gentlemen are to dine with the officers."

Lydia remarked on the visit to the officers, but Mrs. Bennet was concerned about the lack of Mr. Bingley. "Dining out," said Mrs. Bennet, frowning, "that is very unlucky."

"Can I have the carriage?" asked Jane.

Mrs. Bennet glanced again out the window. "No, my dear, you had better go on horseback, because it seems likely to rain; and then you must stay all night."

"That would be a good scheme," said Elizabeth, "if you were sure that they would not offer to send her home."

Mrs. Bennet, with her quick mind, had already considered this. "Oh! but the gentlemen will have Mr. Bingley's chaise to go to Meryton, and the Hursts have no horses to theirs."

Jane said she would prefer the coach, but Mrs. Bennet argued the horses were wanted in the farm. Mr. Bennet finally admitted the horses were in the farm that day, and that they could not be spared. Mrs. Bennet saw her eldest daughter depart on horseback, and she was pleased when it rained hard – and even more pleased as the rain continued to pour.

"This was a lucky idea of mine," said Mrs. Bennet, happier than she had ever been with bad weather.

"Mamma, I am worried about her," said Elizabeth, standing beside Kitty at the window.

"She may be wet through," remarked Kitty, pulling her shawl closer.

"Would you have Jane ride three miles to Netherfield – and another three in return – and *not* see Mr. Bingley?" asked Mrs. Bennet. "What is the point of that? Miss Bingley cannot make Jane an offer of marriage."

Even at tea, when the skies were darkening, rain still fell; Jane could not return.

Mrs. Bennet's Advice

I went downstairs to the kitchen and switched on the coffee machine. "You think you were clever."

"I did not make it rain, but I used it to Jane's advantage."

"She got wet," I objected, as I placed a cup beneath the machine's spigot. Then, after I pushed the button, I added: "Your scheme would not work today." And I told her about precise weather forecasts and cars and cell phones.

"Weather never gets in the way?" asked Mrs. Bennet, and she said my generation must be very soft, if weather was never a challenge.

As I poured cream into my coffee. I told her some weather problems remained serious. We had hurricanes, tornadoes, severe cold and severe heat, droughts and floods. Also, sometimes forecasts were not accurate, despite the satellites and the monitoring stations and all the data that had been collected.

"How interesting," said Mrs. Bennet, but her tone made it clear the weather of my time was anything but interesting. "Anyway, Young Lady, sometimes you need to risk rain for love."

I put the cream back into the fridge and picked up my coffee cup.

"Let's keep going," said Mrs. Bennet.

I went back upstairs to my office.

CHAPTER 10

The following morning the Bennets were again at breakfast, this time without Jane, when another note arrived from Netherfield. This note was addressed to Elizabeth, who read the message aloud. It came from Jane, explaining she was unwell, thanks to her having been drenched during her ride the day before. She would remain at Netherfield until her health improved.

Mrs. Bennet was delighted: Jane staying at Netherfield for a few days! This would give Mr. Bingley the time he needed to fall so deeply in love that he would want to install her permanently.

"Well, my dear," said Mr. Bennet, "if your daughter should have a dangerous fit of illness — if she should die, it would be a comfort to know that it was all in pursuit of Mr. Bingley, and under your orders."

"Oh! I am not afraid of her dying. People do not die of little trifling colds. She will be taken good care of. As long as she stays there, it is all very well. I would go and see her if I could have the carriage." Mrs. Bennet thought her going would be useful, as it would let her see Jane, and advise her to complain as little as possible (not that Jane *needed* to be told that; she was not a complainer, but Mr. Bingley had to be made to appreciate the excellence of Jane's temper).

The horses, however, were engaged in the farm for the day, so going to Netherfield was not possible for the concerned mother.

Then Elizabeth announced *her* intention to go, to see how Jane was. As she was no horsewoman – besides, the horse Jane had ridden was at Netherfield – she planned to walk.

Mrs. Bennet glanced out the window. The skies were clear, so Elizabeth did not risk getting rained upon, but the ground was full of puddles and mud. "How can you be so silly as to think of such a thing, in all this dirt? You will not be fit to be seen when you get there."

"I shall be very fit to see Jane — which is all I want."

Mrs. Bennet's favorite daughter was usually Lydia – Mrs. Bennet often shifted her favorite, giving each girl attention as required – but Mr. Bennet's preference was decidedly Elizabeth (and not, to Mrs. Bennet's surprise, the bookish Mary). Mr. Bennet would not recall the horses in order for his wife to take the carriage, but he offered to recall them for Elizabeth.

Elizabeth maintained the distance was only three miles, nothing to her – she was an excellent walker – and her father could keep the horses at the farm.

Mrs. Bennet thought Elizabeth's plan to walk to Netherfield was a waste of time, as it was home to only two single gentlemen. Mr. Bingley belonged to Jane, and Mr. Darcy had already announced an aversion to Elizabeth.

However, Mrs. Bennet always supported the affection between her two oldest daughters. Besides, if Mrs. Bennet could not go herself, she wanted someone else to report on Jane's health, spirits, and situation. So, although Mrs. Bennet objected, she did not strongly oppose Elizabeth's resolution.

Mrs. Bennet watched Elizabeth set off, with Kitty and Lydia, who were planning to accompany her the first mile, as far as Meryton. Mrs. Bennet was left with only one daughter at home, Mary. She encouraged that daughter to practice the pianoforte, then enjoyed a visit with Lady Lucas, who called with her daughter Maria. Kitty and Lydia returned, but the mother kept watching for Elizabeth.

As the clock struck four, the chaise from Netherfield arrived. Mrs. Bennet expected it to bring Jane and Elizabeth, or at least Elizabeth, but the vehicle contained neither Miss Bennet. Instead, it carried a servant bringing a note from Elizabeth, explaining she planned to stay at Netherfield for a few days to nurse Jane. Would Mrs. Bennet please arrange for some clothes?

Mrs. Bennet, reading the note, sprang into action. Fortunately, she knew the contents of her daughters' wardrobes better than they did themselves. With the assistance of Hill, calling out orders to her three youngest daughters, outfits were quickly chosen and packed, with Mrs. Bennet being aware that Jane was ill and required something pretty to sleep in, while Elizabeth had walked three miles in mud and would need a clean pair of shoes, stockings and a petticoat. During this time Mrs. Bennet kept an eye on the clock, because the attire had to reach Netherfield in sufficient time for Elizabeth to make an elegant appearance at dinner.

Soon all was put together, placed in the Netherfield carriage, which turned around and went on its way.

Mrs. Bennet's Advice

I was cleaning surfaces in the kitchen; Mrs. Bennet hovered close by.

"I admit, I never thought about the clothes that were sent to Netherfield," I said as I sprayed the surface of the fridge.

"Of course, you did not," said Mrs. Bennet. "Nor, I expect, did Miss Jane Austen, but I had to act quickly."

I scrubbed a stubborn spot on the handle. "I don't think most authors would give it much thought. They just expect it to happen."

"Aye, just like so many authors – and so many people – a wave of a hand, the penning of half a sentence, without any consideration of all the trouble! Everything taken for granted! Unless, of course, something goes wrong, at which point there are complaints, but never any thanks for when things go well. Imagine if anyone else had been asked to do this; imagine, for example, if I had been visiting my sister when Lizzy's note arrived?

MRS. BENNET'S ADVICE TO YOUNG LADIES

What if the task had been left to Mr. Bennet? My dear husband would have left out Jane's dressing-gown, and he certainly would have forgotten Lizzy had been wading through mud. He would not have thought of the outfit she needed to wear at dinner and the more casual dress for the morning. These things are just expected to happen without anyone giving them mind!"

"Weren't tasks like this often left to servants?" I asked, as I pulled appliances forward so I could wash behind them. "Although servants are people, too, and so the work would fall to someone."

"Of course, in a wealthier household, if my girls had their own maids, servants would have taken care of the problem," said Mrs. Bennet. "But this had to be executed so quickly! And I had to make sure it was done right, and that my daughters had what they needed. Netherfield was so important."

"So, what should I learn from this?" I said, as I looked around the kitchen with satisfaction.

"Oh! Be ready to act quickly when your children – or your friends – need something." Then Mrs. Bennet added, "And give thanks to those who assist you! Miss Jane Austen never acknowledged it!"

CHAPTER 11

Although only three Miss Bennets were at Longbourn House that evening, its drawing-room was not any quieter. Lydia had much to relate about the officers – including praise Mr. Bingley had made of Jane while dining with them – and then Mary asked her parents to listen to a concerto she was learning.

"No one can dance to that, Mary," Lydia complained.

"Will you play something else?" asked Kitty.

Mary obliged and the two youngest practiced their steps, bowing to each other and walking up and down the room.

Mrs. Bennet was concerned about Elizabeth's being at Netherfield. Elizabeth was pretty, elegant and very fond of Jane, but Mr. Darcy did not like her. What if that dislike influenced his friend? Alas, Mrs. Bennet could do nothing about the situation that evening.

The next day, however, another note arrived from Netherfield, in which Elizabeth asked Mrs. Bennet to come and judge Jane for herself. This request was enough for Mr. Bennet to finally let his wife have the carriage for the morning.

Mary wished to stay home in order to practice the difficult passages of the concerto, but Mrs. Bennet persuaded her two youngest daughters to join her instead of going to Meryton to call on the wife of an officer. "It seems as if the whole family is moving to Netherfield," remarked Mr. Bennet, stepping out into the sunshine as the horses pulled the Bennet carriage up the drive.

Mrs. Bennet chatted eagerly with her younger daughters until the carriage approached their destination. From the carriage, her view was limited, but what she could see of the estate pleased her: some dilapidated fencing had finally been repaired and some overgrown shrubbery had been pruned back. She supposed as Mr. Bingley was only a tenant and not the owner, the improvements he could make were limited. But Jane, even as a tenant mistress, would manage to make it truly elegant.

Mrs. Bennet was informed Mr. Bingley and his friends were still at breakfast, but they were not her first object. She asked to be taken directly to her invalid daughter. Trailed by Lydia and Kitty – whom she hushed, because their noise might disturb the inhabitants of Netherfield as well as poor Jane – she entered her eldest daughter's sickroom.

Jane gave a weak smile at the appearance of her mother and even Elizabeth expressed relief. Mrs. Bennet asked several questions; while Elizabeth and Jane were making their report, Mr. Jones, the apothecary, arrived, which was useful as the information did not need to be repeated twice. Jane had been especially miserable the previous evening, but she had slept deeply the second half of the night and was feeling a little better.

"I should so like to go home with you, Mamma," she said. "You have the carriage, do you not?"

"Dear Jane! I know it is more pleasant to be at home when you are ill, but the ride could bring back the symptoms you felt just last night."

"Miss Bennet, I must agree with your mother," said Mr. Jones. "Your health will be safer if you remain here."

Jane attempted to convince the apothecary, but he and her mother were firm. Mrs. Bennet, who put more stock in her own opinions than in the apothecary's – *she* was familiar with the progress of Jane's colds, and she was certain her daughter was already on the mend – nevertheless welcomed his words, as they conveniently supported her own plans. Jane, ill in her room, had not even seen Mr. Bingley yet; but Mr. Jones's opinion would give them the chance to interact.

The apothecary gave Jane a draught and then departed, leaving Mrs. Bennet, Elizabeth, Kitty and Lydia alone with Jane.

Mrs. Bennet scolded Elizabeth a little for the state of Jane's hair, and then instructed Kitty and Lydia to comb out the knots. The younger girls set about the task, while Mrs. Bennet moistened a cloth and wiped her daughter's face and arms with it. "That will make you feel better," she said, and indeed, with the ministrations under Mrs. Bennet's guidance, Jane's appearance improved substantially.

"Mamma, please allow me to come home," repeated Jane. "I am certain I am well enough for the journey."

"Nonsense. You heard Mr. Jones, did you not? He thinks your removal would be too dangerous."

"I do not like being a burden on my friends."

"Sweet Jane! As if *you* could be a burden on anyone. Besides, how terrible do you think they would feel if you overtaxed your strength by returning to Longbourn and you became seriously ill?"

A servant knocked on the door, inviting Mrs. Bennet and her daughters to join the Netherfield party in the breakfast-parlor. Mrs. Bennet thought the Bingley household kept rather late hours, but Mr. Bingley, as just a tenant, did not have the same responsibilities as Mr. Bennet.

Mrs. Bennet, confident Jane would make a complete recovery, told her eldest daughter to get some rest, and, with Kitty and Lydia in tow, followed Elizabeth to the Netherfield breakfast-parlor.

Mr. Bingley's friends and family stared at the invasion of so many Bennets, but Mr. Bingley greeted them warmly and asked Mrs. Bennet if her daughter were better or worse than she had anticipated.

Mrs. Bennet, who had already considered her answer, said she had found her eldest daughter to be in worse health than expected, and then continued: "She is a great deal too ill to be moved. Mr. Jones says we must not think of moving her. We must trespass a little longer on your kindness." How grateful she was to the apothecary for having reached the conclusion she desired!

"Removed!" cried Bingley. "It must not be thought of. My sister, I am sure, will not hear of her removal."

Up to this point Miss Bingley had been silent, but called by her brother to speak, assured Mrs. Bennet that Miss Bennet would receive every possible attention.

Mrs. Bennet thanked the Bingleys profusely. "If it was not for such good friends, I do not know what would become of her, for she is very ill indeed!" Then, thinking this might be sketching too unattractive a portrait of her daughter, Mrs. Bennet continued: "She suffers a great deal, though with the greatest patience in the world, which is always the way with her, for she has, without exception, the sweetest temper I have ever met with. I often tell my other girls they are nothing to *her*."

Three other Miss Bennets were in the room, but they neither affirmed nor contradicted their mother.

Mrs. Bennet thought she had said enough, for the moment, about Jane. As no one else was speaking, she introduced another topic herself. "You have a sweet room here, Mr. Bingley, and a charming prospect over the gravel walk. I do not know a place in the country that is equal to Netherfield. You will not think of quitting it in a hurry, I hope, though you have but a short lease?" Mrs. Bennet knew the lease was long enough for Mr. Bingley to make an offer, if he were so inclined, but she also wanted to know how long she could count on her eldest daughter remaining in the neighborhood if Jane became Mrs. Bingley.

"Whatever I do is done in a hurry," said the young gentleman, "therefore if I should resolve to quit Netherfield, I should probably be off in five minutes. At present, however, I consider myself as quite fixed here."

Elizabeth joined the conversation. "That is exactly what I should have supposed of you," she observed.

"You begin to comprehend me, do you?" asked Mr. Bingley.

To Mrs. Bennet's horror, Elizabeth continued in this vein. "Oh! yes – I understand you perfectly."

Mr. Bingley was clearly disappointed. "I wish I might take this for a compliment; but to be so easily seen through I am afraid is pitiful."

"That is as it happens. It does not follow that a deep, intricate character is more or less estimable than such a one as yours."

Even though Mrs. Bennet did not like to scold any of her daughters in public, she felt she *had* to restrain Elizabeth from saying anything more that would injure Jane's prospects. Elizabeth did not need to put forward her fancies, and besides, her penetration of Mr. Bingley could be as inaccurate as it was offensive. "Lizzy," warned Mrs. Bennet, "remember where you are, and do not run on in the wild manner that you are suffered to do at home."

Fortunately, the conversation shifted into the less personal, with an exchange between Bingley and Elizabeth about the study of character. Then Mr. Darcy, who had been silent until that moment, offered the following: "The country can in general supply but a few subjects for such a study. In a country neighborhood you move in a very confined and unvarying society."

"But people themselves alter so much, that there is something new to be observed in them forever."

"Yes, indeed," cried Mrs. Bennet, whose goal was to persuade Mr. Bingley to remain in the country as long as possible. "I assure you there is quite as much of *that* going on in the country as in town. I cannot see that London has any great advantage over the country, for my part, except the shops and public places. The country is a vast deal pleasanter, is it not, Mr. Bingley?"

Mr. Bingley smiled at her. "When I am in the country, I never wish to leave it; and when I am in town it is pretty much the same. They have each their advantages, and I can be equally happy in either."

Mrs. Bennet was delighted to hear that Mr. Bingley could be happy in the country. "Aye – that is because you have the right disposition. But that gentleman," and she glanced at Mr. Darcy, "seemed to think the country was nothing at all."

"Indeed, Mamma, you are mistaken," said Elizabeth. "You quite mistook Mr. Darcy. He only meant that there was not such a variety of people to be met with in the country as in the town, which you must acknowledge to be true."

"Certainly, my dear, nobody said there were, but as to not meeting with many people in this neighborhood, I believe there are few neighborhoods larger. I know we dine with four-and-twenty families." With that, Mrs. Bennet was convinced that she had made the argument that the area around Meryton would offer Mr. Bingley sufficient society.

Elizabeth asked if Charlotte had called at Longbourn since her coming away.

Mrs. Bennet said she had, and then spoke of Charlotte's father. "What an agreeable man Sir William is, Mr. Bingley, is not he? So much the man of fashion! So genteel and easy! He has always something to say to everybody. *That* is my idea of good breeding; and those persons who fancy themselves very important, and never open their mouths, quite mistake the matter." The criticism was aimed chiefly at Mr. Darcy, but it could apply just as well to Miss Bingley and to Mr. and Mrs. Hurst.

The conversation continued a while on the subjects of Charlotte, cooking and poetry. Elizabeth's notion about the penning of a sonnet causing a man to fall out of love was such fanciful nonsense that Mrs. Bennet decided she had better depart or she would be tempted to scold Elizabeth again. She thanked Mr. Bingley again for taking care of Jane, and especially apologizing for burdening him with Elizabeth, who, at the time, Mrs. Bennet felt, was a burden. She then ordered her carriage. At this, Lydia, who had been uncharacteristically silent all this time, asked Mr. Bingley if he would keep to his word and hold a ball at Netherfield.

Mr. Bingley's reply was the most satisfactory utterance Mrs. Bennet could imagine. "I am perfectly ready, I assure you, to keep my engagement; and when your sister is recovered, you shall, if you please, name the very day of the ball. But you would not wish to be dancing when she is ill."

Lydia agreed they could wait until Jane was better.

Mrs. Bennet was informed the carriage was ready, and she and her two youngest daughters departed.

"Netherfield is so pleasant," said Mrs. Bennet, glancing at the fine house through the carriage window. "I am sure we will come here often."

Mrs. Bennet's Advice

Although it was still officially winter, the day was sunny and warm, so I was pacing behind my house, walking there so as to avoid others while the disease ran rampant in my part of the world. Mrs. Bennet, although no fan of exercise, joined me, and we discussed the last scene.

"Although Elizabeth does not always agree with you, she still turned to you to get your opinion with respect to Jane's condition."

"Of course! What could be more natural? I am Jane and Lizzy's *mother*. And before I arrived, I *was* a little anxious. I had nursed Jane through many colds before, and it sounded like one of those, but you never know, do you? But the moment I saw her, I relaxed. She had already survived the worst of it. I could give Jane the reassurances, the comfort, that only a mother can give."

I stopped to pull a few weeds out of a flower box. "Would Jane's illness have gotten worse if she had ridden back to Longbourn with you in the carriage?"

Mrs. Bennet shrugged. "Who knows? That is what Mr. Jones said, and it was better to be safe than sorry."

I had brought a copy of the text outside with me, because I wanted to discuss Mrs. Bennet's conversation with Mr. Bingley in the breakfast-parlor. "Have you read Jane Austen's words? After you spoke about dining with four-and-twenty families, this is what she wrote:"

MRS. BENNET'S ADVICE TO YOUNG LADIES

Nothing but concern for Elizabeth could enable Bingley to keep his countenance. His sister was less delicate, and directed her eyes towards Mr. Darcy with a very expressive smile.

"That Miss Jane Austen!" exclaimed Mrs. Bennet. "Always worried about Lizzy being embarrassed! As you know, Young Lady, I wanted Mr. Bingley to remain in the country, but Mr. Darcy was giving Mr. Bingley reasons to leave. I had to assure Mr. Bingley that Hertfordshire could provide him with any society he desired."

I understood her point of view. Her speech had not been delicate, but not everyone is capable of delicacy – and delicacy does not reach everyone. I moved to a passage in the scene in which Mrs. Bennet was talking about Sir William.

He has always something to say to everybody. That *is my idea of good breeding; and those persons who fancy themselves very important, and never open their mouths, quite mistake the matter.*

I summarized: "You were apparently praising Sir William, but in reality, you were criticizing Mr. Darcy."

"Oh! Indeed, I was. I make no apology for it."

"Elizabeth was embarrassed, and Mr. Bingley's sisters would later mock you for it." I put down the text and resumed my steps by my wall of flowers and weeds.

"Mr. Darcy needed to hear these truths! He needed to correct his behavior! And, it is not as if I was alone in my opinion. Mr. Bingley addressed Mr. Darcy about this before, when he insulted Lizzy, but Mr. Bingley's reproaches did not have the desired effect. As you know, Lizzy herself will say far more, and far more bluntly, later."

Pulling out a weed, I nodded, for I knew she was right.

Mrs. Bennet continued: "Sometimes you have to repeat yourself. We cannot expect others to change overnight, much as we would like them too. And gentlemen, especially rich gentlemen, can be very dense; they need to hear truths over and over. A lesson is more likely to be learned if it comes from different people. Mr. Darcy heard from Mr. Bingley at the assembly-room, from me in the Netherfield breakfast-parlor, and he will hear from Lizzy later."

Moving to a new patch of weeds, I observed that her remarks applied to more than rich gentlemen.

"I suppose. Now, I have something to add: it is most unfair that *I* have been mocked for more than two centuries for saying what needed to be said, while Lizzy, who will say the very same things later in the story, is given credit for being lively and outspoken! But that is all right. I do not

MRS. BENNET'S ADVICE TO YOUNG LADIES

regret my daughter getting credit; I just hope *you* give me some."

I was doing exactly that, still, I thought her outspokenness was risky: by offending Mr. Darcy, she could also harm Jane's relationship with Mr. Bingley.

"There is always a risk," admitted Mrs. Bennet, and she sighed. "My poor nerves! Miss Jane Austen delights in making me suffer!"

CHAPTER 12

The Longbourn carriage took Mrs. Bennet away from Netherfield. She had seen enough of Mr. Bingley's concern for Jane for Mrs. Bennet to be content the young gentleman was in love with her eldest daughter.

Mrs. Bennet's visit to Netherfield was made on a Thursday; on Saturday morning, a servant came from that estate, bringing a note from Elizabeth. It arrived while the Bennets were not at breakfast, which gave Mrs. Bennet a chance to read the note without anyone else asking what was in it.

Elizabeth reported Jane was considerably better – of course she was, thought Mrs. Bennet; it was only a trifling cold, but she was still happy that her eldest daughter was healthy again. Then Elizabeth continued with the request that, in view of this development, both she and Jane would appreciate the Longbourn carriage being sent to Netherfield so they could return home.

"Oh!" cried Mrs. Bennet. "What foolish girls!"

Her remark was overheard by Mr. Bennet in his library, who came out to see what she was talking about. "Foolish girls? Do you now share my opinion regarding our two youngest?"

"What? No" – and then she said aye, he might have a point, and excused herself, in order to answer Elizabeth's letter. She engaged in a little deception, for she did not want her husband to realize a note had arrived from Netherfield. Mr. Bennet missed his two eldest daughters, whose conversation he preferred to the others'; if he were to see the note, he might send the carriage to fetch them.

Fortunately for Mrs. Bennet, Mr. Bennet was insufficiently curious to follow her as she went to a desk, dipped a pen in ink, and replied to her daughter in a firm hand that the Longbourn carriage was not available that day, and that she could not guarantee its being available until Tuesday at the earliest. In a postscript she added that if they were invited to stay longer, she could do very well without them. Out of respect for her husband's feelings, she wrote the last bit in her name only, but Mr. Bennet, she thought, would have to become accustomed to the prospect of Jane being at Netherfield all the time. And wherever Jane went, Elizabeth would surely follow.

Mrs. Bennet handed the note to the servant, and he carried it away. For the rest of the day, she imagined Jane, and even Elizabeth, strolling through the corridors of Netherfield. What a lucky idea she had had, sending Jane to Netherfield in the rain! A few more days should do the trick.

But to Mrs. Bennet's great disappointment – although it pleased Mr.

Bennet – on Sunday, the following day, the Netherfield carriage appeared, bringing Jane and Elizabeth back to Longbourn House.

Mrs. Bennet's Advice

I woke up from a nap to find Mrs. Bennet hovering beside me. She told me to get up as we still had plenty to cover.

After making myself a coffee and reviewing the prior scene, I had a question for Mrs. Bennet. "What happened to the horse?"

"What horse?"

"The horse Jane rode over to Netherfield. As she returned to Longbourn in the Netherfield carriage, she did not ride it back."

Mrs. Bennet confessed she did not remember. It could have been ridden back by a servant; it could have been brought alongside by the Netherfield coachman when he brought the Miss Bennets home. Mrs. Bennet's domain was the house, not the stables, but she was sure the animal had returned to Longbourn House. "I was not concerned about the horse. I was concerned about my daughters. They returned too early."

I did not agree with her. Jane was well enough to survive a journey in the carriage, and her visit to Netherfield, which was supposed to last an afternoon, had already gone on for several days, and had roped in Elizabeth.

"Oh! My dear Young Lady," cried Mrs. Bennet. "Remember the object! And ask yourself if it has been achieved!" She reminded me she wanted Mr. Bingley to propose to Jane, but even though she had been under his roof since Tuesday, Mrs. Bennet was certain they could not have spent much time together. "Jane was confined to her sickroom, and Mr. Bingley would not have entered except in case of an emergency. Besides, I wanted him to see her at her prettiest, without her having a red nose or coughing."

"They did not want to impose on their friends," I argued.

"With four or five thousand a year, how could a few extra days' stay be any imposition? It is not as if Jane or Lizzy consume much in food and drink, and in that large house, they were not in the way."

"I could imagine that too much of Jane could put off Bingley."

Mrs. Bennet was even more indignant. "Nonsense! No sensible man could tire of Jane's company, and if Mr. Bingley *did* tire of her, it would be a sign he was not worthy of her. Her haste to leave made it appear as if she wanted to go, or at least, as if she did not want to stay with him."

I said nothing for a few minutes, because the novel contained other hints that Mr. Bingley was unaware of Jane's feelings for him. In chapter 6 of the *Pride & Prejudice* text, Elizabeth told Charlotte Lucas that Jane's feelings were unlikely to be perceived by others. Charlotte responded thus:

"*It may perhaps be pleasant,*" replied Charlotte, "*to be able to impose on the public in such a case; but it is sometimes a disadvantage to be so very guarded. If a woman conceals her affection with the same skill from the object of it, she may lose the opportunity of fixing him; and it will then be but poor consolation to believe the world equally in the dark. There is so much of gratitude or vanity in almost every attachment, that it is not safe to leave any to itself. We can all begin freely — a slight preference is natural enough; but there are very few of us who have heart enough to be really in love without encouragement. In nine cases out of ten a woman had better show more affection than she feels. Bingley likes your sister undoubtedly; but he may never do more than like her, if she does not help him on.*"

After I read this passage to Mrs. Bennet, she was triumphant. "Yes, exactly! If Jane had been more encouraging, she might not have experienced a twelvemonth of heartache. If Lizzy had not made Jane borrow Mr. Bingley's carriage, then they might have reached an understanding by the following Tuesday! Instead of waiting for an entire year! A year of sorrow and uncertainty!"

I pointed out this made the novel more interesting, full of suspense, but this was no consolation to Mrs. Bennet. "Making my dear Jane suffer just to make her story more interesting! How cruel!"

I did not want to argue about Jane Austen, whom, despite Mrs. Bennet's obvious resentment, I still admired. "What should I learn from this, Mrs. Bennet?"

"Oh!" she cried. "My advice is the same that I would give to Lizzy. Listen to your mother!"

I jotted down her words, and then we returned to the story.

CHAPTER 13

The day after Jane and Elizabeth returned from Netherfield was a Monday, and this time Mr. Bennet had his own announcement to make at the breakfast table. He told Mrs. Bennet that he hoped she had ordered a good dinner, because a stranger – a gentleman! – would be joining them.

Mrs. Bennet assumed it was Mr. Bingley and congratulated Jane, then realized the menu was insufficient; they had no fish. "Lydia, my love, ring the bell – I must speak to Hill this moment."

But Mr. Bennet stopped her. "It is *not* Mr. Bingley," he said. "It is a person whom I never saw in the whole course of my life."

"Oh! Mr. Bennet, who could it be?" cried Mrs. Bennet, and Kitty and Lydia named several officers their father had not yet met. Jane and Elizabeth added their speculations, and even Mary appeared interested.

Mr. Bennet finally satisfied their curiosity. The visitor had been announced by a letter, which Mr. Bennet removed from a pocket with a flourish. "It is from my cousin, Mr. Collins, who, when I am dead, may turn you all out of this house as soon as he pleases."

Mrs. Bennet had long given up getting her husband to inform her immediately with respect to events, and so she did not scold Mr. Bennet for not telling her earlier of Mr. Collins's impending visit. The name, however, elicited other emotions in the mistress of Longbourn. "Oh! my dear," cried his wife, "I cannot bear to hear that mentioned. Pray do not talk of that odious man. I do think it is the hardest thing in the world, that your estate should be entailed away from your own children; and I am sure, if I had been you, I should have tried long ago to do something or other about it."

Mrs. Bennet's reproach was unfair; Mr. Bennet had consulted more than one solicitor; none could find a way to break the entail. Mr. Bennet likewise had been disappointed with Mrs. Bennet; why had she failed to provide him with a son?

Mr. Bennet, to his credit, did not mention the lack of Bennet sons but returned to the letter. "It certainly is a most iniquitous affair," said he, "and nothing can clear Mr. Collins from the guilt of inheriting Longbourn. But if you will listen to his letter, you may perhaps be a little softened by his manner of expressing himself."

Mrs. Bennet, however, was vehemently opposed to even the idea of the man. "No, that I am sure I shall not; and I think it is very impertinent of him to write to you at all, and very hypocritical. I hate such false friends. Why could he not keep on quarreling with you, as his father did before him?"

Mr. Bennet, nevertheless, insisted on reading the letter to his wife and daughters. And despite Mrs. Bennet's prejudice, she listened carefully, for it came from a man who could, in the future, evict her and her daughters from their home, if he so chose.

As her husband had said, his young cousin's letter was politeness itself. Mrs. Bennet found the following passage especially intriguing:

As a clergyman, moreover, I feel it my duty to promote and establish the blessing of peace in all families within the reach of my influence; and on these grounds I flatter myself that my present overtures are highly commendable, and that the circumstance of my being next in the entail of Longbourn estate will be kindly overlooked on your side, and not lead you to reject the offered olive-branch. I cannot be otherwise than concerned at being the means of injuring your amiable daughters, and beg leave to apologize for it, as well as to assure you of my readiness to make them every possible amends – but of this hereafter.

Readiness to make possible amends to their amiable daughters! Mrs. Bennet was certain, from these words, that Mr. Collins's plans included choosing one of his fair cousins to be his wife.

While Mrs. Bennet enjoyed this wonderful realization, that the villain threatening their future might turn into its savior, the rest of the family commented on other aspects of the letter: Jane wondering what sort of atonement Mr. Collins could have in mind; Elizabeth finding Mr. Collins's style rather odd; and Mary admired the reference to an olive-branch. Kitty and Lydia were only interested in speaking about officers.

Mrs. Bennet was surprised the other members of her family did not see what was so obvious to her. At any rate, she noted the time of his arrival and the length of his intended stay and considered what activities they could manage during his visit to keep him amused. In the meantime, she arranged a good dinner, chose the chamber in which he would sleep, and otherwise made sure Longbourn was ready to receive him.

Mrs. Bennet's Advice

I was washing the windows, almost as if I, like Mrs. Bennet, was expecting a visitor. As it happened, I was not, but the windows were very dirty.

Mrs. Bennet joined me and remarked that it was a pity I did not have servants to do this.

I agreed with her, and then said, "I find it remarkable that only you noticed Mr. Collins hoped to marry one of your daughters. I thought his letter made his intentions quite clear."

"Sometimes my dear family is not very forward-thinking. I have always been essential to their well-being."

MRS. BENNET'S ADVICE TO YOUNG LADIES

I used a screwdriver to open the casement window so I could clean between the panes. "On the other hand, perhaps assuming that a man who had never been seen before could be coming to court one of your daughters seemed presumptuous."

"Obviously not! And even if Mr. Collins had not been coming with that in mind – if he had only been hoping to mend the breach with Mr. Bennet, his visit still would have been an opportunity. A single gentleman, perfectly eligible, especially as his marriage to one of my daughters would preserve our futures. And even though I believed that was why he had chosen to visit, I did not speak my hope aloud. See? Despite what Miss Jane Austen and her readers may think, I *am* capable of holding my tongue."

Then Mrs. Bennet wondered how so much dust – and even a cobweb! – had managed to gather between the panes, as they were normally fastened shut.

As I used a hand-held vacuum to get rid of the worst of the dirt, I told her I wondered the same thing. When the vacuuming was finished and I was spraying cleaner on the glass, I reverted to the topic of Mr. Collins. "I noticed you were ready to make him welcome."

"Why should I hold a grudge? We had never met Mr. William Collins, and hatred should not be inherited."

I laughed. "Those are pretty words, Mrs. Bennet, but that was not your opinion until you heard his letter. You thought Mr. Collins should keep quarreling with Mr. Bennet as his father had. You only changed your attitude when you thought he might court one of your daughters."

Mrs. Bennet owned I was right, but the hypocrisy did not bother her. "Remember how important it was for me to find husbands for my daughters. That was my object, and it was enough to convince me to reconsider."

At least she had changed her opinion, I thought, as I worked on a stubborn spot. I knew of many people who clung to irrational resentments, despite being given plenty of reason to change. Even I sometimes fell into this unhealthy behavior. "Is that your lesson for me?" I asked, as I started fastening the window pieces back together.

"Yes. It is a simple one, and seems straightforward enough, but not all Young Ladies can manage it. Be willing to change your opinion when offered good enough reason."

CHAPTER 14

At four in the afternoon, as expected, Mr. Bennet's long-estranged cousin arrived. Mr. Collins was about twenty-five, tall, and a little heavy. He might not be as handsome as Mr. Bingley, but many men were far more repulsive. Mrs. Bennet could tolerate him, she decided, as a son-in-law.

They all, including Mr. Bennet, were extremely curious, and welcomed the arrival into Longbourn House. Mr. Collins was all politeness. He complimented everyone and everything, words that would be dear to Mrs. Bennet's heart – unless, as the heir to the estate, he was regarding everything as the future proprietor.

Mrs. Bennet was more of a talker than Mr. Bennet, so it fell to her to conduct most of the conversation with Mr. Collins. Mr. Bennet might sit by and store up witty observations for later, but someone needed to fill the requirements of civility. She inquired about his journey and then introduced him to her daughters.

"Such lovely young ladies," said Mr. Collins, after meeting all the Miss Bennets. "Indeed, their beauty exceeds their reputation, and that is already impressive. I trust my fair cousins will find husbands to take good care of them."

Mrs. Bennet could see her daughters were discomfited by these words: Lydia gaped; Elizabeth held up her hand to hide a smile; and the eyes of the others widened. Although Mr. Collins's manner was formal, his meaning was clear to Mrs. Bennet; he wanted to know if they were available. "You are very kind, I am sure; and I wish with all my heart it may prove so, for else they will be destitute enough. Things are settled so oddly."

"You allude, perhaps, to the entail of this estate."

"Ah! sir, I do indeed. It is a grievous affair to my poor girls, you must confess. Not that I mean to find fault with *you*, for such things I know are all chance in this world. There is no knowing how estates will go when once they come to be entailed." These sentences were the most forgiving that Mrs. Bennet had ever uttered with respect to the entail; she did not want to offend Mr. Collins.

"I am very sensible, madam, of the hardship to my fair cousins, and could say much on the subject, but that I am cautious of appearing forward and precipitate. But I can assure the young ladies that I come prepared to admire them. At present I will not say more; but, perhaps, when we are better acquainted—"

They were summoned to dinner, but Mr. Collins's words were balm to Mrs. Bennet's anxious heart, and she consumed the soup and the fish with more pleasure than usual. After the servants withdrew, Mr. Bennet, who so far had left most of the speaking to Mrs. Bennet, asked about Mr. Collins's patroness, Lady Catherine de Bourgh. The young clergyman was eloquent, praising her affability and condescension, detailing his relationship with her – one Saturday she had invited him to Rosings to play quadrille! – and even describing how liberal her ladyship was with advice on every subject, from house improvements to recommending he marry, if he could find someone suitable.

Mrs. Bennet was certain Mr. Collins had journeyed to Longbourn to follow Lady Catherine's advice. "That is all very proper and civil, I am sure," Mrs. Bennet said, "and I dare say she is a very agreeable woman. It is a pity that great ladies in general are not more like her. Does she live near you, sir?"

"The garden in which stands my humble abode is separated only by a lane from Rosings Park, her ladyship's residence." Mr. Collins took great pride in his home's proximity to Lady Catherine's estate.

"I think you said she was a widow, sir? Has she any family?" Mrs. Bennet continued her inquiries, partly because the subject was so pleasing to her guest, but also because, if Mr. Collins were to marry one of her daughters, understanding the situation would be useful.

"She has only one daughter, the heiress of Rosings, and of very extensive property," replied the visitor.

"Ah!" said Mrs. Bennet, shaking her head, who would have preferred to hear that Lady Catherine had a few unmarried sons. "Then she is better off than many girls. And what sort of young lady is she? Is she handsome?"

Mr. Collins kept speaking on this favorite topic, answering questions posed to him mostly by Mr. Bennet. After tea, when they were gathered by the fireplace, Mr. Collins was invited to read aloud. He was first offered a novel – this he rejected, saying he never read novels – and selected a book of sermons, which he read loudly and solemnly. After three pages Lydia interrupted, talking about the officers, and announcing she planned to walk to Meryton on the morrow – an excursion that had been postponed because of Mr. Collins's imminent arrival.

Although Jane and Elizabeth scolded Lydia for speaking out of turn, Mr. Collins closed the book and set it down. Mrs. Bennet was horrified! Mr. Collins was a relative, a potential suitor, and the man who could turn them out of their house whenever Mr. Bennet dropped dead. She apologized profusely for Lydia and begged their guest to continue reading. However, despite Mrs. Bennet's promise that Lydia would not speak out of turn again, Mr. Collins refused to resume his reading, but instead offered to play backgammon with Mr. Bennet.

Mrs. Bennet's Advice

Clouds had come; the temperature had sunk; walking outside had become unpleasant. Instead, I took several turns about my room, which made me think of Elizabeth and Miss Bingley at Netherfield.

However, Mrs. Bennet and I were in a different part of the story. As I paced, we discussed the Bennets' first encounter with Mr. Collins.

"Jane Austen did not care for Mr. Collins," I said. "She made him a non-reader of novels."

"Of course, Miss Jane Austen preferred those who praise novels to those who insult them. Novels were her business! And I enjoy having them read to me as well. But despite this failing, Mr. Collins was not so bad. He was always polite. He was good-natured enough. He stopped reading the sermons aloud after Lydia's misbehavior. He did not judge Lydia harshly – at least not then – he recognized she was still only fifteen."

I reached the end of the room, turned, and went in the other direction. "What should we learn from this?"

"Oh! Now that I think on it, I was so impressed by Mr. Collins's description of Lady Catherine. *There* is a woman who is not afraid to tell others what to do. She is a great lady."

As the room was not large, I turned again. "You admire Lady Catherine?"

"People listen to her! Mr. Collins came to Hertfordshire, only because her ladyship told him he needed a wife!"

I pointed out that in other parts of the text, Lady Catherine's advice was not always appreciated.

"Good advice is often not appreciated," said Mrs. Bennet, and she added that hers was often rejected, even by her own daughters. "Still, the worst way to advise people is to say nothing at all."

I tried to console her. "*My* opinion is that Mr. Collins appreciated Lady Catherine's advice because he was grateful that she had given him a living. Also, he was awed by her title."

Mrs. Bennet admitted that money and rank garnered respect, and, compared with Lady Catherine, she had less wealth and no title. "But is that reason for me to be silent?"

I agreed it was not.

"To be a great lady, Young Lady, you must act like a great lady."

I decided I had crossed the living-room carpet a sufficient number of times. We returned to the story.

CHAPTER 15

Mrs. Bennet's conviction that Mr. Collins had journeyed to Longbourn to find a wife among her daughters put him solidly in her good graces. How reassuring it would be, to have one of her daughters as the future mistress of Longbourn!

However, as she lay in her bed the night after Mr. Collins's arrival, the current mistress of Longbourn contemplated what she could do to help this hoped-for event happen. First, they had to be as agreeable to Mr. Collins as they could, so that he would welcome a closer alliance with their family.

Second, there was the important question: *which* daughter should marry Mr. Collins? Lydia was too young, and Lydia had already disqualified herself by her rude outburst. Mrs. Bennet was certain Mr. Collins would not even consider Lydia.

Jane, the eldest and the loveliest, attracted the eyes of every man, and imagining her oldest daughter as eventually taking her place as mistress of Longbourn pleased Mrs. Bennet considerably. However, the notion of Jane's being mistress of Netherfield pleased Mrs. Bennet even more. After all, Mr. Bingley's income was more than twice Mr. Bennet's! Besides, Jane and Mr. Bingley were in love, and Mrs. Bennet was, whenever she could manage it, a romantic.

With the exclusion of her eldest and her youngest daughters, Elizabeth, Mary and Kitty remained available to Mr. Collins. Kitty was also young. Mrs. Bennet had no objection to Mr. Collins choosing Kitty, but it seemed unlikely, and not especially wise, as Kitty was not yet ready to supervise a household. That left Elizabeth and Mary. Mary had already expressed some admiration of Mr. Collins, but Elizabeth was much prettier, and men usually preferred pretty women. Furthermore, Elizabeth had joined Jane in rebuking Lydia's rude interruption.

The next morning, Mrs. Bennet met with Mr. Collins before breakfast and engaged him in conversation. When he expressed his hope to find a mistress for his parsonage at Longbourn, she smiled but had to direct him. "As to my *younger* daughters, I cannot say – I do not *know* of any prepossession. However, I must mention that my *eldest* daughter, dear Jane, is likely to be very soon engaged."

From his expression, Mrs. Bennet saw the hint had been necessary. She picked up a poker and used it to adjust the fire, giving her visitor a moment to adjust his plans.

"What about my fair cousin Elizabeth?" asked Mr. Collins.

"Lizzy has no prior attachments," said Mrs. Bennet.

Mrs. Bennet then excused herself and went upstairs to make sure her daughters were not experiencing any difficulties with their morning preparations. What a good day! Soon her *two* eldest daughters would be married, their futures provided for, simultaneously assuring the other girls would also be safe. Jane's match would be a true blessing in every sense: money, love, character and so close and so eligible.

Mrs. Bennet then contemplated Mr. Collins as a husband for Elizabeth. Elizabeth had shown no inclination for Mr. Collins, which caused Mrs. Bennet a little uneasiness. On the other hand, the clergyman had been with them for less than twenty-four hours, so the romance could develop later. Besides, Elizabeth, with her intelligence, seemed unlikely, in Mrs. Bennet's opinion, to fall in love with anyone.

Furthermore, Elizabeth, with her quickness, would realize the benefit of such an alliance to her family. They could remain at Longbourn House. Elizabeth might have to go to Kent for a few years, but that was not a big sacrifice for Mrs. Bennet, as Elizabeth was usually the least favorite of her daughters. Possibly *Mr.* Bennet would not be entirely happy about it; he would miss her. Nevertheless, he would likewise be consoled at the prospect of Elizabeth as Longbourn's future mistress.

Mrs. Bennet was ecstatic. She counted the days until Mr. Collins's scheduled departure. Less than two weeks remained, which was not long to conclude an engagement, but a man who had made his intentions so clear to the mother could not fail to make them clear to his object. He had traveled to Longbourn to find a bride, in part, Mrs. Bennet was sure, to please his patroness; he would not want to leave without happy news to tell her.

Within a few months, Mrs. Bennet would achieve what she had been desperate to achieve ever since realizing she would never produce a son. What had seemed so difficult, even impossible, now seemed inevitable.

Mrs. Bennet's Advice

Witnessing Mrs. Bennet's joy was difficult, as I knew how disappointed she soon would be. "As I know what will happen—" I began.

"It *could* have gone the way I expected," interrupted Mrs. Bennet. "It *should* have gone the way I expected."

"I do not know what advice you can give me, unless it is to tell me that trying to matchmake is almost impossible."

Mrs. Bennet agreed matchmaking was challenging, but far too important for her daughters to leave to chance. "This is one of the times, Young Lady, when you should learn from my failure instead of my success. When you should learn what I should have done."

"And what is that?" I inquired.

"I always believed my biggest challenge was finding suitors for my daughters. What I did not so was sufficiently impress on my daughters the necessity of accepting – or at least not refusing out of hand – any offers of marriage that came their way."

"I do not believe you would have ever convinced Elizabeth."

Mrs. Bennet acknowledged I had a point. She said that, she, too, should not have been so hasty as to settle Mr. Collins on Elizabeth without consulting her daughters' inclinations. "After speaking with Mr. Collins, I should have gone up and spoken with Lizzy, Mary and Kitty about his intentions, and determined which one of them would have found him most acceptable. If Lizzy had made her distaste clear, I would have instructed Mary on the steps she needed to take to catch him. If she had put herself forward, if she had spoken to him and listened to him, she might have done very well."

"Why did you not speak to them immediately?"

Mrs. Bennet shook her head. "I do not know. It seems like such an obvious step now. But it did not occur to me then, and it never occurs to me when I pass through that scene."

"Do you blame Jane Austen?" I asked.

"Oh! yes, I do; it is all her fault! How I wish I could take Miss Jane Austen's pen from her and rewrite that scene!"

I pitied Mrs. Bennet, because she was so frustrated, and because I knew more frustration was headed her way. However, she was the one who had insisted on this project. "Let's continue," I said.

CHAPTER 16

Mrs. Bennet was all smiles as she encouraged Mr. Collins to spend time with her daughters, particularly Elizabeth. So, when Lydia announced she was walking to Meryton, and all her sisters except for Mary chose to accompany her, Mr. Collins went as well. Mrs. Bennet told Elizabeth to pay especial attention to Mr. Collins, who, she was certain, would start his courtship in earnest.

Mrs. Bennet, as she did not go to Meryton that morning with her daughters, was not present when they met Mr. Wickham for the first time, or when Mr. Bingley and Mr. Darcy rode down the street on their horses and Mr. Bingley stopped to chat with Jane. Mrs. Bennet likewise missed the signs of deep disgust between Wickham and Darcy, indicating an old but hostile acquaintance. No, she had to elicit these details from her daughters. As Mrs. Bennet was still angry with Mr. Darcy for calling Elizabeth merely 'tolerable,' she chose – as Elizabeth did – to assume that the guilt belonged entirely to the wealthy gentleman from Derbyshire.

Mrs. Bennet stayed home the next evening as well, when the Longbourn carriage conveyed all five Miss Bennets and their cousin to Meryton for an evening with Mr. and Mrs. Phillips and various officers. Mrs. Bennet would have liked to go, but the carriage would be crowded as it was, and both Mr. and Mrs. Bennet had their reasons for insisting that Mr. Collins take advantage of the invitation. Mrs. Bennet, of course, wanted Mr. Collins to spend time with Elizabeth, while Mr. Bennet had had enough of his cousin's company and wanted Mr. Collins to be anywhere but Longbourn, if only for a few hours.

Although Mrs. Bennet did not go, the next day she learned that her sister Phillips was most impressed by Mr. Collins, who, although a wretched whist player, was most flattering in his comparison of her rooms with Rosings Park, and most amiable about the fact that he had lost repeatedly at cards. "Lizzy will do very well by him," said Mrs. Phillips, after Mrs. Bennet confided her hopes. Mrs. Bennet, at that point, had not yet seen the handsome, charming Mr. Wickham. Lydia and Kitty spoke non-stop about him, so she knew he had impressed her two youngest, but the mother was unaware the new gentleman had also captivated Elizabeth.

Just after Mrs. Phillips's departure, something wonderful happened: Mr. Bingley and his sisters called! Mrs. Bennet rushed to fetch Jane and Elizabeth from the shrubbery. She made sure Jane was as blooming as ever, smoothing her daughter's hair, pinching her cheeks to make them rosy, and then she hastily ushered her eldest daughters back in the house.

Mr. Bingley, Miss Bingley, and Mrs. Hurst had brought the most welcome news: the invitation to a ball at Netherfield! For the following

Tuesday! And instead of merely sending a note by a servant, they had called to make the request. Mrs. Bennet accepted on behalf of the family, and ripples of joy spread throughout Longbourn House. A ball at Netherfield was bound to be more sumptuous than the monthly dances at the assembly-room in Meryton: Mr. Bingley had the means to make it so, and Mrs. Hurst and Miss Bingley took pride in their elegance. All the Miss Bennets inspected their attire for dancing, from their gowns and their shoes to what they would wear in their hair; Mary speculated on the musicians Mr. Bingley would employ; and even Mr. Bennet anticipated an excellent meal.

Then, Mrs. Bennet's happiness was increased by an exchange between Elizabeth and Mr. Collins. Elizabeth asked Mr. Collins if he planned to attend the ball, and if he did, would he dare to dance, or would he think that too undignified for a clergyman? Would Lady Catherine approve?

But Mr. Collins assured Elizabeth he had no problem partaking of an amusement being given by a respectable gentleman. Then he asked Elizabeth to do him the honor of standing up with him for the first two dances.

Elizabeth, Mrs. Bennet was pleased to hear, said yes.

Mrs. Bennet's Advice

When we discussed this last passage, I was putting my breakfast, scrambled eggs with mushrooms and cheese, on the table. "At this point in the story, you were confident your two oldest daughters were on the brink of marriage."

Mrs. Bennet, too full of the emotions she had experienced during that time to remain still, followed me as I went back into the kitchen. "Indeed, I was! How could I not be? Mr. Collins's intentions were obvious: he had come to Longbourn House to select a wife from among his cousins."

"And Mr. Bingley?" I placed my coffee cup on the machine and pressed the button.

Mrs. Bennet waited for the machine's loud grinding noise to finish before she continued. "Oh! My dear Young Lady, how can you ask? Again, Mr. Bingley's hopes were as clear as day. Let us remember that call of Mr. Bingley with his sisters at Longbourn House. Instead of sending a servant with a card, they came themselves. Why? There are so many reasons! First, Mr. Bingley wanted to see Jane. Because he was in love with her, he wanted to see her all the time. Second, Mr. Bingley and his sisters, by calling on her to give the invitation, wanted to honor Jane and to make it clear they were honoring her and her family. Third, we know Mr. Bingley cared about our family because it was Lydia, not Jane, who begged Mr. Bingley to hold a ball. Fourth, Mr. Bingley did not want to go to the considerable effort of arranging a ball at Netherfield without being secure in the knowledge that

Jane would attend! He was holding the ball for *her*."

I poured cream into my coffee, stirred it, and then carried it to the dining area and sat down. As I swallowed a forkful of eggs, Mrs. Bennet, inspired by my meal said, "Unfortunately, I was counting my chickens before they hatched." She elaborated: "I had the eggs – the two suitors who wanted to propose to two of my daughters. They were necessary, but they were not enough."

"Necessary but not sufficient," I said, and I took another bite of breakfast.

"What?" she asked.

"Mathematics," I mumbled, and then added, "sorry."

"I think I understand you. At any rate, I had found two eligible suitors for my two eldest daughters. With the gentlemen, there were no problems. I should have looked for problems elsewhere."

"Even with Mr. Bingley and Jane?"

Mrs. Bennet spoke while I ate. "Not *between* Mr. Bingley and Jane. Those two were so happy together, whenever they met! I later learned his sisters, even though they were fond of Jane – who could not be fond of Jane? – were not keen on the match. I suppose she was not rich enough for them – each of them had dowries of 20,000£. On the day they came to deliver the invitation, they did hurry him away. But I put their haste down to the many things they needed to do – perhaps additional calls – and not to their dislike of the alliance. Even then, I would not have suspected them of interference!

I dropped a piece of bread into the toaster. "What about Elizabeth and Mr. Collins?"

Mrs. Bennet inspected the appliance with interest and then answered my question. "Oh! Lizzy! I *assumed* Elizabeth, who everyone thought was so clever, would see the full advantages of the match! She loved her family, and I thought she would willingly do whatever she could to make sure her mother and her sisters were never homeless. I did tell her Mr. Collins was considering her for a wife, and how pleased I would be by her accepting him. But I did not make her promise to accept him."

I checked the text; in chapter 17 I read:

> *...it was not long before her mother gave her to understand that the probability of their [Mr. Collins and Elizabeth's] marriage was extremely agreeable to her. Elizabeth, however, did not choose to take the hint, being well aware that a serious dispute must be the consequence of any reply. Mr. Collins might never make the offer, and till he did, it was useless to quarrel about him.*

Mrs. Bennet sat down across from me. "You see! If Lizzy had told me how she felt, I would have steered him in Mary's direction, and we would not have wasted a suitor. Instead, Lizzy was polite to Mr. Collins, as I had taught her to be. I thought she would tolerate him very well – and manage him successfully."

I wondered if Mrs. Bennet would have really steered Mr. Collins in Mary's direction, or if the serious dispute Elizabeth had feared would have erupted at Longbourn House. Not wanting a serious dispute with Mrs. Bennet myself, I turned to watch the toaster, hiding my face, and therefore keeping my opinion to myself.

"Besides, as you know, Young Lady, there were circumstances of which I was not aware at the time. Lizzy's heart was already taken."

"By whom?" I asked, taking out the toast and buttering it. "At the time Elizabeth disliked Mr. Darcy."

"You are jumping ahead in the story," said Mrs. Bennet. "Not Mr. Darcy, but Mr. Wickham!"

"Ah, yes, Mr. Wickham," I said, and then took a bite.

"At that time, I had not met that future son-in-law, and the only descriptions I had heard came from Kitty and Lydia; Lizzy had kept quiet. With her attraction to Mr. Wickham completely unknown to me, I had every reason to believe her heart was free."

"What lesson should I take from this?"

"If achieving something is important, do not take *anything* surrounding it for granted."

I nodded. I finished my breakfast, cleared the dishes, and we returned to the story.

CHAPTER 17

Over the next few days, rain fell from dawn to dusk, forcing all the Bennets to stay inside. Only the anticipation of the Netherfield ball kept up their spirits, and in preparation, Mrs. Bennet fussed over each daughter's toilette. Jane, of course, was of the most concern, but Mrs. Bennet made sure the others were very pretty too.

Fortunately, on Tuesday, the skies finally let up, which meant that Mr. Bennet and Mr. Collins, although they would have to sit on the outside of the carriage – leaving the inside to the ladies – would not get wet.

As soon as they arrived, Mr. Bingley asked Jane for the first two dances, delighting Mrs. Bennet. Mrs. Bennet then told Lydia and Kitty to introduce her to the handsome Mr. Wickham, but he could not be found. Shortly afterwards, Mrs. Bennet learned Mr. Wickham *had* been invited, along with the rest of the officers, but he had had to go to London. Later, others added to this reason by saying Mr. Wickham had only 'had' to go to London so he could avoid any encounter with Mr. Darcy. Both Lydia and Kitty were quite disappointed and Mrs. Bennet, on behalf of her younger daughters, increased her resentment of Mr. Darcy.

As the music began, Mrs. Bennet watched with satisfaction as Mr. Collins led Elizabeth to the floor and as Mr. Bingley opened the ball with Jane! The next time Netherfield held a ball, she expected Jane to be welcoming her. No, not that; as Mrs. Bingley's mother, Mrs. Bennet would arrive a day or two in advance to assist with the preparations.

But on this occasion Mrs. Bennet was not responsible, and after giving her compliments to Miss Bingley on the arrangements, and making certain all her daughters were positioned to enjoy themselves, Mrs. Bennet could relax. She took some punch and settled between Lady Lucas and Mrs. Long, whom, because of the rain, she had not seen for a week. They had many questions about Mr. Collins, who, as the future owner of Longbourn House, could be expected to live in the neighborhood eventually.

"Mr. Collins has taken a great interest in Lizzy," said Mrs. Bennet.

"He is not the best dancer, is he?" observed Mrs. Long, as Mr. Collins turned the wrong way on the floor.

"That does not matter," said Lady Lucas. "If Elizabeth is concerned about his dancing ability, she can always improve him."

Mrs. Bennet agreed, and she turned her gaze to Jane and Mr. Bingley. That couple danced with elegance, and she told Mrs. Long and Lady Lucas about her hopes for their relationship. The subject was so satisfactory, so animating, that she continued at length.

As Mary joined them, Mrs. Long asked her for her opinion on the music.

MRS. BENNET'S ADVICE TO YOUNG LADIES

"They are playing well enough," said Mary, "but it is not especially sophisticated. It is music to dance to, not to listen to."

"You are so fortunate, Mrs. Bennet, to have a daughter who plays as well as Mary," said Mrs. Long. "Alas, my nieces are not at all musical."

"Oh! My! Look at that!" remarked Lady Lucas. "Mr. Darcy is dancing with Elizabeth!"

"Mr. Darcy and Elizabeth? Impossible!" cried Mrs. Bennet, but Lady Lucas insisted, and Mrs. Bennet turned her gaze in the direction of the dancers. The tall Mr. Darcy was easy to spot, and she recognized her daughter.

"Did not Elizabeth declare she would never dance with him?" asked Lady Lucas.

Mrs. Long observed that Mr. Darcy's dancing was far superior to Mr. Collins's.

Mrs. Bennet could not understand why, exactly, Elizabeth was dancing with Mr. Darcy, when she ought to be encouraging the attentions of her cousin. Of course, Mrs. Bennet would never discourage any potential husband for one of her daughters, but though Mr. Darcy was tall, handsome and undeniably rich, she had difficulty imagining him as a suitor for Elizabeth. Mr. Darcy, who had called Elizabeth merely tolerable the first time he saw her! Still, she was sufficiently curious to study the expressions of the pair. Elizabeth, of course, she knew quite well, and Mrs. Bennet could tell her daughter was unhappy with her partner. Mr. Darcy, so tall, was easy to see, but his face was more difficult to read – until Mrs. Bennet detected actual disgust. No, *he* could not be a suitor! The question then became, what on earth were they doing on the floor together? Of course, they were at a ball, given by Mr. Darcy's friend Mr. Bingley, whom he could hardly insult by refusing to dance the entire evening. Mrs. Bennet recalled that, as Elizabeth had been at Netherfield while Jane was ill, Mr. Darcy was better acquainted with Elizabeth than he was with most of the other local young ladies. As he had to dance, he invited the hand of someone he knew rather than someone he did not.

Mrs. Bennet expressed these ideas to her friends.

"I think they make a handsome couple," said Lady Lucas.

"What man would not look good with Miss Elizabeth as a partner?" asked Mrs. Long.

The matrons watched as the dance ended, and Mr. Darcy escorted Elizabeth off the floor, neither of them appearing particularly pleased by their experience. Instead of lingering for conversation, they parted quickly, and Elizabeth was rejoined by Mr. Collins.

Mrs. Bennet's Advice

The dishwasher bell went off, letting me know the cycle had ended. I opened the machine to let the contents cool, then began by removing the plastic containers, which retained less heat and so were not too hot to touch.

"You were wrong about Mr. Darcy," I said. "He *was* attracted to Elizabeth."

"Everyone was wrong about Mr. Darcy," said Mrs. Bennet. "Besides, when I observed them, they did not appear a happy couple."

I opened the door to a cupboard and started putting plates into it. "When they had those sour expressions, it was because they were speaking about Mr. Wickham." I wiped my hands dry, and then turned to the text on my tablet. "The pertinent paragraphs are from chapter 18," I announced.

He [Mr. Darcy] made no answer, and they were again silent till they had gone down the dance, when he asked her if she [Elizabeth] and her sisters did not very often walk to Meryton. She answered in the affirmative, and, unable to resist the temptation, added, "When you met us there the other day, we had just been forming a new acquaintance."

The effect was immediate. A deeper shade of hauteur overspread his features, but he said not a word, and Elizabeth, though blaming herself for her own weakness, could not go on. At length Darcy spoke, and in a constrained manner said, "Mr. Wickham is blessed with such happy manners as may ensure his making friends — whether he may be equally capable of retaining them, is less certain."

"Ah!" said Mrs. Bennet. "That explains it! So many people – Mr. Bennet, Miss Jane Austen, and readers – praise Lizzy for her cleverness, but in my opinion, Lizzy should *not* have mentioned Mr. Wickham to Mr. Darcy while they were dancing. It is unwise to provoke your partner while on the dance floor."

I thought that was good advice. I finished unloading the dishwasher, then Mrs. Bennet and I returned to the ball.

CHAPTER 18

Mrs. Bennet, despite Lady Lucas's remarks that Mr. Darcy and Elizabeth made a handsome couple, still disliked that gentleman on her daughter's behalf. The fact that he had danced with her now did not make up for his refusal to dance with her before. Besides, Elizabeth's displeased expression when she left the floor – and Mr. Darcy, instead of remaining to converse with her, strode away on his long legs as if he could not escape quickly enough – confirmed Mrs. Bennet's opinion.

No, Mrs. Bennet was not foolish enough to set her sights on Mr. Darcy, who might be tall and handsome and the richest man in Derbyshire, but who, after dancing with Elizabeth, did not find her company sufficiently tolerable to exchange ten words with. Instead, the mother was happy to watch as that more reliable prospect, Mr. Collins, stayed by Elizabeth's side and engaged her in conversation. Miss Lucas joined them too, for which Mrs. Bennet was grateful. Mr. Collins, Mrs. Bennet acknowledged, could be tedious, but Elizabeth and Charlotte Lucas were close friends, and their chat would keep Mr. Collins amused.

Mrs. Bennet spent much of the evening indulging in Mr. Bingley's fine wines while watching Jane and Mr. Bingley – there would be a great match! – and telling Mrs. Long and Lady Lucas about her expectations for her two eldest daughters. Unlike everyone in her family, the two other matrons understood how important this achievement was.

When the musicians paused, Mary Bennet entertained the guests by playing and singing, only to have her performance cruelly stopped by her own father. Mrs. Bennet made a point of comforting her middle daughter afterwards, while thinking of the rich men that her younger daughters would meet through Jane's alliance with Bingley. Even Mary would find a young man who appreciated her concertos!

Mrs. Bennet – by having spoken with her coachman before – maneuvered to have the Longbourn carriage come last. She hoped Mr. Bingley, flushed and happy from having Jane in his arms for so much of the evening – he had even neglected to take turns with several young ladies – would finally make her an offer. Mrs. Bennet made sure the rest of them stood apart, giving Mr. Bingley and Jane what privacy she could, but the young man did not take advantage of the situation to propose. Perhaps he needed more privacy than was available in the shadows in the vestibule, in which everyone else – not buoyed by love – was yawning.

The Longbourn coach finally arrived, and they were forced to leave Netherfield without an engagement between Mr. Bingley and Jane. Still, as Mrs. Bennet climbed into the coach with her daughters, she was convinced that match would soon happen.

Mrs. Bennet's Advice

I appreciated Mrs. Bennet's interpretation of the events at the ball, but I could not allow her the last word. "Others had very different views of what happened at Netherfield," I said.

"That Miss Jane Austen! Abusing my character again! What exactly does she say?"

"These paragraphs are in chapter 18," I explained, and then I read:

Her mother's thoughts she [Elizabeth] plainly saw were bent the same way, and she determined not to venture near her, lest she might hear too much. When they sat down to supper, therefore, she considered it a most unlucky perverseness which placed them within one of each other; and deeply was she vexed to find that her mother was talking to that one person (Lady Lucas) freely, openly, and of nothing else but her expectation that Jane would soon be married to Mr. Bingley. ... She [Mrs. Bennet] concluded with many good wishes that Lady Lucas might soon be equally fortunate, though evidently and triumphantly believing there was no chance of it.

In vain did Elizabeth endeavor to check the rapidity of her mother's words, or persuade her to describe her felicity in a less audible whisper; for, to her inexpressible vexation, she could perceive that the chief of it was overheard by Mr. Darcy, who sat opposite to them. Her mother only scolded her for being nonsensical.

"What is Mr. Darcy to me, pray, that I should be afraid of him? I am sure we owe him no such particular civility as to be obliged to say nothing he may not like to hear."

"For heaven's sake, madam, speak lower. What advantage can it be for you to offend Mr. Darcy? You will never recommend yourself to his friend by so doing!"

I explained how the text described how embarrassed Elizabeth was by Mary's singing – "Elizabeth was never fair to Mary, deciding she was a better musician even though Mary worked so much harder," interjected Mrs. Bennet – Mr. Collins's deciding to introduce himself to Mr. Darcy, as Mr. Darcy was a nephew to Mr. Collins's patroness, Lady Catherine – "And what is wrong with that? Quite right of Mr. Collins to let Mr. Darcy know his aunt was in good health, although Mr. Darcy certainly did not deserve the attention" – and at the frolic of Lydia and Kitty – "Sometimes I think Elizabeth was born eighty instead of twenty," remarked Mrs. Bennet, words that had to be taken metaphorically in real life, but which could be literal when applied to a character in a novel.

Nevertheless, Jane Austen's passage wounded Mrs. Bennet. My literary mentor did not embarrass easily, but she did feel deeply. She still believed her ideas had been correct, her judgment appropriate, but she wished she had not spoken so loudly or so liberally.

"What advice would you give me?" I asked her.

"When managing something important – and I was trying to marry two daughters, and although circumstances were promising, no promises had yet been made – do not loosen your tongue with wine."

"Wine?" I asked.

She sighed. "Mr. Bingley served excellent bottles at his ball, and I spoke too freely."

CHAPTER 19

Although Mrs. Bennet had not been able to arrange for Mr. Bingley to propose to Jane at the Netherfield ball, she was content that match would happen soon. The following morning she was more concerned about Mr. Collins, as it was already the second Wednesday of his visit. The clergyman could only stay with them until Saturday, when he needed to rise early so that he could return to his parsonage in Hunsford in order to read the service to Lady Catherine de Bourgh on Sunday. If he did not make an offer by Friday, it would be too late.

Mrs. Bennet's mind was busy, considering how to get Mr. Collins to the point. Should she encourage Elizabeth and Mr. Collins to go for a walk? The sun was coming out, but it was not warm, and the paths were muddy from the many days of rain. Elizabeth might not mind the dirt, but Mr. Collins seemed to prefer to keep his shoes neat.

How did one encourage a man to propose? Mrs. Bennet had her own experience, and she had heard the details of proposals to her friends and relatives – her sister, Mrs. Phillips; her sister-in-law, Mrs. Gardiner; and even how her friend Isabel received an offer to become Mrs. Lucas – but those examples did not seem to apply here.

However, Mrs. Bennet did not need to worry. After breakfast, when she was sitting with Kitty, Elizabeth and Mr. Collins in the sunny parlor, the workbasket in her lap as she determined which garment to mend, Mr. Collins took a seat near her. "May I hope, madam, for your interest with your fair daughter Elizabeth, when I solicit for the honor of a private audience with her in the course of this morning?"

A thrill of happiness went through Mrs. Bennet. It was happening; at long last, it was happening! "Oh dear! – yes – certainly. I am sure Lizzy will be very happy – I am sure she can have no objection. Come, Kitty, I want you upstairs." She lifted the workbasket and rose.

Mrs. Bennet was hastening away, when Elizabeth called out: "Dear madam, do not go. I beg you will not go. Mr. Collins must excuse me. He can have nothing to say to me that anybody need not hear. I am going away myself."

"No, no, nonsense, Lizzy. I desire you to stay where you are." And then, realizing Elizabeth truly wished to run away, Mrs. Bennet added: "Lizzy, I *insist* upon your staying and hearing Mr. Collins."

Elizabeth sat back down, and Mrs. Bennet ushered Kitty out of the room.

"Why must we go upstairs, Mamma?" Kitty asked.

"I have something to show you, my dear," said Mrs. Bennet, and led her fourth daughter away. They passed the library, where Mr. Bennet with some of the accounts; a small study, where Jane was working on accounts; the music room, where Mary was practicing, and encountered Lydia on the stairs. Lydia, after the late night at Netherfield, had slept past the breakfast hour. Mrs. Bennet told Lydia to leave the breakfast-parlor alone and to ask for tea and a tray of bread and jam to be brought to Mrs. Bennet's rooms.

"Why?" asked Lydia.

"Do exactly as you are told, Lydia, and I will explain later."

In a few minutes they were in Mrs. Bennet's apartment and she explained to her younger daughters that Mr. Collins was making Elizabeth an offer of marriage.

"Mr. Collins?" asked Kitty, who had apparently not even noticed their cousin's courtship during the last few days.

"Oh! Poor Lizzy!" cried Lydia. "Mr. Collins is so dull!"

"And his dancing is abominable," added Kitty, who had suffered through two terrible dances with Mr. Collins at Netherfield, as had every Miss Bennet. "He trod on my dress and tore it."

Mrs. Bennet tried to impress on Kitty and Lydia that there was no 'poor Lizzy' about this. "Perhaps Mr. Collins does not have the appeal of a red coat, but he is a very respectable man, with an adequate income now and the promise of Longbourn House and the entire estate in the future." She set Lydia and Kitty about mending Kitty's gown, then said she would go attend to the lovers.

"I have given them enough time," said Mrs. Bennet. She went down to the vestibule and saw the door to the breakfast-parlor was still closed. She wanted to burst through and to congratulate them, but she decided to give Elizabeth and Mr. Collins a little more privacy. A proposal, an acceptance, it was such a moment! – she supposed she should arrange something special for dinner that day in order to celebrate. She considered ringing for the cook at that moment, and then decided to wait, because she wanted to be the first to congratulate her new son-in-law.

Mrs. Bennet's hearing was not good enough to discern the words that were being said. Mr. Collins spoke at length, and finally Elizabeth responded. The voices increased in volume – and then Elizabeth slipped out the door, and ran up the stairs, as if she had not seen her mother standing there. Mrs. Bennet supposed Elizabeth wanted first to speak to Jane – she, Fanny, had confided in Agnes as her own romance with Mr. Bennet had progressed – and she went into the room to speak to Mr. Collins.

From the expression on his face all seemed well, and so she congratulated him and herself at the prospect of having a son at last.

"I thank you, Mrs. Bennet," said Mr. Collins. "I am sure it will end well, at the last." And then he proceeded to tell her that Elizabeth had refused him, a device he deemed as a ploy by an elegant female to increase his love for her.

Mrs. Bennet could not believe her ears. "You say, Mr. Collins, that Lizzy refused you?"

"Yes, but with the express blessing from you and Mr. Bennet, I am sure she will understand the advantages of the match and I will soon bring my new bride to Kent."

Mrs. Bennet was horrified, and she did not think Elizabeth, who could be as frank as her mother, would behave in such a manner. "But, depend upon it, Mr. Collins," she added, "that Lizzy shall be brought to reason. I will speak to her about it directly. She is a very headstrong, foolish girl, and does not know her own interest but I will *make* her know it."

Mrs. Bennet's description of Elizabeth alarmed Mr. Collins; he did not want a headstrong, foolish wife.

"Sir, you quite misunderstand me," said Mrs. Bennet, realizing she had said too much. "Lizzy is only headstrong in such matters as these. In everything else she is as good-natured a girl as ever lived. I will go directly to Mr. Bennet, and we shall very soon settle it with her, I am sure."

She did not give him time to reply, but hurried instantly to her husband, calling out as she entered the library, "Oh! Mr. Bennet, you are wanted immediately; we are all in an uproar. You must come and make Lizzy marry Mr. Collins, for she vows she will not have him, and if you do not make haste, he will change his mind and not have *her*."

Mr. Bennet, who was deep in a book, required an explanation, which Mrs. Bennet impatiently gave. She demanded he speak with Lizzy.

Elizabeth was sent for; she soon entered her father's library. Mrs. Bennet recognized Elizabeth's expression as defiant, but she was certain Mr. Bennet would talk sense into her.

Mr. Bennet's beginning was promising. "I have sent for you on an affair of importance. I understand that Mr. Collins has made you an offer of marriage. Is it true?"

"Yes, sir, he has."

"Very well," continued Mr. Bennet, "—and this offer of marriage you have refused?"

"I have, sir."

"Your mother insists upon your accepting it. Is it not so, Mrs. Bennet?"

"Yes!" cried Mrs. Bennet, then added, "or I will never see her again."

Mr. Bennet's tone became even more serious. "An unhappy alternative is before you, Elizabeth. From this day you must be a stranger to one of your parents. Your mother will never see you again if you do *not* marry Mr. Collins, and I will never see you again if you *do*."

Elizabeth smiled in triumph, but Mrs. Bennet, who had believed her husband regarded the affair as she wished, felt betrayed. "What do you mean, Mr. Bennet, in talking this way? You promised me to *insist* upon her marrying him."

"My dear," replied her husband, "I have two small favors to request. First, that you will allow me the free use of my understanding on the present occasion; and secondly, of my room. I shall be glad to have the library to myself as soon as may be."

Mrs. Bennet realized she would receive no assistance from Mr. Bennet, but she could not let the issue, so materially important to their security, drop. She harangued Elizabeth to change her mind; she attempted to enlist Jane's assistance in persuading Elizabeth – but Jane declined. Mrs. Bennet even encouraged her three younger daughters to implore Lizzy to save their home and secure their future, but Mary, who would have appreciated Mr. Collins's attentions herself, was too resentful to participate; Lydia declared marriage to Mr. Collins would be intolerable, even for Lizzy; and Kitty, the most persuadable, had no talent for persuading others. Mrs. Bennet even asked Charlotte Lucas, who called that morning, to intervene. All of Longbourn House was in confusion as Mrs. Bennet realized the prospect of Mr. Collins as a son-in-law was evaporating. It ended when Mr. Collins himself asked Mrs. Bennet to cease her efforts on his behalf.

Mr. Collins was unfailingly polite. "I trust I am resigned. Perhaps not the less so from feeling a doubt of my positive happiness had my fair cousin honored me with her hand; for I have often observed that resignation is never so perfect as when the blessing denied begins to lose somewhat of its value in our estimation. You will not, I hope, consider me as showing any disrespect to your family, my dear madam, by thus withdrawing my pretensions to your daughter's favor, without having paid yourself and Mr. Bennet the compliment of requesting you to interpose your authority in my behalf. My conduct may, I fear, be objectionable in having accepted my dismission from your daughter's lips instead of your own." He apologized several times.

"Oh! Mr. Collins," cried Mrs. Bennet, as she realized she had failed.

Mrs. Bennet's Advice

Mrs. Bennet was beside me, as I carried the laundry to the washing machine and started sorting through it. "That day was very difficult for you," I said.

"Oh! My dear Young Lady, it was! My own family betrayed me. Mr. Bennet and Lizzy conspired to thwart me."

I divided my things into sturdy and delicate, as I considered how to express my objections. "But – and this is certainly true now, but it was true in your day as well – don't you believe a woman should be allowed to make her own choice in marriage?"

"As long as it is not a foolish one! If your daughter is near a cliff, do you let her throw herself off? Even if she ought to be old enough to know better?"

"No, of course not! But the situations are not the same. Elizabeth actively disliked Mr. Collins." I stopped sorting socks and turned to chapter 19:

You could not make me happy, and I am convinced that I am the last woman in the world who could make you so.

I put down the text and returned to the laundry. "Elizabeth was most adamant in her dislike."

"She was. So young! So foolish! And, I suppose, a romantic – something I had not realized before," said Mrs. Bennet.

I continued. "I'm not sure Elizabeth's refusal was due to girlish caprice. Mr. Bennet was also against the marriage."

"Oh! Mr. Bennet! Why should *his* judgment have so much weight in the matter? Of course, I come from a time when husbands and fathers had the last word. It is most unfair."

I opened the washer and started loading dirty clothes. In this, I agreed with Mrs. Bennet. Men, at least in the past, had held too much power over women. I asked her what I should learn from her experience.

"Oh! my dear Young Lady, you must realize that sometimes those you love will work against you. Sometimes you must give in with good grace."

My lips twisted as I reached for the detergent. Mrs. Bennet had not given in with good grace.

"No, perhaps not," she conceded. "I just said that *sometimes* you must give in with good grace. Considering what I knew at the time, I could not think well of Lizzy's refusal. So, other times you must persist in working for those you care about, even when they resist."

Adding detergent to the machine, I considered her words. In my own life I could think of several examples where her advice applied. When we first married, my husband had objected to my habit of walking, but eventually he joined me, experiencing a significant improvement in his health and stamina. Then, back in my twenties, I had compelled an acquaintance to stop cutting class – if I had not done so, he might not have graduated.

As I closed the washer and chose a setting, Mrs. Bennet continued. "A mother persists – it is what she, or any concerned lady – or rational being – would do."

I hit the start button, then waited a moment to make sure the washer was working.

"Perhaps I was wrong about Mr. Collins," Mrs. Bennet said. "But at the time, I was convinced I was right. And as I was convinced, I could not stop working to prevent my daughters from being ruined."

CHAPTER 20

Despite his unsuccessful suit, Mr. Collins did not leave Longbourn House at once, nor did he make any preparations to depart before the original day, Saturday. Lady Catherine had always expected him back at a certain time, even arranging for him to be fetched by her carriage – *one* of her carriages – and Mr. Collins was not about to do anything that could injure his relationship with her ladyship, as he prized that alliance above everything else.

As Mr. Collins would not depart from Longbourn House, several Miss Bennets made their escape from him and walked to Meryton. Lydia said she wanted to tell their aunt Phillips all about the Netherfield ball, as she had not attended it.

"You just want to find out if Wickham has returned," said Kitty.

"I will join you," said Elizabeth, who had more reason than anyone else to flee the estate.

Shortly after her daughters departed, Charlotte Lucas called. Mrs. Bennet poured out her heart to the daughter of her best friend. "I am ill-used by everyone," cried Mrs. Bennet.

They were joined by Mr. Collins, who was happy to speak to Miss Lucas, who proved to be a good listener, especially on the subject of his patroness, Lady Catherine.

"I quite understand," said Miss Lucas. "You should do everything not to inconvenience her ladyship, not when she has been so gracious to you."

Mrs. Bennet wondered why Elizabeth could not be more like Charlotte.

Miss Lucas added that Mr. Collins, although he might not have found a partner in Elizabeth Bennet, obviously appreciated his relationship with the Bennets. "Mr. Bennet is, after all, your cousin. All the Miss Bennets are your cousins."

"Very true," said Mr. Collins. "I do not have so many relatives in the world."

"And eventually, you can expect to reside in the area. You should become familiar with the neighborhood, now that the weather is better." And Charlotte invited Mr. Collins, and all the Bennets, to dinner at Lucas Lodge the next day.

That was how to do it, thought Mrs. Bennet. She summoned Mary, thinking *she* might manage to attract Mr. Collins's notice, and compelled that daughter to sit with her, their cousin and Charlotte.

The other Bennet girls returned from Meryton, bringing several officers with them back to Longbourn for tea, and Mrs. Bennet finally met the much talked-of Mr. Wickham.

Mr. Wickham was tall – nearly as tall as Mr. Darcy, but much better looking, because he smiled instead of frowned and because he chatted instead of staying silent. Mr. Wickham said he was delighted to meet Mrs. Bennet. All the officers in the regiment had spoken of nothing but the beauty of the Miss Bennets, and of course he had witnessed that for himself, but he had been eager to view the original.

"You flatter me, sir," said Mrs. Bennet.

"Not at all, mum," replied the handsome lieutenant as he bent over her hand to kiss it. Even Mrs. Bennet, who believed that with five grown-up daughters, she ought to be beyond such things, experienced a thrill as he gazed at her with his dark eyes.

And then Mrs. Bennet, watching Elizabeth speaking to Mr. Wickham, observing the smiles, the laughter, the animated conversation, realized what had thwarted her plans for Elizabeth and Mr. Collins. Elizabeth was infatuated with this young soldier, and from how Lieutenant Wickham behaved, *he* was just as interested in her. No wonder Elizabeth refused her cousin!

Mrs. Bennet, never forgetting her object, told Mary to speak more with Mr. Collins. She could not let a potential suitor go to waste; she still had five daughters who needed husbands. Mary and Charlotte Lucas listened to him, keeping him from feeling slighted by all the attention paid to the red coats, although he was a dull wren in a flock of pheasants.

The following day was Thursday; Elizabeth, Kitty and Lydia walked again to Meryton in the morning. Mrs. Bennet, preoccupied by Mr. Collins, had not thought about Mr. Bingley on Wednesday, except to send a note of thanks to Netherfield. Besides, Mr. Bingley, Mrs. Bennet recalled, had had a matter of business to tend to in London. However, Thursday morning Jane received a letter from Miss Bingley. The note's delivery put a smile back on Mrs. Bennet's face. She might have failed with Mr. Collins, but there was always Mr. Bingley, and there was no doubt but that Jane was interested in him! Elizabeth might be unreliable, but sweet Jane, conscientious Jane, the responsible eldest, the beauty – *she* would do what was best for her family and not refuse an offer.

The sparkle in Jane's eyes, however, vanished as she read Miss Bingley's letter. She explained the whole party had left Netherfield for London.

"That cannot be," cried Mrs. Bennet, and she took the note from Jane and read it herself. Then, because she could not bear another disappointment, she tried to look at it in the most favorable manner. Just because Mr. Bingley's friends had gone to London did not mean he had to remain there himself. London was only a half day away. He would return and court Jane in peace, without the distraction of his sisters and the despicable Mr. Darcy.

That day, the Bennets were to dine at Lucas Lodge; they walked there with Mr. Collins. All the Bennets were relieved to enjoy the hospitality of their friends. Mrs. Bennet spent the time relating her grievances to Lady Lucas, and even Mr. Collins's mood, as he spoke with various Collinses, improved.

Mr. Collins was departing early on Saturday morning, and so he made his farewells to the Bennets on Friday evening. After the niceties, in which Mr. Collins expressed his thanks for their hospitality, and his good wishes for the health and success of all his dear relations – "not excepting my cousin Elizabeth" – Mrs. Bennet made the usual statement of his being welcome again at Longbourn House should he ever venture their way again.

Mr. Collins indicated he hoped to visit them again quite soon, naming a date only a few weeks away. This surprised all of the Bennets, and not all of them were pleased. Mr. Bennet tried to dissuade his cousin. "But is there not danger of Lady Catherine's disapprobation here, my good sir? You had better neglect your relations than run the risk of offending your patroness."

"My dear sir," replied Mr. Collins, "I am particularly obliged to you for this friendly caution, and you may depend upon my not taking so material a step without her ladyship's concurrence."

"You cannot be too much upon your guard," said Mr. Bennet. "Risk anything rather than her displeasure; and if you find it likely to be raised by your coming to us again, which I should think exceedingly probable, stay quietly at home, and be satisfied that *we* shall take no offence."

But Mr. Collins would not be dissuaded. He wished them all health and happiness and again, promised a letter of thanks.

Before the sun rose on Saturday, Mr. Collins left Longbourn House as scheduled, but the prospect of an early return was so dismaying to Mr. Bennet that he remarked on it to Mrs. Bennet at breakfast. "I used to regret not having more intercourse with my relatives, but Mr. Collins has cured me of that particular disappointment."

"He was not so much trouble," said Mrs. Bennet. "If you had only encouraged Lizzy" –

"She did not wish to marry him," said Mr. Bennet. "I will not force any of my daughters into an unhappy alliance. Let there be an end to this, Mrs. Bennet!"

"I insist on the discussion of one more matter," said Mrs. Bennet. "If one of our daughters were to accept him with pleasure, would you permit the engagement?" She was thinking, of course, of Mary. Mary had to be the reason Mr. Collins was planning to return so soon to their neighborhood.

Mr. Bennet said he would not interfere, not if he were convinced a daughter truly wished to marry the clergyman. Then he reiterated that he did not want to speak any more about Mr. Collins and any possible nuptials.

Mr. Bennet, however, was out of luck. The topic of Mr. Collins's marriage plans could not be dropped, for a few hours later that day Sir William Lucas called at Longbourn House to make an announcement. Mr.

Collins had proposed to Charlotte Lucas – and she had said yes!

Mrs. Bennet's Advice

The washer had finished, and as I rarely used the dryer, I was hanging up the clothes in the laundry room. It occurred to me this task, at least, had changed little since Mrs. Bennet's time. "Hearing about the engagement of Mr. Collins and Charlotte Lucas must have been difficult," I said to her, as I shook out a wet shirt and placed it on a hanger.

"I did not believe it. None of us believed it," said Mrs. Bennet.

"Except Elizabeth."

"That is because Charlotte called earlier in the day and told her before Sir William came to tell us."

I used clothespins to fasten my socks on some lines so they could dry.

"Besides, it was preposterous! Mr. Collins proposed to Lizzy on Wednesday; what was he doing, making an offer of marriage to another woman on Friday? Charlotte – I know she is our dear friend, or at least she was before all this – Charlotte dresses as well as she can, but she is plain. You must admit she is very plain, especially when compared to any of my girls – even when compared to Mary! How could a man, any man with eyes, prefer the eldest Miss Lucas to any Miss Bennet? She had scars from the smallpox in her youth that carried away her brother and her sister; they were faded, but they were there."

"Looks matter, but they are not everything," I said.

"And Charlotte – she was twenty-seven to Mr. Collins's twenty-five!"

"That age difference is not important—" I began, but Mrs. Bennet had more to say.

"Mr. Collins belonged rightly to the Bennet family; the idea that he could take himself down the road to form an alliance with a Lucas was so unfair! So improper! The Lucases must have done something to charm him to betray his new-found family."

"Charlotte decided to marry him if she could," I said. I hung up a turtleneck, then turned to the text to read from chapter 22:

> *The Bennets were engaged to dine with the Lucases and again during the chief of the day was Miss Lucas so kind as to listen to Mr. Collins. Elizabeth took an opportunity of thanking her. ... Charlotte assured her friend of her satisfaction in being useful, and that it amply repaid her for the little sacrifice of her time. This was very amiable, but Charlotte's kindness extended farther than Elizabeth had any conception of; its object was nothing else than to secure her from any return of Mr. Collins's addresses, by engaging them towards herself.*

"Aye!" cried Mrs. Bennet. "Charlotte worked her wiles on him, by listening to him – which my daughters refused to do. After all my kindness to her throughout the years, for her to use me so ill!"

I had always liked Charlotte Lucas, so I attempted to defend her. From the same chapter, I shared another passage:

Charlotte herself was tolerably composed. She had gained her point, and had time to consider of it. Her reflections were in general satisfactory. Mr. Collins, to be sure, was neither sensible nor agreeable; his society was irksome, and his attachment to her must be imaginary. But still he would be her husband. Without thinking highly either of men or matrimony, marriage had always been her object; it was the only provision for well-educated young women of small fortune, and however uncertain of giving happiness, must be their pleasantest preservative from want. This preservative she had now obtained; and at the age of twenty-seven, without having ever been handsome, she felt all the good luck of it.

"You should not be angry with her. You wanted your own daughters to make the same decision. And your daughters were younger and much more attractive. They were not desperate enough to settle for Mr. Collins."

Mrs. Bennet calmed down a little. She watched as I resumed hanging up garments to dry, interested in the peculiar fashions of my time.

"What advice do you have for me?" I asked, using a hanger with clips for a pair of jeans.

"Oh! Do you not know? You have said it yourself. Timing is important," she said.

"What do you mean?"

"My daughters, as you say, were not ready to marry Mr. Collins. On the other hand, Mr. Collins was available because *he* was ready – he had come to Longbourn House in order to find a wife. Charlotte, at twenty-seven, *knew* she was not likely ever to receive a better offer."

Reaching into the washer for stray socks, I nodded.

"Timing matters, but not just *your* timing. You must take advantage of opportunities when they appear."

"As Charlotte did."

Mrs. Bennet sighed. "Yes."

CHAPTER 21

Mrs. Bennet did not want to believe that Mr. Collins had made an offer of marriage to Charlotte Lucas. However, Sir William Lucas and his daughter insisted it was so, and Elizabeth maintained Charlotte had told her of the engagement earlier. Still, Mrs. Bennet clung to the hope that it could all be a mistake – at least until Mr. Collins's letter of thanks for their generous hospitality arrived on Tuesday. In that letter, after expressing his gratitude, he wrote he had been successful in his suit of their amiable neighbor, Miss Lucas, hence his desire to return soon to Longbourn House in order to be near his betrothed. He reported, too, Lady Catherine approved the match, so he hoped his dear Charlotte would let him name an early date on which he would be made the "happiest of men."

"So, you see, Mrs. Bennet, the information from the Lucases is true," said Mr. Bennet, after reading the letter to her and to their daughters. "I always thought Charlotte Lucas was tolerably sensible, but it appears I was mistaken, for she has, indeed, agreed to marry my cousin."

"I cannot understand it," said Elizabeth, whose opinion of Mr. Collins was so poor that she could not comprehend any woman of sense agreeing to wed him. "It is disappointing."

"It is disappointing," agreed Mrs. Bennet, "but it did not need to be. I should not have let Charlotte Lucas outwit me, and that would not have happened, if my own family had not been against me!"

"Madam—" began Elizabeth.

"You, Lizzy, should have made a different decision! How will you feel when Charlotte and Mr. Collins inherit this house, and we are forced to crowd in with your uncle Phillips in Meryton or my brother Gardiner in London?"

"I should like to go to London," said Lydia.

"I like London, too," Mrs. Bennet admitted, "but it is one thing to visit and another to live there as a poor relation."

Mr. Bennet attempted to soothe her. "Come, come, Mrs. Bennet, there is no need to worry about events like this."

"You are right. I am done trying to find husbands for all of you; you will have to find them on your own!" cried Mrs. Bennet, but the declaration had to substitute for the deed, because Mrs. Bennet could not truly abandon her life's purpose. She asked Jane if she had heard from Miss Bingley.

"No, Mamma, not yet," said Jane.

"My aunt Phillips says that she spoke to the realtor and he does not believe Mr. Bingley will be back this winter," reported Kitty.

"I do not believe it," said Mrs. Bennet, but worry overwhelmed her. If she could lose Mr. Collins to the Lucases, then she could also lose Mr.

Bingley. "And I cannot bear that Mr. Collins should return to Longbourn House! Why, if he is engaged to Charlotte Lucas, does he not stay at Lucas Lodge? His coming here is most inconvenient and inconsiderate!"

Mr. Bennet said he would prefer that arrangement as well.

Mrs. Bennet considered telling her husband to write to Mr. Collins to make that very suggestion, but then it occurred to her that she had better be hospitable to Mr. Collins, as he might be in a position to decide *her* future living arrangements. Besides, persuading Mr. Bennet to write any letter was always difficult.

"Mamma, it is so dull," said Lydia. "Why do we not invite some of the officers?"

Mrs. Bennet was amenable to the suggestion, but Mr. Bennet protested. "My library time was under siege during Mr. Collins's visit, and as this letter has informed us, he will return in only a fortnight. Let me enjoy some peace."

Mrs. Bennet told Lydia to ask Mr. and Mrs. Phillips to arrange several amusements; Mrs. Bennet went occasionally herself, and was distracted, at least, by the sight of so many red coats. Mr. Wickham, always ready with a compliment or an anecdote, was especially good at dispelling the gloom.

Still, for Mrs. Bennet, the November days were bleak. Jane received a letter from Mr. Bingley's sister, in which Miss Bingley made it clear the family planned to remain in London for the winter. Wintering in London was not unusual, but a man as violently in love as Mr. Bingley had shown himself to be ought not to be able to resist returning. Could his business be so pressing? Or had he met another young lady, with a large fortune? Mrs. Bennet heard Mr. Darcy had a younger sister, and that Miss Darcy had a dowry of 30,000£, giving Mrs. Bennet yet another reason to hate the name Darcy.

Mr. Bingley stayed away, but as promised, Mr. Collins returned. Mrs. Bennet succeeded in being polite to him, yet her feelings required release, and so when Mr. Collins left to spend his days at Lucas Lodge, she scolded Elizabeth.

The circumstances continued to try Mrs. Bennet's poor nerves. Normally she would have confided in Lady Lucas, but as she was angry with her friend, she could not. Nevertheless, avoiding the Lucases completely was now impossible, given their families would be allied by marriage. After a dinner at Lucas Lodge, Mr. and Mrs. Bennet returned to Longbourn House, and Mrs. Bennet expressed her frustration to her husband. "Indeed, Mr. Bennet," said she, as the servant took her coat, "it is very hard to think that Charlotte Lucas should ever be mistress of this house, that *I* should be forced to make way for *her*, and live to see her take her place in it!"

Mr. Bennet went with her into the drawing-room, where a cheerful blaze lit the fireplace, and held his hands before it to warm them. "My dear, do not give way to such gloomy thoughts. Let us hope for better things. Let us flatter ourselves that *I* may be the survivor."

As Mrs. Bennet was several years younger than Mr. Bennet, this idea was not consoling. It was not the prospect of Death, which, as a Christian, she was not supposed to fear, but the idea of leaving her daughters only to be protected by their father. In his cool, rational way, Mr. Bennet cared for them, but he would make no effort to secure them husbands and he could not break up the estate to give them dowries of any substance.

Unable to correct the defects in Mr. Bennet, Mrs. Bennet returned to the subject of Mr. Collins and his intended. "I cannot bear to think that *they* should have all this estate. If it was not for the entail, I should not mind it."

"What should not you mind?"

Mrs. Bennet imagined that blissful world, in which the entail did not exist, and where she did not have to worry about her daughters sinking into poverty. "Oh! If it were not for the entail, I should not mind anything at all."

"Let us be thankful that you are preserved from a state of such insensibility."

He was attempting a joke, but in Mrs. Bennet's opinion, the matter was too serious for levity. "I never can be thankful, Mr. Bennet, for *anything* about the entail. How anyone could have the conscience to entail away an estate from one's own daughters, I cannot understand; and all for the sake of Mr. Collins, too! Why should *he* have it more than anybody else?"

To that, Mr. Bennet could make no useful answer. "I leave it to yourself to determine," he said.

Mrs. Bennet's Advice

I was cleaning up a nook near the fireplace. The inclement weather made a cheerful blaze appealing, but it would be more pleasant if the area near it were free of dirt.

Mrs. Bennet joined me. She was still upset by her inability to catch either of the suitors for her daughters.

"That time must have been distressing for you," I said to Mrs. Bennet.

"Oh! It was bleak, very bleak. Two engagements that had seemed so secure, both of which had failed! And I was concerned about my two daughters. It broke my heart to see Jane so unhappy. She had never cared for a man the way she cared for Mr. Bingley. Yet he was gone off to London, without so much as saying farewell, and although Jane waited eagerly for Miss Bingley's letters, when they arrived, they never made her happier. The only good thing was my dear Jane retained her looks. I was afraid being crossed in love would make Jane lose her bloom, but despite the blow to her spirits, she was as beautiful as ever."

"Elizabeth's spirit, however, was not disturbed by the end of Mr. Collins's courtship," I said, moving the magazine rack and the tools for the fireplace from the corner.

"It is just as you say. Lizzy did not regret her refusal of Mr. Collins. But she was very unhappy with Charlotte Lucas, who had always been her closest friend in the neighborhood. Instead of questioning her own judgment, which Lizzy should have done, she questioned Charlotte's decision. Jane tried to reconcile her to the match, but even Jane could not persuade her."

Mrs. Bennet was correct. I paused in my project to share this conversation between Jane and Elizabeth, from chapter 24.

"My dear Lizzy, do not give way to such feelings as these. They will ruin your happiness. You do not make allowance enough for difference of situation and temper. Consider Mr. Collins's respectability, and Charlotte's steady, prudent character. Remember that she is one of a large family; that as to fortune, it is a most eligible match."

"To oblige you, I would try to believe almost anything, but no one else could be benefited by such a belief as this; for were I persuaded that Charlotte had any regard for him, I should only think worse of her understanding than I now do of her heart. My dear Jane, Mr. Collins is a conceited, pompous, narrow-minded, silly man; you know he is, as well as I do; and you must feel, as well as I do, that the woman who married him cannot have a proper way of thinking. You shall not defend her, though it is Charlotte Lucas. You shall not, for the sake of one individual, change the meaning of principle and integrity, nor endeavor to persuade yourself or me, that selfishness is prudence, and insensibility of danger security for happiness."

"You see?" cried Mrs. Bennet, as I put down the text. "It was a difficult time for me, for Jane, and even for Elizabeth. We all struggled with our spirits." Then she inspected the nook near the fireplace. "My goodness, that is filthy."

She was right about the mess. Not only was there dust and dirt, but sometime, possibly years ago, something made of glass had fallen and had broken to bits behind the overflowing magazine rack. The shards were dangerously sharp; I needed a special container to hold them. I found a small cardboard box, and carefully placed the shards within. I then fetched the vacuum. I asked Mrs. Bennet what I should learn from these last scenes, but she did not answer until the machine had stopped making its noise.

"Sometimes, when you attempt a great project, you will be disappointed."

At first, I smiled at her calling finding husbands for daughters a great project. But then I checked myself, for finding a good partner was a challenge in any age, while finding five partners for five different daughters would be especially difficult.

"This does not mean you should give up – but you may need to take steps to restore your spirits," said Mrs. Bennet. "Only then can you return to your business."

I mostly agreed with her. There were situations, of course, in which one needed time to grieve, and we were learning these days that much depression had physical origins. "What did you do?" I asked.

"Oh! I am revived by time with friends."

I put the fire utensils back and admired my work; the space had not looked this good in years.

I washed my hands and returned to Mrs. Bennet. "Let's continue."

CHAPTER 22

The gloom experienced by Mrs. Bennet was severe, but the distractions of the everyday and the fact that their lives were not so very different than what they had been before the appearance of Mr. Bingley and Mr. Collins in their lives gradually returned Mrs. Bennet to her usual self. Only Jane, still attached to Mr. Bingley, could not be cheered, but Jane took pains to hide her dejection.

The best antidote to the melancholy of the short days and the long nights was Mr. Wickham, who had a talent for entertaining them and everyone else. His handsome face and his pleasant conversation made him welcome everywhere. Moreover, he was an excellent dancer, moving with spirit and elegance. Elizabeth seemed especially attached to him, but he was a favorite with Lydia as well.

"Mind you do not refuse him, too, should he propose!" Mrs. Bennet advised Elizabeth. "But remember, too, Wickham is popular everywhere and you have competition."

Mr. Collins departed again, and a few days later Mr. and Mrs. Gardiner arrived from London in order to spend Christmas with them. After welcoming them both, Mrs. Bennet turned to her sister-in-law for conversation. Mrs. Bennet was not a great correspondent, so, unlike her daughters, she had not communicated her troubles by letter to her sister-in-law, but she *was* a great talker, and she spent an hour unburdening her heart to her brother's wife. Two of her girls had been upon the point of marriage, which would have been so satisfying! But after all, there was nothing in it; her efforts and her exertions had been for naught.

"I do not blame Jane," she continued, "for Jane would have got Mr. Bingley if she could. But Lizzy! Oh, sister! It is very hard to think that she might have been Mr. Collins's wife by this time, had it not been for her own perverseness. He made her an offer in this very room, and she refused him. The consequence of it is, that Lady Lucas will have a daughter married before I have, and that the Longbourn estate is just as much entailed as ever."

Mrs. Gardiner attempted to speak, but Mrs. Bennet had more to say, this time complaining about her neighbors, friends who had been a part of her life as long as she could remember, but who had betrayed her. "The Lucases are very artful people indeed, sister. They are all for what they can get. I am sorry to say it of them, but so it is. It makes me very nervous and poorly, to be thwarted so in my own family, and to have neighbors who think of themselves before anybody else."

Mrs. Bennet decided she had gone on long enough on the subject. She poured more tea, handed a cup to her sister-in-law, and said, "Your coming just at this time is the greatest of comforts, and I am very glad to hear what you tell us, of long sleeves."

"Do you not have something planned with the Lucases?" asked Mrs. Gardiner.

"Yes, on Wednesday. I could not avoid it; the Lucases knew you were visiting and insisted on inviting you to dinner. Sir William has always been fond of Edward. And, as their daughter is to marry Mr. Collins, the families will be connected. Oh! What a terrible day that will be, when Charlotte Lucas turns me out of my own home."

Mrs. Gardiner assured Mrs. Bennet there was no reason to worry; if that happened – and she was not sure it would – Mr. Gardiner would provide for his sister and his nieces. They might not be able to stay at Longbourn House, but they would not be reduced to poverty.

These words provided great comfort to Mrs. Bennet. "Oh! sister, you are too kind, sister! But I hope it will never come to that. I do not want to be a burden and come to live with you and Edward."

Mrs. Gardiner's eyebrows rose, as if she were not sure she wanted Mrs. Bennet to come live with her either. "If such an event happens, Mr. Gardiner will find an arrangement, I am sure, that will be satisfactory to all. We hope, however, that Mr. Bennet will live for many more years. Besides telling you about long sleeves, Mrs. Bennet, is there anything I can do for you today?"

Mrs. Bennet never forgot her main object. "My daughters need husbands. That is the best way to keep them from ever being encumbrances on you in the future. Jane, especially, has met every eligible young man in the area, and has been admired by many, but she has only fallen in love with one – and he has left the country. If you could take her to London and introduce her to some young men, then that would be helpful."

Mrs. Gardiner said Jane was always welcome to visit them in Gracechurch Street, but she could not promise a supply of eligible young men. Their style of living – the Gardiners had several young children – did not let them partake much of society.

"Still, it may happen in London," said Mrs. Bennet. "Perhaps Edward will meet someone suitable through business and bring him to Gracechurch Street for tea. Unlike my other girls, Jane is not charmed by the officers."

"And she will not encounter this Mr. Bingley by chance, if that is what you hope," Mrs. Gardiner warned. "We are not in the same social circle."

"No! I do not expect that," cried Mrs. Bennet, although that was indeed what she hoped. "However, they are more likely to meet if Jane is there than if she remains here, and he was so struck by her beauty before. I am a partial mother, but I do not think her looks have lessened, do you, sister?"

Mrs. Gardiner agreed Miss Bennet was as lovely as ever.

"It is not easy to find husbands for daughters," said Mrs. Bennet. "I cannot ask you to succeed when I have failed. However, I would appreciate it if you try, or at least if you take Jane away from here for a bit – I believe that being in the same rooms where she met Mr. Bingley is too dispiriting for her. But, my dear sister, let the idea seem to come from you."

Mrs. Gardiner said she needed to speak to Mr. Gardiner, but she was certain he would agree.

"I cannot ask more," said Mrs. Bennet.

"Now, tell me about these officers," said Mrs. Gardiner.

"Oh! The officers," cried Mrs. Bennet. "They add so much to Meryton. There is no shortage of gentlemen at the assemblies these days, which means that none of the girls need sit out the dances. But the most agreeable, the handsomest of them all, is Mr. Wickham."

Mrs. Bennet's Advice

The night was unexpectedly cold, so after I rose, I set about making a fire in the fireplace, an activity far more pleasant since I had cleaned up the nearby corner. I opened the chimney damper and arranged for a draft, laid some wood, cardboard and lit a match.

Mrs. Bennet was interested in the match. "Mr. Bennet has heard of such things, but I have never seen one."

After the wood started to burn, I put the screen before the blaze and resumed our discussion of the story. "*You* were responsible for sending Jane to London? I always thought it was Mrs. Gardiner's idea. This is what she said to Elizabeth," I said, and I read to her from chapter 25.

"Poor Jane! I am sorry for her, because, with her disposition, she may not get over it immediately. It had better have happened to you, Lizzy; you would have laughed yourself out of it sooner. But do you think she would be prevailed upon to go back with us? Change of scene might be of service—and perhaps a little relief from home may be as useful as anything."

Elizabeth was exceedingly pleased with this proposal, and felt persuaded of her sister's ready acquiescence.

"I hope," added Mrs. Gardiner, *"that no consideration with regard to this young man will influence her. We live in so different a part of town, all our connections are so different, and, as you well know, we go out so little, that it is very improbable that they should meet at all, unless he really comes to see her."*

Mrs. Bennet defended her taking credit. "You will notice, Young Lady, Mrs. Gardiner does not say it was *not* my idea," said Mrs. Bennet. "Mrs. Gardiner was wise enough to notice the awkwardness between Lizzy and me, so something being *my* idea would not be a recommendation. But really, arranging a visit for Jane to London was obvious, so how can it be a surprise that it occurred to me as well as to Mrs. Gardiner?"

Considering Mrs. Bennet's personality, and her scheming in other situations, her claim to have done what she could to advance Jane's visit to London did not strike me as improbable.

"I did not know if Jane and Mr. Bingley would meet," said Mrs. Bennet. "As Mrs. Gardiner said, there was no guarantee; it was even unlikely, but the chances were *better* if Jane were in London. And if not, she might meet someone else."

I took the poker in my hand and used it to push back a burning log that had rolled forward. "What should I learn from this?"

"Oh! When you are out of options, ask for help from others."

CHAPTER 23

For Mrs. Bennet, the week with Mr. and Mrs. Gardiner flew by. She used her brother's visit as an excuse to increase their engagements. Mr. Bennet would normally protest against so much society, but in the Christmas week he was resigned. Besides, he enjoyed Mr. Gardiner's company. So, not only did they dine at the Lucases, but they also dined with Mr. and Mrs. Phillips, as Mrs. Phillips was also eager to spend time with her brother.

And, whenever they were not invited elsewhere, Mrs. Bennet made sure they had company: Mrs. Long and her nieces; Mr. Robinson; and, of course, a large helping of officers. Mr. Wickham was invited often, and to Mrs. Bennet's satisfaction, he was as handsome and as charming as she had promised. He had some commonalities with Mrs. Gardiner, who before her marriage had spent several years in Derbyshire, which was where Pemberley, Mr. Darcy's estate, was located. Mr. Wickham's residence in that part of the country was more recent than Mrs. Gardiner's, and she was happy to learn of improvements he could tell her about Lambton, a town only five miles from Pemberley.

"The late Mr. Darcy was an excellent man," said Mrs. Gardiner. "I recall he started a school in Lambton for boys and his wife, Lady Anne, arranged one for the girls."

"Yes, they did," said Mr. Wickham, and he related several instances of the generosity of old Mr. Darcy, who had been his godfather and for whom he was named.

"What do you think of Mr. Wickham, sister?" Mrs. Bennet asked, after the officers had departed from Longbourn.

"He is as agreeable as you said he would be," said Mrs. Gardiner.

"What do you think of him as a husband for one of the girls?"

"For that, I do not have enough information," said Mrs. Gardiner. "Do you know his income?"

Mrs. Bennet spoke of what Mr. Wickham's income *ought* to be, if the late Mr. Darcy's wishes had been fulfilled properly and he had received a particular living. Of course, if Wickham had become a clergyman, he would not now be an officer, and they would not have the pleasure of his company. She explained that their brother Phillips said Mr. Wickham provided good custom with all the tradesmen of Meryton.

"That is all well and good, as long as he pays his bills," said Mrs. Gardiner. "Does he?"

Mrs. Bennet did not know.

"Let us ask our brother," said Mrs. Gardiner. She inquired of Mr. Phillips, who was in the room with them, and he reported that one or two tradesmen had complained about Mr. Wickham's being behindhand in

MRS. BENNET'S ADVICE TO YOUNG LADIES

settling a few bills with them.

"Colonel Forster will straighten him out," said Mr. Phillips. "He cannot allow the reputation of the regiment to suffer."

"I hope not," said Mrs. Gardiner.

"Oh! Wickham will find the money if he needs it. Who could deny him anything?" Mrs. Bennet sympathized with the young officer, as she also had a desire to spend more than Mr. Bennet thought she should.

"Still, I will warn Lizzy," said Mrs. Gardiner.

Mrs. Bennet said that if Elizabeth and Mr. Wickham truly loved each other, they would find a way. However, she did not object to Mrs. Gardiner giving Lizzy counsel.

"Lizzy is but twenty. She still has time to find a husband," said Mrs. Gardiner. And she changed the subject to power loom weaving, a method of creating much better and yet less expensive cloth.

The Gardiners' visit was soon over. Before they climbed into their coach, Mrs. Bennet kissed her brother and her sister farewell. She clung a moment to her oldest daughter, who was going with them.

"Jane, my love, you are such a beautiful young lady – it will all turn out all right."

Mrs. Bennet remained in the driveway even after the carriage pulled away. She hoped her words of encouragement to her daughter would prove true.

Mrs. Bennet's Advice

After sleeping poorly the night before, I needed a nap, so I went to the bedroom and stretched out. Nevertheless, I had a few questions for Mrs. Bennet.

"There was talk about Mr. Wickham's extravagant habits?"

"A little."

"Why did you not follow up on this?" I asked. After all, Mrs. Bennet had examined every detail she could find on Mr. Bingley.

"Why should I?" asked Mrs. Bennet. "His financial situation was not important to me! Mrs. Gardiner warned Lizzy to stay away from him, and at the time he showed no particular interest in any of my other girls. Also, Mr. Wickham did not owe Mr. Bennet any money. Besides, the regiment attempted to hush up his problems."

"And you asked Mrs. Gardiner to give advice to Elizabeth?"

"Do you doubt me?"

I did; Mrs. Bennet seemed to be ready to take credit for everything. On the other hand, she was ungrudgingly generous towards her girls, willing to send Jane to London for months, even though Jane assisted with running Longbourn House.

Mrs. Bennet pointed out that Jane was of more assistance to Mr. Bennet than to herself, but otherwise she was ready to sacrifice anything for her daughters. "At that time, Lizzy would not heed my advice, and Mr. Bennet, although he loves Lizzy, was not always in a position to understand a young lady's needs. So, I encouraged Mrs. Gardiner to give her counsel."

Drifting to sleep, I closed my eyes, but I could still hear Mrs. Bennet's voice.

"If your children will not take your advice, find someone trustworthy whose advice they will take."

CHAPTER 24

Jane and the Gardiners were gone. The church bells rang in the New Year, and then, early in January, Charlotte Lucas became Mrs. Collins. She asked, most earnestly, Elizabeth to visit her at Hunsford, by joining her sister Maria and her father Sir William Lucas when they made the journey in March. Elizabeth, although fond of Charlotte, was reluctant to go and still hesitating shortly before they were to leave.

"Aye, of course you do not want to go," said Mrs. Bennet. "You do not want to see your friend's wonderful situation, which could have been yours."

The family was sitting around the fireplace for tea. "I have no fear of regretting my decision," said Elizabeth, who was playing backgammon with Kitty. "But I have taken pains, as you know, to avoid spending time with Mr. Collins, and this visit will put me in his company for several weeks."

"*I* would prefer for you to stay here," said Mr. Bennet. "But do you not wish to see the great chimney piece at Rosings?"

"You can go eat their food for a while," declared Mrs. Bennet. "Mr. Collins was such a burden, staying with us all those times and marrying Charlotte instead of you."

"I am also not sure I feel the same way about Charlotte as I did before."

"Now that she is Mrs. Collins instead of Charlotte Lucas?" asked Mrs. Bennet. "Aye, *that* I understand. It was such a betrayal. But that never would have happened had *you* accepted Mr. Collins's offer, Lizzy."

Elizabeth shook her head and rolled the dice.

"Charlotte will want to see you," Kitty said softly. "She is your dearest friend, is she not?"

"She always was," said Elizabeth, moving her pieces and winning the game.

Mary, who was studying some music, said, "Friendship is to be treasured, in adversity as well as in prosperity."

Lydia, who was altering one of her gowns to match the long sleeves worn by Mrs. Gardiner, looked up from her work. "You might as well go to Hunsford with Maria, Lizzy. Wickham is now dancing attendance on Mary King."

Miss King was another young lady in the neighborhood. She had reddish hair and freckles, which prevented her from being considered a local beauty – certainly not in comparison with the Miss Bennets! Miss King, however, had one undeniable asset: a relative had died recently and bequeathed her a handsome sum.

"It is so unfair. Mary King is so plain!" cried Kitty.

"Even Wickham cannot make her pretty. How can he bear to look at her, when he himself is so handsome? Mrs. Forster does not understand it," said Lydia.

Mrs. Forster was the new bride of Colonel Forster; she and Lydia had just met.

"Are you very upset by his defection, Lizzy?" asked Kitty, rising.

"I will survive," said Elizabeth. "Papa, would you care for a round of backgammon?"

Mrs. Bennet believed that, despite her second daughter's brave words, she *was* upset. "Ah, Lizzy, I am sorry for you, even though you do not deserve my pity. We all miss Wickham. What a charming man! And I agree he would be far happier with any Miss Bennet than with Miss Mary King. *That* is obvious."

"I wish *I* had a grandfather who would die and leave me ten thousand pounds!" cried Lydia.

Mr. Bennet took Kitty's place at the backgammon board. "I would not mind an additional ten thousand pounds myself."

"You should go, Lizzy," said Mrs. Bennet. "And who knows? Perhaps you will meet someone interesting at Rosings Park."

"Very well," said Elizabeth. "I will write to Charlotte and tell her I will join her father and her sister in their visit to Mr. Collins's parsonage. We can call on my aunt and uncle on the way."

Elizabeth's intention to accompany Sir William Lucas and his daughter Maria to visit the Collinses in Kent spread through the neighborhood and even the regiment. The news brought them an unexpected but welcome visitor: Lieutenant Wickham! He called the day before Elizabeth's planned departure, and charmed them all, especially Elizabeth.

If only Elizabeth had ten thousand pounds! thought Mrs. Bennet, as she made sure Lieutenant Wickham was well supplied with tea and cake. There was no question; Elizabeth *did* like him – he told her what he remembered of Lady Catherine de Bourgh in the most amusing manner, making them laugh – and although Lieutenant Wickham had been paying attention to Mary King, he had not yet made Miss King an offer.

Mrs. Bennet hoped something would happen to separate Miss King from Mr. Wickham, so that he would be available for one of her daughters. What an addition he made to their family circle! It was a pity to give him up to another.

The officers left, and early the next day, so did Elizabeth. Shortly after sunrise she kissed her family good-bye and climbed into the Lucas carriage.

Mrs. Bennet's Advice

Before I could move from my computer, Mrs. Bennet started speaking. "You are going to ask me, Young Lady, what you should take from this scene. In my opinion, the wisdom comes from two of my younger daughters, Kitty and Mary, and it is about friendship. Although I was angry with Mrs. Collins, Charlotte and Lizzy were close friends for years. You should treasure friendships, and put effort into them, especially when it is hardest."

I thought of times I had let friendships lapse, either because of a difference of opinion or because one of us moved away.

I rose and gathered my cup and saucer, carrying them to the kitchen.

"Lizzy's friendship is so important to Mrs. Collins. And the alliance had so many other possible benefits, not just to Mrs. Collins, but to Elizabeth and the rest of the family!"

I turned on the faucet in order to rinse my cup. "Really? What benefits are you talking about?"

"Oh! Is that not obvious? Mrs. Collins, in all likelihood, could expect to be mistress of Longbourn House herself. If Elizabeth maintains her friendship with Charlotte – and behaves in such a way that she no longer offends Mr. Collins – then, when the time comes, there is a chance they may make a provision for her rather than putting her out to fend for herself in the fields."

"So, you only care about friendships if they benefit you?"

"How can you say that? True affection between friends should be valued for its own sake. Mr. Bennet is a good husband, in his way, but my heart often opens more easily to my sister Phillips and to Lady Lucas and to Mrs. Long. Still, 'tis folly not to recognize when friends can help us in more material areas."

I opened the dishwasher and started stacking dirty dishes inside it.

"Also, Lizzy needed to be away just then. Although she pretended otherwise, watching Wickham court Mary King hurt her. I thought her heart would recover better if she were away."

Reflecting on what Mrs. Bennet said, I resolved to contact an old friend, and to arrange a conversation. We had been extremely close for years, but different time zones and work schedules made talking difficult. But if I rose early, we could manage it.

I went back to my desk and my computer and turned to Mrs. Bennet, for we had a little problem with the story. "Because Jane Austen wrote mostly from the point of view of Elizabeth, she did not write much about you when Elizabeth was at Hunsford."

"Oh! I know! Whenever Lizzy was away, Miss Jane Austen ignored us, as if everyone in Longbourn House had turned to stone."

"I want you to tell me about that time," I told her. "However, I'll also want your opinion of the scenes at Hunsford."

Mrs. Bennet was always willing to give her opinion.

"Let's start with Longbourn," I said, and she agreed.

CHAPTER 25

After Elizabeth departed, the weather improved as spring took hold. Mr. Bennet attended to the farm, supervising the planting of crops, while Mrs. Bennet used the carriage whenever she could to make more frequent excursions to Meryton.

A week after Elizabeth's departure, Sir William Lucas, who had his own business to tend to in Meryton and who could not make long visits to other places, returned to the neighborhood and reported on the situation at Hunsford. Sir William also carried two letters from Elizabeth, one addressed explicitly to her father and the other directed to her mother. Mr. Bennet read his letter aloud to Mrs. Bennet; Elizabeth said that Mrs. Collins seemed happy enough and that Lady Catherine de Bourgh fulfilled all their expectations – as did the chimney piece and the large number of windows at Rosings. To her mother, Elizabeth reported on Jane's situation – on their way to Hunsford, Elizabeth and the Lucases had stopped one night at the Gardiners – letting Mrs. Bennet know that Mr. Bingley had *not* called on Jane while she was in London, and that Miss Bingley, when she had come to Gracechurch Street, had been cold and distant.

Mrs. Bennet understood, from the letter from her second daughter, Elizabeth was trying to put an end to her hopes for a match between Jane and Mr. Bingley. But the mention of Miss Bingley and how she had dropped her friendship with Jane made her suspicions grow.

Mrs. Bennet was as convinced as ever that Mr. Bingley had been violently in love with Jane. What if Miss Bingley had interfered with that relationship? Mrs. Bennet recalled how, after the Netherfield ball, Mr. Bingley had left the next day for London on business – only to be followed the day after by Miss Bingley, the Hursts and Mr. Darcy.

Mrs. Bennet told Lydia to bring her Jane's correspondence. Lydia did so, and Mrs. Bennet flipped through the letters Jane had received from various friends until she found those from Miss Bingley. She studied the letters from Miss Bingley. Then she asked Lydia to bring her Elizabeth's correspondence, too. In a letter from Jane to Elizabeth, Mrs. Bennet read the following:

My dearest Lizzy will, I am sure, be incapable of triumphing in her better judgement, at my expense, when I confess myself to have been entirely deceived in Miss Bingley's regard for me. But, my dear sister, though the event has proved you right, do not think me obstinate if I still assert that, considering what her behavior was, my confidence was as natural as your suspicion. I do not at all comprehend her reason for wishing to be intimate with me; but if the same circumstances were to happen again, I am sure I should be deceived again. Caroline did not return my visit till yesterday; and not a note, not a line, did I receive in the meantime. When she did come, it was very evident that she had no pleasure in it; she made a slight, formal apology, for not calling before, said not a word of wishing to see me again, and was in every respect so altered a creature, that when she went away I was perfectly resolved to continue the acquaintance no longer.

The tone and the manner persuaded Mrs. Bennet that Miss Bingley and the rest of the party of Netherfield had departed in order to separate Mr. Bingley from Jane.

Mrs. Bennet could not decide who was most to blame for this – Miss Bingley? Mr. Darcy? Miss Bingley, at least, had been a willing participant even if she were not the instigator.

But why would Miss Bingley do such a thing? Mrs. Bennet discussed this with her sister, Mrs. Phillips.

"Are you sure?" asked Mrs. Phillips. "You told me Miss Bingley seemed especially fond of Jane."

"I always thought she was. I do not understand it."

Mrs. Phillips considered, then offered a speculation. Miss Bingley, as her brother had no wife, had served as the mistress of Netherfield. She might like Jane as a friend but not want to be supplanted in her brother's household.

"Oh! sister! You may be right," said Mrs. Bennet. She knew how worried she was about her position at Longbourn House being taken over by Mrs. Collins; why should Miss Bingley not have similar feelings? "What can we do about it?"

But neither Mrs. Bennet nor Mrs. Phillips had any idea what they could do. "If Miss Bingley were to marry someone else – like Mr. Darcy – that would take her out of Mr. Bingley's way, and he would no longer be under his sister's influence."

"That is what we should hope for," said Mrs. Phillips. "Although if Miss Bingley *is* responsible for separating Mr. Bingley from Jane, it seems too kind to Miss Bingley, to let her marry Mr. Darcy. He is so handsome! And so rich!"

"And so disagreeable," said Mrs. Bennet. "Being married to Mr. Darcy would be punishment for any woman. And Miss Bingley deserves to be punished, after making poor Jane suffer." She looked out the window, and her gaze landed on Mr. Wickham and Miss King. Mr. Wickham! Another defector!

Mrs. Phillips glanced too. "That sight is disappointing," she pronounced.

"Wickham looks wretched!" exclaimed Mrs. Bennet.

If Mrs. Bennet had been a disinterested observer, she might have not discovered any clues of dissatisfaction in the handsome lieutenant's demeanor. His behavior towards Miss King was solicitous; he helped her avoid a patch of mud, and he appeared to listen to her conversation with pleasure. But Mrs. Bennet had observed Mr. Wickham when he had been at his liveliest, laughing with animation with Elizabeth. No, Mr. Wickham was not, in her opinion, in love with Mary King.

They would never be happy together. If only she could stop that union!

If Miss Bingley could interfere to separate her brother from Jane, why could not Mrs. Bennet apply the same strategy? Was there anything Mrs. Bennet could do to separate Wickham from Miss King?

Mrs. Bennet asked her sister if she thought Wickham and Mary King made a good match. As Mr. Phillips was Miss King's attorney, Mrs. Phillips would not speak against the young lady, even though she was red-haired and freckled, but Mrs. Phillips did have some details she could share. "Now that her grandfather is dead, Mary King has an uncle who has invited her to stay with him," Mrs. Phillips reported.

Mrs. Bennet wondered if Mr. Phillips could encourage the niece to move to her uncle's house. And when Mr. Phillips arrived for a cup of tea and a slice of cake, Mrs. Bennet suggested it to her brother.

"I have to do whatever is in the best interest of my client," said Mr. Phillips.

"It *would* be in Mary King's best interest," said Mrs. Bennet. "Mr. Wickham does not love her."

Mr. Phillips said he would consider his sister's request, and several weeks later he did press the uncle to take in Mary King. His action, however, was motivated by information to which Mrs. Bennet was not privy. Mr. Phillips, responsible for advising Miss King with respect to the recently inherited ten thousand pounds, was asked by Miss King to settle some local debts for Lieutenant Wickham.

"What sort of debts?" asked Mr. Phillips.

Miss King had a list of expenditures made by Mr. Wickham at several taverns, the local inn, a tailor and a bootmaker.

"Why does Lieutenant Wickham not pay these expenses himself? He receives a salary from the militia!"

"Not a large one," whispered Mary King. Then she added, as if she had rehearsed the words before: "Please, Mr. Phillips, it is my money, is it not? I love him and I fear he will not marry me unless I pay these bills!"

Mr. Phillips, generally affable, noticed the warning signs of a man planning to spend the fortune of a betrothed – only Miss King and Lieutenant Wickham were not actually betrothed. Although the attorney enjoyed the amusing officer's company more than he did the insipid Miss King's, Miss King was his client, and Mr. Phillips was always mindful of his client. "I must strongly counsel you against marrying this officer."

Miss King wavered, but she was not yet against Wickham. "Please, Mr. Phillips. I promised."

Mr. Phillips pretended to relent, but he explained he could not give her the money immediately. He said it took time to transfer funds and to investigate the expenses.

"How long?" asked Miss King.

"It depends," said Mr. Phillips. In truth, he could have settled things immediately, but he wanted time to protect his young client. "Perhaps a week?"

As soon as Miss King left his office, Mr. Phillips sent an express to her uncle, who was at his London home, and warned him that his niece was being preyed on by a fortune-hunter. Two days later the uncle arrived, bringing his daughter with him, and the uncle and the cousin packed up Miss King and took her away. Instead of returning to London, they continued to Liverpool, to make sure Miss King and Mr. Wickham were further apart.

Mrs. Bennet was not aware of these developments until after they happened. She was chatting with Lady Lucas, who had called to say when Elizabeth and Maria would return from Hunsford, when Lydia and Kitty, fresh from a visit to Meryton, returned to Longbourn House with part of the news.

"Mary King has left Meryton!" Lydia announced. "Without a wedding, without so much as an engagement! Wickham is a free man."

Kitty said that if Mary King was in love with the lieutenant, she ought not to have let her uncle take her away.

"No one cares about Mary King's feelings!" cried Lydia. "What matters is Wickham!"

Lady Lucas inquired if Lydia had any information on the matter; Lydia had spoken at length with Mrs. Forster. Wickham, although apparently *surprised* by Miss King's departure, had not behaved like a man with a broken heart. He had joined his fellow officers in a drink and a game of cards.

"Oh! That is good news," said Mrs. Bennet, wondering if her conversation with Mr. Phillips had played a role in events.

"But none of this matters," said Kitty, "because the militia is leaving as well. They are going to Brighton."

"Can *we* go to Brighton for the summer? Please, Mamma?" begged Lydia.

Mrs. Bennet agreed Brighton would be great fun – she had always wanted to try sea-bathing; it would settle her nerves – and she promised to speak to Mr. Bennet on the subject.

"Sir William says Meryton will miss the custom," said Lady Lucas.

"Anyway, Mrs. Bennet, you now know when our daughters plan to return. Can you arrange for your carriage to fetch them?"

Mrs. Bennet promised to send the carriage for Maria Lucas and Elizabeth on the appointed day. She then ordered it for herself for that afternoon and went to Meryton to see if her brother and sister could tell her anything about Miss King's departure.

Mr. Phillips explained what had happened. Mrs. Bennet was not alarmed by what her brother said about Wickham's debts, mostly because she herself tended to run up accounts with the draper and the milliner. What interested her was Wickham. "Is his heart free?" she asked.

"Oh, I do not think the lieutenant's heart was touched by Miss King," said Mr. Phillips. "And I think Miss King will benefit from the guidance of a guardian."

Mrs. Bennet went home, convinced she had played a role, however small, in keeping Mr. Wickham safe from Mary King. She felt a little guilty on Miss King's behalf, but she always put her daughters first. "Lizzy ought to thank me," she said to herself, but she knew she would never tell her.

Mrs. Bennet's Advice

Spring was in the air; daffodils bloomed in a sunny spot beneath the cherry tree. The weather was not exactly warm, but it was warmer than it had been. I was outside clearing the bits of dry leaves that had been trapped beneath the snow.

"You wanted Wickham and Mary King to separate?" I asked, for Mrs. Bennet had joined me.

"Of course! We all did. Wickham did not love Mary King; he would never have been happy with her."

"What about Mary King's feelings?" I asked, sweeping the leaves into a pile.

Mrs. Bennet admitted Miss King might have suffered, for which she was sorry, but Mrs. Bennet had done nothing to influence Wickham's feelings. As Wickham had not loved her, their marriage would have been miserable. "Better to suffer a few months of unhappiness than to be stuck with a bad partner for life."

Besides, Mrs. Bennet said her role in the matter had been tiny, inconsequential; all she had done was to make a suggestion to Mr. Phillips.

"I know you are supposed to be giving me advice," I said, picking up an armful of leaves and moving them to a pile, "but I think *you* feel guilty for what you did. Perhaps Mary King *was* better off without Mr. Wickham; in fact, I believe she was. But you did not separate them in order to protect Miss King."

Mrs. Bennet said nothing.

"You separated them, the way others separated Mr. Bingley and Jane."

"That was my intention," she said. "But if Wickham truly loved Miss King, he could have pursued her to Liverpool. If Miss King had cared enough, she could have insisted on staying in Meryton."

"If you believe the arguments you are making, then you should ask yourself why Mr. Bingley did not return to Netherfield sooner," I said. "Especially as the journey from London was shorter for him than it would be for Wickham to go to Liverpool. Bingley's income, too, made such travel easier."

"I know," said Mrs. Bennet. "That is why I was so worried about Mr. Bingley, why I did not understand it. Back in November, at the Netherfield ball, he was obviously in love with Jane – his feelings were much deeper than any Wickham ever had for Mary King. So, why did Mr. Bingley stay away?"

I had finished cleaning up the leaves; I put away the rake and peeled off my gardening gloves. "Let's go back inside and continue the story."

CHAPTER 26

Jane and Elizabeth returned to Longbourn. Mr. Bennet was especially happy to have his favorite daughter back home and Mrs. Bennet – although disappointed that neither girl had caught a husband – was relieved to see Jane as beautiful as ever. Jane's lovely smile and her sweet nature brightened every room she entered.

Mrs. Bennet then observed Elizabeth, noting that daughter no longer cared to socialize with the officers and was against the scheme to go to Brighton. Mrs. Bennet was concerned and decided to speak with her. Elizabeth, however, had always been the most difficult of her daughters to reach, but Mrs. Bennet was determined to try. When she saw Elizabeth take a book with her to read on a bench in the shrubbery, Mrs. Bennet decided to follow her. Besides, Mrs. Bennet wanted to consult Elizabeth about Jane.

"Well, Lizzy," said Mrs. Bennet, "what is your opinion *now* of this sad business of Jane's? For my part, I am determined never to speak of it again to anybody. I told my sister Phillips so the other day. But I cannot find out that Jane saw anything of him in London. Well, he is a very undeserving young man – and I do not suppose there's the least chance in the world of her ever getting him now. There is no talk of his coming to Netherfield again in the summer; and I have enquired of everybody, too, who is likely to know."

Elizabeth closed the book. "I do not believe he will ever live at Netherfield anymore."

Mrs. Bennet joined her daughter on the bench. "Oh well! it is just as he chooses. Nobody wants him to come. Though I shall always say he used my daughter extremely ill; and if I was her, I would not have put up with it."

Elizabeth said nothing to this, so Mrs. Bennet changed the subject. "So, the Collinses live very comfortable, do they? Well, well, I only hope it will last. And what sort of table do they keep? Charlotte is an excellent manager, I dare say. If she is half as sharp as her mother, she is saving enough. There is nothing extravagant in *their* housekeeping, I dare say."

Elizabeth agreed the Collinses were not extravagant.

Mrs. Bennet detected some dissatisfaction on her daughter's part. Something had happened. Elizabeth seemed to have matured, become more reserved, since her visit to Hunsford. Was it merely the realization that Charlotte had made the right choice in choosing to marry Mr. Collins, establishing herself for life? Mrs. Bennet probed a little further, but Elizabeth's replies were not revealing. Mrs. Bennet did not think she had found the answer.

Mrs. Bennet's Advice

With the sun shining, the pansies in my flower boxes were flourishing, but so were the weeds. Mrs. Bennet joined me as I pulled up the plants I did not want. "You were correct that something happened in Kent. While Elizabeth was visiting the Collinses in Hunsford, Mr. Darcy arrived at Rosings in order to visit his aunt, Lady Catherine de Bourgh. After a few weeks, Mr. Darcy made Elizabeth an offer of marriage."

"Oh! Could you remind me of those passages?" Mrs. Bennet said those scenes were some of the furthest from her own, and hence the hardest for her to reach.

I put down the trowel, picked up a copy of the text, and explained that in this scene, which took place in chapter 34, Elizabeth was alone at the Hunsford parsonage. To Mrs. Bennet I read:

...her spirits were very differently affected, when, to her utter amazement, she saw Mr. Darcy walk into the room. In an hurried manner he immediately began an enquiry after her health, imputing his visit to a wish of hearing that she were better. She answered him with cold civility. He sat down for a few moments, and then getting up, walked about the room. Elizabeth was surprised, but said not a word. After a silence of several minutes, he came towards her in an agitated manner, and thus began:

"In vain I have struggled. It will not do. My feelings will not be repressed. You must allow me to tell you how ardently I admire and love you."

Elizabeth's astonishment was beyond expression. She stared, coloured, doubted, and was silent. This he considered sufficient encouragement; and the avowal of all that he felt, and had long felt for her, immediately followed. He spoke well; but there were feelings besides those of the heart to be detailed; and he was not more eloquent on the subject of tenderness than of pride. His sense of her inferiority — of its being a degradation — of the family obstacles which had always opposed to inclination, were dwelt on with a warmth which seemed due to the consequence he was wounding, but was very unlikely to recommend his suit.

In spite of her deeply-rooted dislike, she could not be insensible to the compliment of such a man's affection, and though her intentions did not vary for an instant, she was at first sorry for the pain he was to receive; till, roused to resentment by his subsequent language, she lost all compassion in anger. She tried, however, to compose herself to answer him with patience, when he should have done. He concluded with representing to her the strength of that attachment which, in spite of all his endeavours, he had found impossible to conquer; and with expressing his hope that it would now be rewarded by her acceptance of his hand. As he said this, she could easily see that he had no doubt of a favourable answer. He spoke of apprehension and anxiety, but his countenance expressed real security. Such a circumstance could only exasperate farther, and, when he ceased, the colour rose into her cheeks, and she said:

MRS. BENNET'S ADVICE TO YOUNG LADIES

"In such cases as this, it is, I believe, the established mode to express a sense of obligation for the sentiments avowed, however unequally they may be returned. It is natural that obligation should be felt, and if I could feel gratitude, I would now thank you. But I cannot — I have never desired your good opinion, and you have certainly bestowed it most unwillingly. I am sorry to have occasioned pain to anyone. It has been most unconsciously done, however, and I hope will be of short duration. The feelings which, you tell me, have long prevented the acknowledgment of your regard, can have little difficulty in overcoming it after this explanation."

"Oh! My word!" cried Mrs. Bennet. "Lizzy was even more cruel to Mr. Darcy than she was to Mr. Collins!"

"She was," I agreed. "But Mr. Collins, even though Elizabeth did not want to marry him, was polite when he proposed. Mr. Darcy was not."

"That was wrong of him," said Mrs. Bennet. "Of course, I knew nothing about it at the time, and I was completely unaware of Mr. Darcy's feelings, and I disliked him as much as Elizabeth did. Still, I believe her refusal was a mistake."

"You do? Mr. Darcy was so rude! And, Mrs. Bennet, far from me to criticize—"

"— you have criticized before! —"

"— she was angry with him. She gets her anger, her readiness to speak sharply, from you. Do you really think *you* could have controlled yourself?"

"She does get her quick temper from me. I am so glad you recognize that. So many readers do not, and they do not understand that Lizzy, no matter how much she wants to deny nature, is very much my daughter. Despite all this, I believe I could have controlled myself. You know my purpose, my first purpose, is to get my daughters married so they will not be paupers."

I thought Mrs. Bennet defended herself very ably. I picked up the trowel again in order to dig up more weeds.

She returned to the details of the scene at the parsonage; despite the tension between her and Elizabeth, Mrs. Bennet adored anything that demonstrated admiration of any of her daughters. "Mr. Darcy was in love with Lizzy, so much in love with her that he proposed!" she exclaimed. "Most gentlemen do not go around proposing every day, so it is not surprising that Mr. Darcy should do it so awkwardly on his first time. Nevertheless, Lizzy should not have refused him the way she did."

I moved over to the next weed-infested flower box. "Besides her dislike of him, and her anger at his rude behavior, Elizabeth had two reasons for doubting Mr. Darcy's character. Elizabeth believed Mr. Darcy had treated Mr. Wickham with cruelty and contempt."

Mrs. Bennet sighed. "I am fond of Wickham; he is the most agreeable of my sons-in-law. But although Wickham is charming, his interpretation of events is not always accurate."

"Wickham's a damned liar!"

"Yes. So, that should not have been a reason for refusing Mr. Darcy. Although I suppose Lizzy did not know the truth about Wickham and Darcy's history at the time."

"Elizabeth also believed – with reason – that Mr. Darcy was instrumental in separating Jane from Mr. Bingley."

"Oh! Yes! But, my dear Young Lady, *that* was absolutely the worst reason to refuse Mr. Darcy!"

"I don't understand you. Unlike Elizabeth's reproach about Mr. Wickham, this accusation was true. Mr. Darcy did help separate Mr. Bingley and Miss Bennet."

"I am not defending Mr. Darcy's conduct. But Lizzy, if she was concerned for Jane, was suddenly in a position to do something about it. If she had accepted Mr. Darcy's offer of marriage, Mr. Bingley, as Mr. Darcy's friend, and Jane, as Lizzy's sister, would have been thrown together. Their romance would have blossomed, and they would have married. The best way for Lizzy to secure Jane's happiness would have been for her to accept Mr. Darcy's offer. But she did not. She refused him, and in such a way that it is amazing that he ever consented to see her again!"

Mrs. Bennet's arguments had some logic, I thought, as I attempted to pull up some weeds without also pulling up a pansy.

Mrs. Bennet continued. "Lizzy, bless her, did not know what she was doing. I must remember she was still young, not yet one and twenty, and while she was in Kent, she did not have her mother to advise her. But how close we were to losing everything – if Lizzy had had her way, and chased off Mr. Darcy permanently, none of my daughters – not Jane, not Lizzy and not even Lydia would be married to their current partners."

"It all turns out all right in the end," I reassured her.

"You say that, but I never know." Mrs. Bennet sighed, and in a quiet voice she added, "When I wander through Miss Jane Austen's story, I often fear things will turn out differently, that none of my daughters will marry, that all my efforts will fail, that Mr. Bennet will fall dead from an apoplectic fit and that Mr. and Mrs. Collins will turn us out as penniless beggars."

Her worry was genuine, and I pitied her. I could not know what it was like to be a character in a story, unsure of the happy ending. On the other hand, in real life, we also did not know our endings. To keep from getting too philosophical, I asked: "From this situation, what advice would you give me? You cannot tell me not to refuse Mr. Darcy. Mr. Darcy will not be proposing to *me*."

"Oh! Is it not obvious?" asked Mrs. Bennet. "No one, and certainly not you, dear Young Lady, should hastily turn down a golden opportunity."

Mrs. Bennet explained she did not mean to say that a person should accept a golden opportunity immediately, either. "Given Mr. Darcy's previous conduct, Lizzy had every right to be *surprised* by his offer, and I could understand her being angry."

"If you are angry, would you not let that person know?" I could think of many instances of Mrs. Bennet showing anger and disapproval, even anger at Mr. Darcy.

"Oh! Of course, I can be angry, but at least I stop when it is foolish to do so," said Mrs. Bennet. She reminded me how much she had hated Mr. Collins, before he wrote the letter announcing his intention to visit Mr. Bennet and Longbourn House. Then she had perceived, as her family had not, that he hoped to marry one of her daughters. She returned to Mr. Darcy's proposal to Elizabeth. "I understand Lizzy's anger with Mr. Darcy. Given what she knew, her ire was justified. Still, she should not have refused him so categorically. She should have let him court her, and she should have encouraged him to earn her good opinion."

"It made for a great scene," I said. Mr. Darcy's insult-laden proposal of Elizabeth Bennet and her spirited rejection was one of the favorites in all literature.

"That may be true, but I do not believe you should base your life choices on what is entertaining in literature."

But I was still entranced by *Pride & Prejudice*. "Without Elizabeth's rejection of Mr. Darcy," I continued, "we would lose half the book. Mr. Darcy's proposal takes place at the exact midpoint of the novel."

"My dear Young Lady, your life does not need to imitate art," said Mrs. Bennet with some asperity. She repeated her advice: "If you are given an unexpected opportunity, do not refuse immediately. Take time to consider – to imagine the possibilities. Ask for advice; consult with someone you trust."

"Get a second opinion," I said.

She nodded, and then asked if we could continue. I put away my gardening things and returned inside.

CHAPTER 27

For a fortnight Mrs. Bennet had all her daughters at Longbourn, and although her mission was to find them husbands, she adored having her girls at home. She could look at Jane's lovely face, listen to Lizzy's laughter, lose herself in Mary's music, and revel in the schemes of Lydia and Kitty.

The fortnight was marred by the anticipation of a sad event – the regiment would be leaving Meryton for Brighton. No more red coats! Fewer men at the dances! And there were some whose company she truly enjoyed! Denny and Captain Carter, Colonel and Mrs. Forster, and most of all, of course, Mr. Wickham.

Mrs. Bennet, with the assistance of Kitty and Lydia, were still trying to persuade Mr. Bennet to take the family to Brighton.

Mr. Bennet, however, kept refusing. "Why should we want to go to Brighton?"

"Oh! Mr. Bennet, why should we not? Other people go on pleasure tours, why should we not as well?"

"I do not think *I* would find any pleasure in Brighton. Why would I wish to trade the comfort of my library for the cramped rooms of an inn?"

"Then we should do it for the girls. They have made such friends among the officers."

"If the officers are such friends with our girls, then the officers should invite them," said Mr. Bennet.

"Our girls never go anywhere!"

"Jane has been in London for several months, while Lizzy has been in Kent – and Lizzy will soon be joining Mr. and Mrs. Gardiner for a tour."

"That is no reason for the rest of us not to go," said Mrs. Bennet.

Mr. Bennet announced he was wanted on the farm, and he left the shade of his library to inspect the fields. The fact that Mr. Bennet had left his library for the fields signaled how little the idea of going to Brighton pleased him. Over the years, Mrs. Bennet had fought many battles with Mr. Bennet and had developed a sense of how they would go; she did not think she would win this one, at least not on her own.

She commiserated with Kitty and Lydia. "I am sure," said she, "I cried for two days together when Colonel Miller's regiment went away. I thought I should have broken my heart."

"I am sure I shall break *mine*," said Lydia.

"If one could but go to Brighton!" observed Mrs. Bennet.

"Oh, yes! — if one could but go to Brighton! But papa is so disagreeable."

"A little sea-bathing would set me up forever."

"And my aunt Phillips is sure it would do *me* a great deal of good," added Kitty.

Mrs. Bennet decided the best strategy to get her way would be to enlist Jane and Elizabeth as allies in her campaign. But both girls had, as Mr. Bennet remarked, just returned from their own journeys.

"Would you not enjoy Brighton, Lizzy? Wickham will be there," said Mrs. Bennet.

"No, Mamma, I think we have had enough of the regiment," said Elizabeth.

To Mrs. Bennet's astonishment, Elizabeth's words were matched by her actions. Elizabeth refused, more than once, to walk into Meryton where she would encounter the officers. When officers came to Longbourn House, she made a late appearance and followed that by an early departure, excusing herself with a headache (but Mrs. Bennet discovered she had been reading, rather than sleeping). When Mr. Wickham attempted to engage her in conversation, Elizabeth usually smiled and moved away.

No, Elizabeth was not pining for Wickham. Mrs. Bennet could not comprehend it, but as the regiment was about depart, it was just as well.

Mrs. Bennet's pity was only required for her two youngest, who were completely miserable at the prospect of the regiment's removal. Then, to Mrs. Bennet's happiness, Lydia was invited by Mrs. Forster, the young bride of Colonel Forster, to join them in Brighton.

"Oh! My dear! What an honor, to be invited by Mrs. Forster herself!" exclaimed Mrs. Bennet.

Lydia flew around Longbourn House, demanding congratulations from everyone, without waiting to listen to their reactions. Jane said she was happy for Lydia, and Mary said she was happy, too, although she added she could not see the attraction of it. Kitty, however, sat down in the drawing-room and cried. "I cannot see why Mrs. Forster should not ask *me* as well as Lydia," said she, "though I am *not* her particular friend. I have just as much right to be asked as she has, and more too, for I am two years older."

"Kitty, you should have spent more time with Mrs. Forster – or another officer's wife – if you wanted an invitation," said Mrs. Bennet. "Lydia has earned her invitation through friendship, just as Lizzy was invited by Mrs. Collins to Hunsford."

Elizabeth, instead of wishing Lydia well, tried to warn her. "Are you sure Papa will give you permission? He has been against any excursion to Brighton."

"Oh! Papa will allow it, I am certain. *He* may not want to go, but he will not care if *I* go."

"You should not celebrate until you have his permission," said Elizabeth.

This situation tried Mrs. Bennet's nerves; she hated it whenever one sister was not happy for another. She could not understand it; she rejoiced in the success of all her daughters. After scolding Kitty, Mrs. Bennet turned to Elizabeth. "Mr. Bennet will give Lydia permission," she said. "You need have no fear on that account, dear Lydia. Come, let us look at your clothes and see if you need anything."

Mrs. Bennet left with Lydia, and they spent a lovely two hours rummaging through gowns, shoes, and ribbons. "My dear, you will be the belle of Brighton!"

"Miss Bennet, the belle of Brighton," repeated Lydia. As none of her older sisters would accompany her, she would be Miss Bennet, *the* Miss Bennet, instead of just Miss Lydia Bennet.

Shortly after that, the regiment had its last day in Meryton. Several officers, including Mr. Wickham and Colonel Forster, dined at Longbourn House. Lydia and her trunk were to leave with the Forsters so that she would be with them as they departed early in the morning.

"Be sure to take every opportunity to enjoy yourself," said Mrs. Bennet, kissing Lydia. "And write to us often!"

"I will. Good-bye!" cried Lydia, and after embracing them all, she climbed into the carriage. Mrs. Bennet wiped away a tear of joy as it pulled away.

Mrs. Bennet's Advice

I was eating my lunch: canned lentil soup that I had improved by adding chopped vegetables and bacon. Mrs. Bennet could not eat anything, but she joined me at the table.

"Did you know Elizabeth tried to stop Lydia from going to Brighton? She spoke to Mr. Bennet about it."

"That must be from pages I do not visit. Remind me, please."

I said the following passage came from chapter 41:

As for Elizabeth herself, this invitation was so far from exciting in her the same feelings as in her mother and Lydia, that she considered it as the death warrant of all possibility of common sense for the latter; and detestable as such a step must make her were it known, she could not help secretly advising her father not to let her go. She represented to him all the improprieties of Lydia's general behaviour, the little advantage she could derive from the friendship of such a woman as Mrs. Forster, and the probability of her being yet more imprudent with such a companion at Brighton, where the temptations must be greater than at home. He heard her attentively, and then said:

"Lydia will never be easy until she has exposed herself in some public place or other, and we can never expect her to do it with so little expense or inconvenience to her family as under the present circumstances."

I skipped ahead, then continued with Elizabeth's speech:

MRS. BENNET'S ADVICE TO YOUNG LADIES

"Our importance, our respectability in the world must be affected by the wild volatility, the assurance and disdain of all restraint which mark Lydia's character. ... In this danger Kitty also is comprehended. She will follow wherever Lydia leads. Vain, ignorant, idle, and absolutely uncontrolled! Oh! my dear father, can you suppose it possible that they will not be censured and despised wherever they are known, and that their sisters will not be often involved in the disgrace?"

*Mr. Bennet saw that her whole heart was in the subject, and affectionately taking her hand said in reply: "Do not make yourself uneasy, my love. Wherever you and Jane are known you must be respected and valued; and you will not appear to less advantage for having a couple of — or I may say, three — very silly sisters. We shall have no peace at Longbourn if Lydia does **not** go to Brighton."*

Mrs. Bennet colored with indignation. "Oh! Lizzy tried to stop Lydia from going to Brighton. How selfish of her! I should not be surprised – but how is it that I did not know?"

I continued by reading from the same chapter:

Had Lydia and her mother known the substance of her conference with her father, their indignation would hardly have found expression in their united volubility.

"Ah, that explains it," Mrs. Bennet said. She told me that as a character from a story, if the author wrote that a character did not know something, ignorance could be hard to overcome. Sometimes she managed it – for example, she had known of Mr. Bennet's visit to Mr. Bingley when that gentleman first took residence at Netherfield – but it was more difficult if the knowledge were too painful. Even after sneaking onto the forbidden pages, she could not recall their events for long. "I have visited that scene in Mr. Bennet's library, and Lizzy's opinion of all of us – Mr. Bennet's opinion, too – hurt to hear. Perhaps it is good I cannot remember them."

I expressed sympathy. "I don't suppose you have any lessons for me from these pages. Perhaps Lydia should not have been permitted to go to Brighton?"

"Oh! That. I do not know, Young Lady, I do not know. I believe, given Miss Jane Austen's opinion of Lydia, not even I could have stopped Lydia from going to Brighton. Miss Jane Austen was determined to send her there."

"Then shall we continue with your side of the story?"

"What about my advice for you? For I have some. We should rejoice when good things happen to our families. Instead of shedding tears for herself, Kitty should have been happy for Lydia, when Mrs. Forster invited her to Brighton."

I agreed that Kitty had not behaved well, but then I reminded Mrs.

Bennet how poorly she had treated Charlotte Lucas, after she accepted Mr. Collins's offer of marriage.

"Oh! Yes! Well, Mr. Collins had proposed to Lizzy only a few days before, was an unexpected blow. And Charlotte Lucas, although a dear neighbor, was not a member of my family. But I suppose I could have been more gracious."

I was surprised to hear Mrs. Bennet speak this way.

"You do not think I am capable of improving? I am, and you will see it at the end. But all you need to know for now, Young Lady, is that we should rejoice in the success of those close to us."

CHAPTER 28

The regiment departed, taking the lively Lydia with it, and Mrs. Bennet tended to the daughters still at home. Jane was indifferent to the departure of the officers – Mrs. Bennet worried about her, but her inquiries about the possible return of Mr. Bingley to Netherfield gleaned no useful information. Mrs. Bennet did not need to worry about Elizabeth; in a few weeks, Elizabeth would take a tour in the north with Mr. and Mrs. Gardiner. And Mary, of course, said she preferred Meryton without red coats on every corner.

Kitty, however, was another matter. "It is not fair," said Kitty. "Why should Lydia have all the fun?"

Mrs. Bennet told her that instead of being angry with Lydia, Kitty should write to her. "Lydia may be able to bring you with her next time, but she will not want to if you are unpleasant."

In the meantime, families who had been in town for the winter returned, helping to fill the gap made by the absence of the officers.

Mrs. Bennet met frequently with her sister. "I still have five unmarried daughters," she complained. "Agnes, what will become of them?"

"They are still young," said Mrs. Phillips.

"Jane will soon be three-and-twenty!"

"That is not old – remember Charlotte was twenty-seven when she married Mr. Collins. And Jane is as beautiful as ever. Perhaps Lydia will marry an officer – or Lizzy will meet someone when she travels. When does Edward arrive, Fanny?"

"Tomorrow. Our nieces and nephews will stay at Longbourn House," said Mrs. Bennet.

"A lot of work for you," said Mrs. Phillips.

"Oh! with Lydia and the regiment away, Longbourn House is almost too quiet. Also, it is good to know Edward's boys can fish at the same river where he fished as a boy. And our nieces and nephews will be a good distraction for Jane."

The next day, Mr. and Mrs. Gardiner arrived, delivering their children to Longbourn House for a month in the country. The day after that they left for their tour of Derbyshire, taking Elizabeth with them.

Mrs. Bennet's Advice

I was weeding again, tackling parts of the garden where the dirt was hard.

"And what am I supposed to learn from this?" I asked, trying to loosen the earth with a cultivator.

"Oh! It is the same advice I gave Kitty. You cannot expect an invitation from your sister if you treat her poorly."

I agreed with her.

"It is all too easy," Mrs. Bennet continued, "to take our relatives for granted, even though there are so many examples when relationships fail, such as Mr. Bennet and the father of the current Mr. Collins. You notice how we welcomed my brother's children to Longbourn for several weeks."

Her words reminded me that I owed one of my nieces an email.

"You are not in the next few scenes," I told Mrs. Bennet. "They are about Elizabeth and the Gardiners in Derbyshire. How shall we cover them?"

"Ah, yes. I have visited those pages, and I heard some details from Lizzy and Mrs. Gardiner. Will you tell me what Miss Jane Austen writes? Then I will tell you what I think."

The ground was as hard as cement; I would not be able to make any progress with it until we had a good rain. I put my tools away and went back in the house, where I stretched out on the sofa with my laptop, while a box of chocolates sat on the coffee table.

"Let's catch you up," I said. "Remember, Mr. Darcy proposed to Elizabeth in Kent – and she refused him and accused him of some pretty bad deeds, as well as calling him rude —"

"— he *was* rude —" interjected Mrs. Bennet.

"— and after Elizabeth's rejection, Mr. Darcy gave her a letter recounting events from his point of view – a letter that had completely altered her opinion of him."

Mrs. Bennet said she would like to read that letter.

"Another time," I promised her, and continued. "Mr. Darcy was from Derbyshire, and when they were in Lambton, Mrs. Gardiner expressed a desire to see Pemberley, his estate." I then turned to the text and read to Mrs. Bennet from chapter 42.

"My love, should not you like to see a place of which you have heard so much?" said her aunt; "a place, too, with which so many of your acquaintances are connected. Wickham passed all his youth there, you know."

Elizabeth was distressed. She felt that she had no business at Pemberley, and was obliged to assume a disinclination for seeing it. She must own that she was tired of seeing great houses; after going over so many, she really had no pleasure in fine carpets or satin curtains.

Mrs. Gardiner abused her stupidity. "If it were merely a fine house richly furnished," said she, "I should not care about it myself; but the grounds are delightful. They have some of the finest woods in the country."

Elizabeth said no more — but her mind could not acquiesce. The possibility of meeting Mr. Darcy, while viewing the place, instantly occurred. It would be dreadful! She blushed at the very idea, and thought it would be better to speak openly to her aunt than to run such a risk. But against this there were objections; and she finally resolved that it could be the last resource, if her private enquiries to the absence of the family were unfavourably answered.

I looked up and grinned at Mrs. Bennet. "What do you say to that?

"Oh! Lizzy, Lizzy!" Mrs. Bennet cried. "My daughter made two mistakes there – deciding to avoid Mr. Darcy if she could, and then, not telling her uncle and aunt what had happened. If she would not take my advice, I wish she had listened to her aunt."

"Would it not be very embarrassing?" I asked.

"Avoiding embarrassment is a poor reason to forgo happiness."

I thought Mrs. Bennet made an excellent point.

"Go on, Young Lady," she said. "Lizzy does not confide in me, so listening to these passages is a treat."

I explained that Pemberley was grand, beautiful, and that the housekeeper spoke well of Mr. Darcy. In chapter 43, Mrs. Reynolds said:

"I have always observed, that they who are good-natured when children, are good-natured when they grow up; and he was always the sweetest-tempered, most generous-hearted boy in the world."

"That is an excellent recommendation," said Mrs. Bennet. "Almost too excellent, if you ask me! Why was Mr. Darcy never sweet-tempered in Meryton? Mr. *Bingley* is sweet-tempered, certainly, but Mr. Darcy?"

"Those are the words in the text," I said.

Mrs. Bennet murmured something unflattering about Miss Jane Austen, then begged me to continue.

When all of the house that was open to general inspection had been seen, they returned downstairs, and, taking leave of the housekeeper, were consigned over to the gardener, who met them at the hall-door.

As they walked across the hall towards the river, Elizabeth turned back to look again; her uncle and aunt stopped also, and while the former was conjecturing as to the date of the building, the owner of it himself suddenly came forward from the road, which led behind it to the stables.

They were within twenty yards of each other, and so abrupt was his appearance, that it was impossible to avoid his sight. Their eyes instantly met, and the cheeks of both were overspread with the deepest blush.

"Oh!" cried Mrs. Bennet, clapping her hands together. "I do love a good blush!"

"Even when it is your daughter who is doing the blushing?"

"Lizzy, although I love her, deserved it. Please, Young Lady, tell me more."

I skipped down a few paragraphs, explaining that Elizabeth and Mr. Darcy had exchanged a few words, then read the following:

At length every idea seemed to fail him; and, after standing a few moments without saying a word, he suddenly recollected himself, and took leave.

The others then joined her, and expressed admiration of his figure; but Elizabeth heard not a word, and wholly engrossed by her own feelings, followed them in silence. She was overpowered by shame and vexation. Her coming there was the most unfortunate, the most ill-judged thing in the world! How strange it must appear to him! In what a disgraceful light might it not strike so vain a man! It might seem as if she had purposely thrown herself in his way again! Oh! why did she come? Or, why did he thus come a day before he was expected? Had they been only ten minutes sooner, they should have been beyond the reach of his discrimination; for it was plain that he was that moment arrived — that moment alighted from his horse or his carriage. She blushed again and again over the perverseness of the meeting. And his behaviour, so strikingly altered — what could it mean? That he should even speak to her was amazing! — but to speak with such civility, to enquire after her family! Never in her life had she seen his manners so little dignified, never had he spoken with such gentleness as on this unexpected meeting. What a contrast did it offer to his last address in Rosings Park, when he put his letter into her hand! She knew not what to think, or how to account for it.

"Ah! There goes Lizzy, being embarrassed again!" exclaimed Mrs. Bennet.

"I think it would be embarrassing, to appear to throw herself at Mr. Darcy."

"But Mr. Darcy was not expected then, was he?" asked Mrs. Bennet.

"No," I said, and read another bit of text, from the same chapter.

After a short silence, the lady first spoke. She wished him to know that she had been assured of his absence before she came to the place, and accordingly began by observing, that his arrival had been very unexpected "—for your housekeeper," she added, "informed us that you would certainly not be here till tomorrow; and indeed, before we left Bakewell, we understood that you were not immediately expected in the country." He acknowledged the truth of it all, and said that business with his steward had occasioned his coming forward a few hours before the rest of the party with whom he had been travelling.

"Miss Jane Austen is so considerate of Lizzy's sensibilities," Mrs. Bennet remarked. "She arranges for Lizzy and Mr. Darcy to meet again, but in such a way that neither had to act as if either were interested in the other. Lizzy was not expecting to see Mr. Darcy at Pemberley – and of course he did not know she was there."

I acknowledged Mrs. Bennet had a point. I reached for a chocolate, then asked: "What if Elizabeth had learned Mr. Darcy would be at home? Would you have told her go?"

"Of course!" Mrs. Bennet looked with longing at my chocolates, but she could not eat them, and she told me to eat an extra one for her. Then Mrs. Bennet continued: "In fact, Lizzy's appearing at Pemberley, even if it cost her some blushes, was just what the gentleman needed – some hope after her rude refusal of him in Kent."

Mrs. Bennet's advice seemed appropriate because we knew, after reading the end of the book, that Mr. Darcy was still in love with Elizabeth. Still, I had my doubts regarding Mrs. Bennet's advice. First, at this point in the story, Elizabeth did not know her feelings for Mr. Darcy. And what if her harsh rejection had caused him to dislike her? What if his pride made him decide to ignore her? I expressed these concerns to Mrs. Bennet. "I know this is all conjecture. And I am not sure she even knew how she felt about him."

"You say Lizzy did not know her own heart. I believe you. But she was more likely to improve her understanding of her feelings if she saw Mr. Darcy than if she hid in the inn at Lambton. As for Mr. Darcy, what if he were angry with her? She would have been no worse off than she already was. But I think, if Mr. Darcy had been nurturing a grudge, his anger would have vanished the moment he saw her."

I could not quarrel with her interpretation.

"Lizzy had been wrong about him – she gets her obstinacy from me – and, what is worse, she had been wrong *to* him. She owed Mr. Darcy some tribute of politeness. She had to make an effort, even though it might have cost her some embarrassment. After all, what did she expect? For him to somehow know, from a distance, that her feelings for him were now different? If your feelings about something change, Young Lady, you cannot expect others to guess it. You have to let people know."

I rather liked this advice. It was so simple, and yet so often ignored.

"Shall we continue with your side of the story?" I asked.

"Yes," said Mrs. Bennet.

CHAPTER 29

While Elizabeth was traveling around Derbyshire with Mr. and Mrs. Gardiner, Mrs. Bennet was at Longbourn. Without Lydia and Lizzy – the liveliest of the Miss Bennets – the house might have been too quiet, except for the four visiting Gardiner children. Jane, who knew them best after her long stay in Gracechurch Street, was most responsible for their supervision, but all the Bennets played parts in their care. Mary sometimes gave them piano lessons and Kitty taught them dances. On rainy days, Mr. Bennet read to them from the books in his library; when the sun shone, he took the boys fishing. Mrs. Bennet encouraged the girls to try on different clothes and sometimes took them to see their other uncle and aunt, Mr. and Mrs. Phillips, in Meryton.

Then, one hot summer night in early August, someone pounded at the front door. It was far too late for a casual caller; the knocking indicated an emergency. Mr. Bennet, dressed in a nightgown – flanked by his family and some of the servants – opened the door.

It was not a neighbor or a tenant, but a man with a letter. His uniform and the horse in the drive made clear he was delivering an express.

"Oh! Mr. Bennet, what is it?" cried Mrs. Bennet, after he paid the letter carrier and opened the missive. Her mind went to her two distant daughters. "Lydia? Or Lizzy?"

"Lydia," announced Mr. Bennet, reading under the light of a candle.

"No! Has something happened to her? Has she drowned in the sea? Mr. Bennet, tell us!" cried the distressed mother.

"Let us go into the drawing-room," said Mr. Bennet. After candles were lit, he passed the note to Jane, who read it aloud. The letter was from Colonel Forster. Lydia had left the Forsters' apartment during the night, in order to elope with Mr. Wickham, who had also departed from the regiment. In a letter left for Mrs. Forster, Lydia announced they were traveling to Scotland to marry.

"Wickham? Lydia!" cried Mrs. Bennet. "Married?" Her life's goal, ever since Jane turned sixteen, was to marry off her daughters, but now that one was doing it, she did not feel the elation she had expected. Perhaps the news was too sudden.

"Why would Wickham marry Lydia?" asked Mr. Bennet.

Kitty, who had received several letters from Lydia – following her mother's advice to mend her relationship with her favorite sister, Kitty had written back – said Wickham and Lydia had been spending time together. "Lydia said they were in love."

"In love?" asked Mr. Bennet. "Wickham, in love with *Lydia*?"

"You never give Lydia enough credit," said Mrs. Bennet, hoping for the best.

"Why should they marry in such haste?" asked Mary. By going to Scotland, the pair could marry immediately, instead of waiting a few weeks as required by the Church of England. "Why not announce it and have a proper wedding?"

To this no one had a satisfactory answer. Mrs. Bennet wondered if Wickham might have had a dream of marrying Scotland – but she also knew, quite well, that Lydia would prefer to marry from Longbourn, and have all her older sisters serve as bridesmaids.

"We will learn more later today," said Jane. "Colonel Forster will arrive to consult with you, Papa, and to bring the things Lydia did not take with her."

"Until then, there is nothing we can do," said Mr. Bennet, and he took the colonel's letter back from Jane and withdrew to his library.

Mrs. Bennet sent her daughters back to bed, but instead of retiring herself, she followed her husband to the library, where he was taking down a volume from one of his shelves.

"Mr. Bennet, what do you make of this?" she asked.

For once her husband spoke without levity. "I am concerned for Lydia. Wickham must know we have no fortune for her, so why would he marry her? I fear his motives are – dishonorable. That he will not marry her."

At the prospect of her favorite daughter being disgraced, Mrs. Bennet could scarcely breathe. "Perhaps he loves her."

"We can hope," said Mr. Bennet, but Mrs. Bennet knew from the way her husband spoke he harbored no such hope.

"You married me," Mrs. Bennet reminded him.

"You are correct, I did – proof that men are capable of making decisions that others cannot understand. Perhaps that is true of Wickham, Mrs. Bennet."

"You should have let me go to Brighton," said Mrs. Bennet. "I would have kept Lydia from doing anything foolish."

"My dear, not even you could have prevented our youngest from doing something foolish. Now, we can do nothing until we know more, and we will not know anything more until Colonel Forster arrives."

Mr. Bennet opened his book, and Mrs. Bennet left the library to return to her own bedroom. Her husband's remark had been unflattering, but she was still convinced, after nearly a quarter century of marriage, she had rescued Mr. Bennet from a dull and lonely life. She knew, too, Lydia's elopement weighed on him heavily; he would not sleep the rest of the night. Of more concern, pressing down on her heart, was Lydia and Wickham. What if they did not marry? Lydia would be ruined and her sisters as well!

No, Mr. Bennet had to be wrong. Lydia would not do such a thing, would she?

Mrs. Bennet was not sure. She respected Mr. Bennet's abilities. He did not spend much time with people, but he was often clever about them. She recalled, too, how Lieutenant Higbee had kissed her years ago, and how tempted she had been to do something that was wrong.

Mrs. Bennet turned in her bed. Why, oh, why, had she not insisted on going with Lydia to Brighton? She could have taken Kitty with her; they would have had an enjoyable summer, and she would not be in this intolerable state of suspense.

No one in Longbourn House slept well that night, not even the servants. They knew, as servants always do, what troubled the family. Everyone rose early, in order to make the hours waiting for Colonel Forster as numerous as possible. At first Mr. Bennet hid in his library, and then he went into the farm to make sure everything was in order, in case he needed to be away for a few days. Jane watched her young cousins, finding time in a spare quarter of an hour to pen a hasty note to Elizabeth. Mary played the piano, but even she was restless. For most of the day, Kitty sat with Mrs. Bennet, ostensibly sewing, but mostly staring out the window.

At last, in the late afternoon, Colonel Forster's carriage appeared. He came to the door, followed by a servant carrying Lydia's trunk.

Colonel Forster, instead of coming into the drawing-room, joined Mr. Bennet in the library. Mrs. Bennet told Kitty to ring the bell for tea, and to order a room prepared for the colonel if he wished to stay. Jane, having left the young Gardiners under the supervision of a maid, entered the drawing-room, and even Mary emerged from the music room.

"What news is there, Mamma?" asked Jane.

"Colonel Forster has arrived," said Mrs. Bennet. "He is speaking with Mr. Bennet now." Her mind ran along possibilities. If all was well, they had to find a way to celebrate. A glass of wine? Wine for everyone, including the servants – that would prevent them from spreading bad gossip!

And if all was not well? – Mrs. Bennet's mind refused to acknowledge it.

Shortly after the tea and cakes arrived, Mr. Bennet and Colonel Forster joined the ladies in the drawing-room.

"Colonel Forster, we thank you for coming," said Mrs. Bennet. "Please, have some tea and tell us your news of Lydia." She gave him her best smile in anticipation of the best news.

Mr. Bennet sat in his usual chair, but Colonel Forster remained standing. He did not take tea; he did not return Mrs. Bennet's smile.

"I come with unpleasant information," said the officer. "Miss Lydia Bennet has put herself into Wickham's hands. And although she believes his intentions are honorable" – he passed a letter to Mrs. Bennet – "Wickham's closest friends say he does not plan to marry her."

"No!" cried Mrs. Bennet. "That is impossible!"

"I am afraid it is the truth, madam," said Colonel Forster, and he detailed conversations he had had with Denny, one of Wickham's intimate friends. The colonel also spoke of debts Wickham had run up at some of the shops in Brighton – debts that gave Wickham a motive to depart from the area, a motive that had nothing to do with marriage to Lydia.

At the prospect of Lydia, her youngest child, her dearest daughter, ruined instead of honorably married, Mrs. Bennet collapsed. She cried out; she accused Colonel Forster for not looking after Lydia – to his credit, Colonel Forster said he felt responsible – and she blamed Mr. Bennet for not allowing them all to go to Brighton. "You must do something to stop it," she urged the men.

Mr. Bennet, who had been silent for all this time, finally spoke. "I do not know what we can do." Her husband was too ready, even in this terrible situation, to do nothing.

"Find her! Save her!" cried Mrs. Bennet.

Colonel Forster, by nature a man of action, had more ideas. "We could attempt to trace her," he suggested. "If we ask questions where they changed horses, someone might know something."

"Yes. Find her. If they are not married, make them marry," ordered Mrs. Bennet. Then, unable to prevent the tears, she started to wail. Her daughters escorted her to her rooms, and there Mrs. Bennet remained.

Mrs. Bennet's Advice

"It was a terrible moment for you," I said to Mrs. Bennet.

"Yes, it was. Could you make a cup of tea? It would settle my nerves."

"You cannot drink it!"

"You can," she said.

I usually drank coffee, not tea, but my husband liked the latter beverage; the house had plenty of supplies.

"Very well," I said, and started preparations.

Mrs. Bennet thanked me. "It is hard, very hard, to go through these scenes again. As a character in a novel, I feel everything as deeply every time. I do not remember it – I relive it. I was so worried for Lydia!"

I turned on the electric kettle. "You are not at all embarrassed by your behavior?"

"What do you mean? Why should *I* be embarrassed?"

I had already learned Mrs. Bennet did not embarrass easily, but I pursued my point. "You made a loud fuss. And you blamed both Colonel Forster and Mr. Bennet, far more than they perhaps deserved."

"No, Young Lady, I am *not* embarrassed by my behavior. My reaction was perfectly natural – my child's life was threatened. Besides, my scolding of Colonel Forster and Mr. Bennet was absolutely necessary."

I did not understand why she considered her behavior not merely excusable but required; Mrs. Bennet was ready to explain. "You, Young Lady, can do many things that were not possible or at least far more difficult for most women when Miss Jane Austen wrote her novel. *I could not go off in pursuit of my daughter. No one would have paid attention to me.*"

I doubted that anyone, ever, could have ignored Mrs. Bennet, but she was right in that women's movements in her era had been severely limited.

Mrs. Bennet continued. "Instead, I needed Colonel Forster and Mr. Bennet to act, and as quickly as possible, before Lydia's situation grew worse. Colonel Forster was a man of action, but Lydia was not his daughter and he had other duties. I *had* to make him feel responsible, to make him feel his own reputation was at stake. If I did not, he might have stayed at the Meryton Inn and returned to Brighton the next day, congratulating himself on having done all he needed to do. Lydia's problems would have soon left his mind."

"And Mr. Bennet?" I asked.

"Mr. Bennet is a good husband in his way, but he has his flaws. He prefers to do as little as possible so he can enjoy a quiet life in the country. But with the violence of my emotion, I made him understand that if he did not do all he could to recover Lydia, a life of peace and quiet at Longbourn House would be impossible."

"The squeaky wheel gets the grease," I said.

Mrs. Bennet was unfamiliar with the expression, so I explained it to her. "Those who call attention to a problem, who make the problem most annoying and impossible to ignore, are most likely to get the problem solved."

"Just so. My making a fuss, as you call it, worked. To get things done, to make others act, often you have to make a big fuss."

"So, you deliberately made a fuss," I said, pouring myself a cup of the tea she had commanded, even though she had calmed down considerably.

"I did not have to pretend. My anxiety was sincere. I was terrified for Lydia, and for the consequences her elopement might have on the rest of my girls. But, making a fuss" – and Mrs. Bennet winked at me – "is one of my talents."

CHAPTER 30

Mrs. Bennet's agitated urging spurred Colonel Forster and Mr. Bennet into action. They were soon on their way, taking Colonel Forster's coach as they sought to determine what could be traced along the Barnet road – the route Wickham and Lydia would have taken if they were continuing to Scotland.

Mrs. Bennet stayed at Longbourn House, not leaving the estate, not even leaving her rooms, but having her meals brought to her as she stared out the window or fidgeted in her chair. Her nerves were too fraught for her to tend to her usual duties.

Mrs. Bennet might remain in her rooms, but the dreadful news spread through the neighborhood. Mrs. Phillips arrived to condole with her sister, but also brought information about Wickham's debts at certain shops in Meryton. "The tradesmen tell of many bills he left unpaid."

Besides the usual debts for food and ale and renting a horse, several caused more concern with respect to Wickham's habits: ribbons for a barmaid; a bonnet for a milkmaid; a basket of fruit for a tradesman's daughter.

Two days later word arrived from Colonel Forster; Jane opened the letter and read it to Mrs. Bennet.

The news was not good. He and Mr. Bennet had not been able to trace the fugitives on the Barnet road, so there was no evidence of their going to Scotland to marry. Instead, they had learned that Wickham and Lydia had changed from a chaise into a hackney coach. Colonel Forster and Mr. Bennet assumed the pair had headed to London.

Colonel Forster, who had other duties – and no Mrs. Bennet at hand to harass him – was returning to Brighton. There he would make inquiries among the officers to determine what could be discovered. Mr. Bennet would continue alone to London and would look for his youngest daughter.

"No!" cried Mrs. Bennet, when she learned Colonel Forster had given up his part in the search. "This is *his* fault; how dare he go back to Brighton? Lydia is not in Brighton!"

"Mamma, he has other things to do," said Jane. "If they are in London, Papa will find her. But my hope is that they continued to Scotland and are now married."

"It is possible, is it not?" asked Kitty. She wanted good news for her favorite sister, partly because she did not want Lydia to suffer disgrace, but mostly because the rest of her family had scolded her for not warning them about Lydia's partiality for Wickham.

"You are too apt to make optimistic assumptions about men," said Mary. "Lydia has never guarded herself against their depraved instincts. Her actions have degraded herself – and the rest of the Miss Bennets."

"Mary! Don't speak so," cried Mrs. Bennet. Mary might, in a perverse way, enjoy the ruin of her least favorite sister, but the dismay on the faces of Jane and Kitty showed this was more than they could bear. "If Mr. Bennet has gone to London without Colonel Forster, he will need assistance. We must ask my brother Gardiner to help him. Edward is capable; Edward is a man of business."

"My uncle Gardiner is in Derbyshire, is he not?" asked Kitty.

"We must get him back. Jane, you must write to Lizzy again. Tell her what we have learned, and beg my brother to end his holiday and to come here. At once, my dear, at once!"

Jane's letter went out that day. It had the desired effect, for as soon as possible after that, the Gardiners' coach pulled up to the Longbourn House front door, bringing Mr. and Mrs. Gardiner and Elizabeth.

After the Gardiners tended to their own children, Mrs. Bennet welcomed her brother, sister and Elizabeth to her apartment. After the exchange of greetings, the Gardiners asked if there were news, and they were told what little had been learned over the past few days. And finally, finally, Mrs. Bennet had an audience for all she wanted to say! "If I had been able," she cried, "to carry my point in going to Brighton, with all my family, *this* would not have happened; but poor dear Lydia had nobody to take care of her. Why did the Forsters ever let her go out of their sight? I am sure there was some great neglect or other on their side, for she is not the kind of girl to do such a thing if she had been well looked after. I always thought they were very unfit to have the charge of her; but I was overruled, as I always am. Poor dear child! And now here's Mr. Bennet gone away, and I know he will fight Wickham, wherever he meets him and then he will be killed, and what is to become of us all? The Collinses will turn us out before he is cold in his grave, and if you are not kind to us, brother, I do not know what we shall do."

"Mamma!" exclaimed Elizabeth. "Papa would never fight Wickham."

"Oh! Yes, he would!" cried Mrs. Bennet. "I know Mr. Bennet better than you do. That is why we need your uncle's assistance. *Edward* has a head for business; Mr. Bennet does not. *Edward* will find Lydia. *Edward* will keep Mr. Bennet from coming to harm, and the rest of us from losing our home."

"Fanny, my dear sister, calm yourself," said Mr. Gardiner. "You can rely on me, but for the sake of your girls, do not give way to useless alarm. Though it is right to be prepared for the worst, there is no occasion to look on it as certain. It is not quite a week since they left Brighton. In a few days more we may gain some news of them; and till we know that they are not married, and have no design of marrying, do not let us give the matter over as lost. As soon as I get to town I shall go to my brother, and make him come home with me to Gracechurch Street; and then we may consult together as to what is to be done."

"Oh! my dear brother," replied Mrs. Bennet, "that is exactly what I could most wish for. And now do, when you get to town, find them out, wherever they may be; and if they are not married already, *make* them marry. And as for wedding clothes, do not let them wait for that, but tell Lydia she shall have as much money as she chooses to buy them, after they are married. And, above all, keep Mr. Bennet from fighting. Tell him what a dreadful state I am in, that I am frighted out of my wits —and have such tremblings, such flutterings, all over me — such spasms in my side and pains in my head, and such beatings at heart, that I can get no rest by night nor by day. And tell my dear Lydia not to give any directions about her clothes till she has seen me, for she does not know which are the best warehouses. Oh, brother, how kind you are! I know you will contrive it all."

Mr. Gardiner and Mrs. Bennet's daughters begged Mrs. Bennet to be moderate in her hopes, as well as in her fears, and then Mr. Gardiner assured her he would leave for London early the next morning.

Mrs. Bennet's Advice

I poured myself a cup of tea from the pot that was sitting on a tea warmer. As the pot was now empty, I snuffed the candle.

"My dear Young Lady, I was so relieved when my brother appeared."

"I'm sure you were," I said, as I added milk and stirred.

"Mr. Bennet means well, but he is not practical, like Edward."

I carried the tea over to the little table by my chair. I commended her on how she had compelled her brother into action by making a fuss; indeed, she had talent. Then I added: "Your imagination was extremely active. What did you think of your brother's counsel to be moderate?"

"Because I imagined the very best as well as the worst?" asked Mrs. Bennet. "I could not help myself, all those days in my rooms. I imagined everything!"

"I think you were wise," I told her.

"You do?"

"Perhaps you were emotional in your speeches, but creating scenarios is a standard technique for risk managers these days."

"I beg your pardon, Young Lady, but I do not know what you mean."

"Imagining the best outcome as well as the worst outcome is a form of preparation – for the best, for the worst, and everything in between."

"Oh! Now I understand you," said Mrs. Bennet. "Yes, it is useful to plan for the worst, as well as the best – and then to do all you can to make the best happen. And I did all I could to get my brother to work for the best. I flattered Edward into believing *he* could find Lydia, and I told him to make them marry if they were not yet married. That was the best. And the worst

– not just Lydia ruined, but Mr. Bennet dead – if that happened, we would need Edward's support."

"What did you think would happen?" I asked.

"What did I think would happen?" repeated Mrs. Bennet. "My dear Young Lady, I had no idea. When I go through that scene, I never have any idea. I am at the mercy of Miss Jane Austen, who does all she can to cross me and to tease me. She does not care about my nerves!"

"Let's keep going," I said hastily, before Mrs. Bennet could vent herself further on my favorite author.

CHAPTER 31

Early the next morning, Mr. Gardiner departed for London, but Mrs. Gardiner and the Gardiner children remained.

With Mrs. Gardiner and Elizabeth at Longbourn, life at the estate became more orderly. Mrs. Bennet, when she took a respite from worrying about Lydia, was glad for Jane that the other ladies had come. Mrs. Gardiner took over the care of her children, so Jane had relief in that area, and Elizabeth assisted Jane with the business that normally fell to both Mr. and Mrs. Bennet.

Elizabeth's dispiritedness concerned Mrs. Bennet. Elizabeth was usually a pillar of strength and good cheer, able to laugh off disappointment, with a general good humor that Mrs. Bennet believed her second daughter had inherited from her. But these days Elizabeth was abrupt in her responses and her face was almost haggard. Kitty reported to her mother that Elizabeth was neither eating nor sleeping.

"She is taking Lydia's situation to heart," said Mrs. Bennet, but her second daughter's gloom was so profound she wondered if Elizabeth's own heart might be bruised. Did she still harbor feelings for Wickham? It was not impossible, but it did not seem likely; Elizabeth had pointedly avoided him just before the regiment left Meryton. Could there be someone else? On one occasion, when Mrs. Bennet was alone with Mrs. Gardiner, she asked her sister-in-law if Elizabeth had met someone new during their holiday.

"Someone new?" repeated Mrs. Gardiner. "No, I am afraid she did not. I hoped to introduce her to my acquaintance at Lambton, but as you know, our stay was cut short."

Mrs. Bennet remained unsure about Elizabeth's situation, but until that daughter confided in her, she felt she could do nothing. Besides, she spent most of her strength worrying about Lydia.

Unlike Mr. Bennet, Mr. Gardiner was a reliable correspondent, so they received daily reports after he left for town. Mr. Gardiner's first letter arrived on a Tuesday; he let them know how Mr. Bennet had been going to all the inns, making inquiries about Wickham and Lydia. So far, unfortunately, Mr. Bennet had discovered nothing. On the Friday of that week Mr. Gardiner's letter informed them that Mr. Bennet would return to Longbourn on Saturday.

"What, is he coming home, and without poor Lydia?" cried Mrs. Bennet, when this letter was read to her. 'Sure, he will not leave London before he has found them! Who is to fight Wickham, and make him marry her, if he comes away?"

"Mamma, my uncle will continue his search for Lydia," said Jane.

"And I do not think we can prevent Papa from returning," added Elizabeth.

But Mrs. Bennet would not be consoled by Jane or made resigned by Elizabeth. If Mr. Bennet, Lydia's father, could not search for his daughter for as long as a fortnight, what hope did they have of ever discovering her? Mr. Gardiner was only an uncle.

Elizabeth was correct; Mr. Bennet could not be stopped from coming home. Mrs. Gardiner, too, wished to go home with her children, and so she and Mr. Bennet traded places in the carriages as he came from London and she returned to it.

Mr. Bennet, when he arrived at Longbourn House, did not come up to Mrs. Bennet's rooms immediately. They were both too full of reproach. Mrs. Bennet was angry with him for not finding Lydia; he was angry with her for not having raised Lydia better. In truth, both partners in the marriage knew they were as responsible as the other; their pain would only increase if they shared it.

Mr. Bennet did, finally, make his way to Mrs. Bennet. He accused her of causing trouble to the household, while she told him her nerves made her incapable of following her usual routine. Besides, she was trying to be discreet by remaining in her rooms.

"Discretion in such a matter is impossible, Mrs. Bennet," said Mr. Bennet. "The whole world knows what our youngest daughter has done."

"Oh! Mr. Bennet, why could you not find her?"

"I assume it is because she does not wish to be found. They are not at any of the inns, and we have nowhere else to look. I think it is time to resume our lives as best we can, Mrs. Bennet."

"Oh! Mr. Bennet! Oh, my dear, sweet Lydia," she said, but this time her voice was full of mourning and not reproach.

Despite Mr. Bennet's recommendation to resume her life, Mrs. Bennet kept to her rooms, waited on by the servants, attended by her daughters, and visited by her sister Mrs. Phillips. The family, excepting Mrs. Bennet, went to church on Sunday, but she received reports from her daughters on the experience. "You were right not to go, Mamma," said Elizabeth. "A sermon about lost sheep and unpleasant remarks from Lady Lucas."

"Lizzy, that is not fair," said Jane. "Lady Lucas meant well."

"My dear girls – what shall become of us?" cried Mrs. Bennet, for she was out of ideas. She had worked so hard to marry off her girls this last year, but the only thing that had happened was that they were all one year older – and Lydia was missing.

On Monday, however, an express arrived from Mr. Gardiner for Mr. Bennet. Mrs. Bennet was sitting with Mary and Kitty in her rooms when Jane and Elizabeth brought the letter to them. Jane read the letter aloud to all.

MRS. BENNET'S ADVICE TO YOUNG LADIES

Soon after you left me on Saturday, I was fortunate enough to find out in what part of London they were. The particulars I reserve till we meet; it is enough to know they are discovered. I have seen them both. They are not married, nor can I find there was any intention of being so; but if you are willing to perform the engagements which I have ventured to make on your side, I hope it will not be long before they are. ... There will not be the smallest occasion for your coming to town again; therefore, stay quiet at Longbourn, and depend on my diligence and care. Send back your answer as fast as you can, and be careful to write explicitly. We have judged it best that my niece should be married from this house, of which I hope you will approve. She comes to us today.

Mrs. Bennet, who, in her darkest moments, had feared that Lydia had been murdered by bandits, was first relieved to hear she had been found. Then – well, Lydia was not yet married, but she was assured it would be happened soon. Mrs. Bennet went from despair to relief to raptures. She listened to the end, then cried out: "My dear, dear Lydia! This is delightful indeed! She will be married! I shall see her again! She will be married at sixteen! My good, kind brother! I knew how it would be. I knew he would manage everything! How I long to see her! and to see dear Wickham too! But the clothes, the wedding clothes! I will write to my sister Gardiner about them directly. Lizzy, my dear, run down to your father, and ask him how much he will give her. Stay, stay, I will go myself. Ring the bell, Kitty, for Hill. I will put on my things in a moment. My dear, dear Lydia! How merry we shall be together when we meet!"

Jane attempted to restrain her, reminding her of how much they owed Mr. Gardiner. "We are persuaded that he has pledged himself to assist Mr. Wickham with money."

This did not trouble Mrs. Bennet. "Who should do it but her own uncle? If he had not had a family of his own, I and my children must have had all his money, you know; and it is the first time we have ever had anything from him, except a few presents. Well! I am so happy! In a short time, I shall have a daughter married. Mrs. Wickham! How well it sounds! And she was only sixteen last June. My dear Jane, I am in such a flutter, that I am sure I can't write; so, I will dictate, and you write for me."

Jane persuaded her to wait until Mr. Bennet could be consulted, and then added that a delay of a day could not matter.

"You are right, my dear, a single day will not matter – and I have other things to do." Mrs. Bennet rose and went to her own closet and pulled out a gown. "I will go to Meryton," said she, "as soon as I am dressed, and tell the good, good news to my sister Philips. And as I come back, I can call on Lady Lucas and Mrs. Long. Kitty, run down and order the carriage. An airing would do me a great deal of good, I am sure. Girls, can I do anything for you in Meryton? Oh! Here comes Hill! My dear Hill, have you heard the good news? Miss Lydia is going to be married; and you shall all have a bowl of punch to make merry at her wedding."

Mrs. Bennet received Hill's congratulations, and then quickly attended to her toilette. Mrs. Bennet, so relieved she was triumphant, soon emerged from her rooms. The carriage pulled up and Mrs. Bennet walked through the doors of Longbourn House to reassume her position in the world.

Mrs. Bennet's Advice

"You were happy that day," I observed, as I took out an onion that I planned to use in my dinner.

"Yes, I was! Why should I not have been?"

I chopped the onion. "Lydia had run off, something frowned upon in her time."

"And she was found, and her situation remedied."

"Even so, she was about to put her life into the hands of Wickham, a man we know is not reliable."

"Even the best unions have some faults. I understand Charlotte manages Mr. Collins very well; I expect Lydia will learn to manage Mr. Wickham."

Turning on the stove, I conceded that was possible.

"Enjoy successes when you can, Young Lady," recommended Mrs. Bennet. "They may not happen exactly as you wish or even as you expect, but they do happen, and when they do, they should be celebrated."

She was eager to continue, so after my food was cooking, I obliged.

CHAPTER 32

After calling on her sister and friends, Mrs. Bennet resumed her place at the dinner table. At last, after so many years, a daughter was on the threshold of marriage! She and Mrs. Phillips had wondered where Mr. and Mrs. Wickham might live, and, during her airing in the carriage, Mrs. Bennet had driven past many of the homes in the neighborhood.

At dinner, she considered possible situations. "Haye Park might do," said she, "if the Gouldings could quit it — or the great house at Stoke, if the drawing-room were larger; but Ashworth is too far off! I could not bear to have her ten miles from me; and as for Pulvis Lodge, the attics are dreadful."

Kitty participated in the conversation with enthusiasm, while the other Miss Bennets spoke little, and Mr. Bennet was as silent as a portrait. Only when the servants were gone did her husband speak. "Mrs. Bennet, before you take any, or all, of these houses for your son and daughter, let us come to a right understanding. Into *one* house in this neighborhood, they shall never have admittance. I will not encourage the impudence of either, by receiving them at Longbourn."

"What? Not receive your own daughter? Mr. Bennet!" cried Mrs. Bennet.

She learned, too, Mr. Bennet was too angry to acknowledge Lydia's nuptials by any mark of generosity. "You may not order clothes for her," he said. "I will not pay for them."

Mrs. Bennet attempted to persuade him, but he was adamant, and eventually he pushed back his chair and went to his library.

"How lucky it is, we did not take the order earlier," said Jane, who would never cross her father.

"I do not think it lucky at all," said Mrs. Bennet. If they had written out an order for material; if she had dropped it off when she went to Meryton, it would be difficult to cancel, and she would have bought Lydia her trousseau. She could have explained to Mr. Bennet that she had assumed he would pay for Lydia's new clothes; every new bride needed them, especially as she could expect dinners and receptions in her honor. Alas, Jane was too honest for Mrs. Bennet to pretend she had already placed an order.

"Mamma, we do not even know their plans," said Elizabeth. "Wickham may wish to go somewhere else."

"True," said Mrs. Bennet. "Well, I say we should have a glass of wine, because your sister will be married, and if we do not celebrate it, who will?"

The wine was poured, and then they left the dining-room. Mrs. Bennet, who had not been downstairs for a fortnight, asked Mary to play for her.

A few days later, another letter arrived from Mr. Gardiner, which detailed the plans of the engaged couple. This time Mr. Bennet read it to his wife and daughters.

It is Mr. Wickham's intention to go into the regulars; and among his former friends, there are still some who are able and willing to assist him in the army. He has the promise of an ensigncy in General ———'s regiment, now quartered in the North. ... Haggerston has our directions, and all will be completed in a week. They will then join his regiment, unless they are first invited to Longbourn; and I understand from Mrs. Gardiner, that my niece is very desirous of seeing you all before she leaves the South. She is well, and begs to be dutifully remembered to you and her mother.

The letter also contained some details about Mr. Bennet's paying Wickham's creditors in Meryton, while Mr. Gardiner pledged compensation for the creditors in Brighton – but Mrs. Bennet was more interested in the other information. Just as she finally, finally had a married daughter, that daughter would be moving far away!

"It will be hard, so very hard!" cried Mrs. Bennet. "Lydia will suffer as well. She is so fond of Mrs. Forster; it will be quite shocking to send her away! And there are several of the young men, too, that she likes very much. The officers may not be so pleasant in General ———'s regiment."

"Papa, you must answer the letter," said Jane.

"Of that I am aware," said Mr. Bennet.

"Will you allow them to visit?" asked Elizabeth.

Mrs. Bennet observed Mr. Bennet closely. He had previously declared, despite all her pleas, that he would not grant Mr. and Mrs. Wickham entrance into Longbourn House. Would he remain hard-hearted, or would he change his mind?

Mrs. Bennet longed to see Lydia, especially after spending so much of the last month worrying about her. Mrs. Bennet opened her mouth to speak, but Mr. Bennet held up his hand to forestall her. "Mrs. Bennet, I am aware of your wishes," he said. "Daughters, what are your opinions?"

The Miss Bennets were silent for a moment. Kitty spoke first: "I should like to see Lydia again," and then she added that Lydia had borrowed several ribbons and a cloak from her before going to Brighton, and she wanted her things back.

Mr. Bennet then looked at Mary; from that daughter, Mrs. Bennet had little hope. "Their sin was unforgivable," said Mary, "therefore, they should not be forgiven."

Mr. Bennet nodded, then turned towards Jane and Elizabeth. "What do the two of you have to say?"

The sisters exchanged a glance; Jane gave her opinion next. "I disagree with Mary; I think they should be forgiven, at least once they have done what they can do to atone for their behavior by getting married. We should encourage them to do what is right by acknowledging them when they have done what is right."

"Lizzy?" asked Mr. Bennet. "What have you to say?"

Mrs. Bennet was afraid of its all coming down to Elizabeth, who had been most upset, far more upset than anyone could have expected, by Lydia's escapade. Elizabeth, too, was the daughter whose opinion Mr. Bennet valued most.

Elizabeth was slow to speak. "I do not think we should remain angry forever," she said. "And I know Mamma would love to see Lydia. After that, Lydia and Wickham will be far away."

Mrs. Bennet breathed more easily. Three of the four daughters had taken her side.

"You think that, do you Lizzy?" asked Mr. Bennet. "Your uncle appears to be of the same opinion."

Mrs. Bennet finally felt free to speak. "Please, Mr. Bennet, I long to see Lydia."

"Very well," said Mr. Bennet. "When I write to your brother, I will give permission. That way Kitty can reclaim her ribbons."

Mr. Bennet rose to return to his library, while Mrs. Bennet, delighted, clapped her hands together with joy.

Mrs. Bennet's Advice

I spooned my dinner into a bowl, and congratulated Mrs. Bennet on her husband changing his mind, so that the Wickhams could visit as soon as they were married.

"Oh! I knew Mr. Bennet would change his mind! Over the years, I have managed to change his mind many times."

"Have you?" I asked, carrying my bowl and some silverware to the table. "He was adamant about not going to Brighton."

"Mr. Bennet is more stubborn when he does not want to do something. *He* did not want to go to Brighton, but he did not prevent Lydia from going."

Which he should have, I thought, sitting down at my place. "Furthermore, with respect to receiving the Wickhams, it seems to me that Elizabeth had the last word in making him change his mind."

"True, Lizzy had the last word – but who had the first? I did. If I had not pleaded before so earnestly for Lydia to be allowed to come, Lizzy might not have sided with me. And that is my advice to you, Young Lady. If *you* cannot persuade someone to do what you want, get another to argue for you."

As I took a bite, I thought of occasions where I knew her advice had had merit; her advice was a standard technique among politicians.

After swallowing, I introduced a new topic. "I have something more to tell you about Lydia. I know what she did was scandalous. But these days, in many places around the world, her reputation would not have been ruined."

"Really!"

"Sex before marriage is not the big issue it used to be, at least not in many cultures. In fact, in some parts of the world, *Wickham* could have gotten in serious trouble for what happened, because Lydia was still so young, below what we call the age of consent."

Mrs. Bennet wished to know more, and I briefed her on various details – different attitudes around the world; how in some cultures a woman would suffer greatly for a premarital relationship; she might even be murdered by her own father, but how in many, no one would care. Lydia's deeds – although they might lead to gossip and they might be a bad idea for other reasons, such as unwise emotional attachments or sexually transmitted diseases – Lydia's deeds would not have ruined her for life, and they would not have damaged the reputation of her sisters.

"But what if there are children?"

I explained how women had reliable methods to keep themselves from getting pregnant. Of course, a young lady had to *use* protection in order for it to work – not all of them did – so there were still unwanted pregnancies.

"My word," said Mrs. Bennet.

I wiped my mouth with a napkin, then took a drink of water.

"This is all amazing," said Mrs. Bennet. "We can agree that Lydia's going off with Wickham was unwise—"

"— yes, he was a liar, a gambler, a predator of young women—"

"—but *her* action was more foolish than evil. She was not cruel or unkind; she did not steal money or hurt others. She needed the support of her parents."

"Yes, if this happened today, she would still need the support of her parents, and given Wickham's character, they would most likely be against the marriage. Or, if Lydia still insisted on marrying him, she would need her parents' support a few years later, when the marriage fell apart."

This pronouncement interested in Mrs. Bennet very much. "For the moment I will ignore what you said about dear Wickham – I know many have a poor opinion of him – but the idea that a young lady could sleep with a man before marriage and not be ruined is both astonishing and yet reassuring. I knew I was right to support Lydia, and not just because she is my daughter."

"The disapproval of the public, however, was useful for creating tension in the story," I said.

I saw Mrs. Bennet was about to utter something unpleasant about Miss Jane Austen, so I hastily suggested we continue.

CHAPTER 33

The details of the visit were quickly arranged. As soon as Mr. and Mrs. Wickham *were* Mr. and Mrs. Wickham, they would climb into the Gardiners' carriage, which would carry them in the direction of Hertfordshire. At the usual spot, the Bennets' carriage would meet them, and they would continue on to Longbourn House.

The rest of her family might continue to frown, but Mrs. Bennet was happy, and determined to remain that way despite the skeptics. She sometimes had flutterings of anxiety – what if Wickham, who had run away from Brighton, fled from Lydia now? – but she reminded herself the financial relief Wickham was to receive by marrying Lydia would be too great for Wickham to desert Lydia before they took their vows. Mrs. Bennet believed that to abandon Lydia now would also hinder his taking a position in the army in the North.

Mrs. Bennet reminded herself of these facts as she sat with Kitty in the breakfast parlor on the day the union was to take place.

As the afternoon wore on, and the Wickhams' arrival ought to be imminent, the rest of the family joined them.

"Why are they not yet here?" inquired Kitty.

Mr. Bennet consulted his pocket-watch. "They are not yet late," he said.

"I ordered Lydia's favorite dish for dinner," said Mrs. Bennet. "And gooseberry tarts – I know Wickham is fond of them."

"They are coming," pronounced Mary, whose hearing was the best among the Bennets.

Jane and Elizabeth said nothing, but the sisters reached out to each other and squeezed each other's hands.

Kitty went to the window. She announced Mr. Wickham had descended from the carriage, and he was helping out Lydia. "She has a new gown," reported Kitty.

Mrs. Bennet smiled. Perhaps Mr. Bennet had refused to advance any guineas towards dresses for his errant daughter, but Lydia had found a way. A present from Mrs. Gardiner? Or even from Mrs. Forster? Also, the last traces of her worry vanished; if Wickham had come with Lydia, they were married!

They could be heard in the vestibule; Mrs. Bennet rose from her chair, just in time to embrace Lydia as she ran into the room. "Lydia, my love!" she cried. "My dear, sweet, girl!"

"You must call me Mrs. Wickham," said Lydia, and Mrs. Bennet did so happily.

"Where is he?" inquired Mrs. Bennet, but before Lydia could reply, Mrs. Bennet's new son-in-law entered the room.

"Just tending to our things, mum," he said, bowing over her hand.

Lydia then went to Mr. Bennet, who acknowledged her coolly. She demanded to hear 'Mrs. Wickham' from each sister. Mr. Wickham was smoother, calling Mrs. Bennet 'our mother' – and saying how wonderful it was to utter those words again, as his own mother had died many years ago. The words warmed Mrs. Bennet's heart.

Mrs. Bennet was aware most of her family was not as pleased to greet the Wickhams as she was – why could they not take joy in this day? – but she was not about to let their sullen moods ruin her own delight. Mrs. Bennet went around the house with Lydia, as her youngest daughter showed her ring to the servants, and then returned with Lydia to the breakfast room to await the summons to dinner.

"Well, Mamma," said Lydia, "and what do you think of my husband? Is not he a charming man? I am sure my sisters must all envy me. I only hope they may have half my good luck. They must all go to Brighton. That is the place to get husbands. What a pity it is, Mamma, we did not all go."

"Very true; and if I had my will, we should. But my dear Lydia, I don't at all like your going such a way off. Must it be so?"

"Oh, lord! yes; there is nothing in that. I shall like it of all things. You and papa, and my sisters, must come down and see us. We shall be at Newcastle all the winter, and I dare say there will be some balls, and I will take care to get good partners for them all."

"I should like it beyond anything!" said Mrs. Bennet.

"And then when you go away, you may leave one or two of my sisters behind you; and I dare say I shall get husbands for them before the winter is over."

"I thank you for my share of the favor," said Elizabeth, "but I do not particularly like your way of getting husbands."

"Lizzy!" remarked Mrs. Bennet in her scolding voice. She saw no reason to mention what was best forgotten.

"Mr. Wickham has received his commission, has he not?" asked Jane, smoothing over the awkward moment by changing the subject.

"Yes, and he must join his regiment at the end of the fortnight," said Lydia. "That is why we cannot remain longer."

"We will make the most of the time you are here," said Mrs. Bennet. "All our friends want to see you."

Mrs. Bennet and Lydia engaged in conversation about which neighbors to invite – the Lucases, the Longs, and the Gouldings – and Kitty made several suggestions. Mrs. Bennet added that Mrs. Phillips planned an evening for her niece and nephew-in-law.

For Mrs. Bennet the ten days passed all too quickly. "Oh! my dear Lydia," she cried, as the trunks – into which she had slipped a few new gowns, ostensibly made for other daughters but always meant for Lydia –

were loaded into the carriage, "when shall we meet again?"

"Oh, lord! I don't know. Not these two or three years, perhaps."

"Write to me very often, my dear."

"As often as I can. But you know, married women have never much time for writing. My sisters may write to *me*. They will have nothing else to do."

Mr. Wickham also made his farewell. "My dear Mr. and Mrs. Bennet – my dear father and mother – I thank you for the warm reception into your family. My dear Miss Bennets – it is a delight to have sisters, true sisters! I hope we will soon meet again."

The Wickhams climbed into the carriage, which pulled away.

"He is as fine a fellow," said Mr. Bennet, as they returned to the house, "as ever I saw. He simpers, and smirks, and makes love to us all. I am prodigiously proud of him. I defy even Sir William Lucas himself to produce a more valuable son-in-law."

Mrs. Bennet's Advice

"Oh! Those were some of the happiest days," pronounced Mrs. Bennet.

"I'm sure they were," I said, scrubbing a pan that had soaked overnight. Mrs. Bennet's best feature was how she rejoiced in the success of any of her daughters.

She continued her raptures. "Lydia was so radiant! Wickham so handsome, and so charming! Even Mr. Bennet softened towards the end of the visit. Did you see how he responded to a letter from Mr. Collins? I believe Miss Austen included it in her text."

The passage was in chapter 57, in a scene between Mr. Bennet and Elizabeth, but Mrs. Bennet had managed to slip onto those pages. In this case there was no authorial prohibition; her husband regularly shared Mr. Collins's letters with her.

After rinsing the pan and flipping it to dry, I retrieved the text. Aloud I read some words uttered by Mr. Bennet:

Mr. Collins moreover adds, 'I am truly rejoiced that my cousin Lydia's sad business has been so well hushed up, and am only concerned that their living together before the marriage took place should be so generally known. I must not, however, neglect the duties of my station, or refrain from declaring my amazement at hearing that you received the young couple into your house as soon as they were married. It was an encouragement of vice; and had I been the rector of Longbourn, I should very strenuously have opposed it. You ought certainly to forgive them, as a Christian, but never to admit them in your sight, or allow their names to be mentioned in your hearing.' That is his notion of Christian forgiveness!

MRS. BENNET'S ADVICE TO YOUNG LADIES

Mrs. Bennet was triumphant. "You see, Mr. Bennet came around! He condemns Mr. Collins as being too unforgiving, even though Mr. Collins's opinion was originally his own."

"True," I said, putting down the text and placing a few items in the dishwasher.

"Also, by letting Lydia come to Longbourn, we were able to distract from her conduct before marriage. We drew attention to the marriage, and not her folly before it."

I agreed she made a good argument. "What words of wisdom are you giving me?"

"Sometimes, if you want a scandal not to matter, you need to behave as if it does not matter."

As I wiped the counters, I considered her advice. I knew of politicians who had done this successfully. Sometimes the accusations were false, or they overcame scandals that were trivial and should never have been deemed scandals in the first place. On other occasions this tactic helped bad people get away with deeds that were cruel or criminal. Would not repentance and restitution be better?

While scrubbing a sticky spot on the counter – I must have spilled some jam – I relayed my objections.

"Oh! I do not say the tactic *should* be used by everyone, only that it works. People who are cruel or dishonest will not change their behavior – it is in their nature – so they will be brought down by future transgressions," said Mrs. Bennet. "But Lydia's situation – and you told me most people today would not care sixpence about her running off with Wickham – Lydia did not deserve the punishment Mr. Collins would have inflicted on her. And, despite what my other daughters may have thought, how they disapproved, by doing what I could to restore Lydia's reputation, I protected their reputations, too."

I thought Mrs. Bennet made an excellent point and I told her so as I put away my cleaning materials and washed my hands. "Lydia is on her way to Newcastle. Let's get back to your other daughters."

CHAPTER 34

A few days after Lydia and her husband departed, leaving Longbourn House more tranquil than it had been since their elopement, Mrs. Phillips called with important news. Mr. Bingley, Mrs. Phillips announced, was expected back at Netherfield! The reason given for his return to the estate was shooting, as it was late September.

Mrs. Bennet saw Jane blush deeply, and she did her best to shield her eldest daughter by continuing the conversation. "He is nothing to us, you know, and I am sure I never want to see him again. But, however, he is very welcome to come to Netherfield, if he likes it. And who knows what may happen? But that is nothing to us. You know, sister, we agreed long ago never to mention a word about it. And so, is it quite certain he is coming?"

"You may depend on it," replied Mrs. Phillips, "for Mrs. Nicholls was in Meryton last night; I saw her passing by and went out myself on purpose to know the truth of it; and she told me that it was certain true. He comes down on Thursday at the latest, very likely on Wednesday. She was going to the butcher's, she told me, on purpose to order in some meat on Wednesday, and she has got three couple of ducks, just fit to be killed."

Although Mrs. Bennet's words to her sister pretended that Mr. Bingley's return was nothing, this time she was determined to catch him, at last, for the lovely, long-suffering Jane. Mrs. Bennet had managed to marry off one daughter; surely, she could repeat her success?

Besides, Mrs. Bennet, having noticed Jane's reaction, was certain Jane still loved him. Mrs. Bennet was persuaded the other members of her family shared her belief, but they were not cooperative. Mr. Bennet refused to lift a finger, even declaring he would not call on Mr. Bingley when he returned, claiming it was an etiquette he despised.

"What can I do about it?" Mrs. Bennet complained to her sister, for this time, knowing Mr. Bennet, she believed he would not go. She was calling on Mrs. Phillips, after stopping at the milliner's shop across the street to see if the shop had any bonnets that would make Jane's beautiful face even more beautiful.

"We will send Mr. Phillips."

"Yes, I will go," said Mr. Phillips, who had joined them for tea. "Besides, Mr. Morris and I need to speak with him, to ask him about his extending the lease."

"That is such a comfort," said Mrs. Bennet. "You do not know how I suffer, Mr. Phillips, when Mr. Bennet will not lift a finger to assist his children!"

"Perhaps it is for the best," remarked Mr. Phillips.

"The best?" cried Mrs. Bennet. "How can it possibly be for the best, if Mr. Bennet will not renew the acquaintance with Mr. Bingley?"

"Yes, Mr. Phillips, how can you talk so?" echoed Mrs. Phillips.

Mr. Phillips opined it might be better to let Mr. Bingley come to Longbourn – as they were long acquainted, no etiquette prevented that – and then they could see if he were still in love with Jane. However, if he were *not* in love with Jane, then would not Jane be better off not seeing him?

"Not in love with Jane! How could Mr. Bingley not be in love with Jane?" Mrs. Bennet exclaimed.

Her brother reminded Mrs. Bennet that Mr. Bingley had been gone for many months. As far as they knew, nothing had prevented him from returning to Netherfield earlier. If he were in love with Jane, why had he stayed away?

"And why is he returning now?" demanded Mrs. Bennet.

"It is his house, Mrs. Bennet, one he has legally rented. And it is the hunting season. Perhaps Mr. Bingley has stayed away all this time, hoping to decrease Jane's affection for him, but now he believes she will no longer be in love with him." Mr. Phillips reached for a piece of cake. "I do not say you should not hope for the best, but it is wise to prepare yourself for all possible contingencies."

"Mr. Phillips has the mind of an attorney," said Mrs. Phillips.

"Yes, he does," said Mrs. Bennet. She did not like Mr. Phillips's theories, but she recognized the importance of preparing for all possibilities. "Well, brother, let me know what you can about Mr. Bingley's circumstances, such as being engaged to another young lady." This, short of being actually married to some woman, not half as deserving as Jane, was the worst she could imagine.

"You may rely on me, Mrs. Bennet," said Mr. Phillips.

Mrs. Bennet knew her brother-in-law meant well, but how could she have any confidence that he, with his attorney's mind, so concerned with contracts and leases, had any insight into the human heart? Could he be too discreet to learn anything? Still, she had to make do with those who were willing.

Immediately after Mr. Bingley's arrival at Netherfield, Mr. Phillips called and returned with the intelligence required. He could not let Mrs. Bennet know the state of Mr. Bingley's heart, but Mr. Bingley had not mentioned a wife or anyone he planned to marry; surely, if he intended such a step, he would be able to speak of nothing else. Mr. Phillips could also tell her no ladies were present or even expected, not even Mr. Bingley's own sisters. Male visitors were expected within a day or two.

No Miss Bingley! No Mrs. Hurst! That was a pity, as Jane had been such good friends with them, Miss Bingley especially. Without a Miss Bingley in residence, Jane could hardly call at Netherfield. But then Mrs. Bennet remembered her suspicions about Miss Bingley, that Miss Bingley had been against the marriage between her brother and Jane, and Mrs. Bennet was happy no ladies were coming.

"Can you tell me anything else, Mr. Phillips?"

Mr. Phillips reported that Mr. Bingley had inquired about the health of the Bennets, including Mr. Phillips's nieces. "I informed him that the youngest, Lydia, had recently married, but that the rest were all at Longbourn."

Now Mrs. Bennet knew, without a doubt, Mr. Bingley knew that Jane was at Longbourn. Would he call or would he stay away?

During the next three days, Mrs. Bennet kept Jane near her, discouraging her from walking into Meryton. What a disaster it would be if Mr. Bingley called and Jane were not home! The young man was obviously faint-hearted; he needed encouragement.

The first day after her report from Mr. Phillips, no Mr. Bingley appeared, nor on the second. Mrs. Bennet was practically in despair, then she recalled how he had told her that Mr. Bingley had been expecting a male visitor during the next day or two. Perhaps Mr. Bingley was staying at home in order to receive some friend. Finally, on the third day she looked out from her dressing-room window and saw Mr. Bingley approaching the house on horseback.

She quickly joined three of her daughters in the drawing-room, informed them of the wonderful event, and summoned them to the window in that room to look. Jane, overwhelmed, remained at the table, but Elizabeth and Kitty joined their mother. Elizabeth, always willful, did not stay at the pane but returned to sit next to Jane. Then Kitty remarked that Mr. Bingley was accompanied by a man on another horse; who could it be?

"Some acquaintance or other, my dear, I suppose; I am sure I do not know," said Mrs. Bennet.

"La!" replied Kitty, "it looks just like that man that used to be with him before. Mr. what's-his-name. That tall, proud man."

Mrs. Bennet, at that point in time, had a low opinion of Mr. Darcy, because she held him responsible for Wickham's relative poverty. Mr. Wickham, she believed, should have been left half of Pemberley. "Good gracious! Mr. Darcy! – and so it does, I vow. Well, any friend of Mr. Bingley's will always be welcome here to be sure; but else I must say that I hate the very sight of him."

Mrs. Bennet's immediate concern was for Jane. Jane was as beautiful as ever, but after Mr. Bingley's long absence – so many months! – the sweet-tempered, sensitive young lady was uneasy, and Mrs. Bennet feared that Jane's silence could discourage the gentleman into departing again. Because of this, when the gentlemen entered, Mrs. Bennet did most of the speaking, letting the embarrassed stay quiet, giving them time to become used to sitting again in the same room. Finding subjects of conversation was not difficult. She informed Mr. Bingley of the changes in the neighborhood, such as the marriages of Miss Lucas and of her youngest, Lydia.

"It is a delightful thing, to be sure, to have a daughter well married," continued Mrs. Bennet, "but at the same time, Mr. Bingley, it is very hard to have her taken such a way from me. They are gone down to Newcastle, a place quite northward, it seems, and there they are to stay I do not know how long. His regiment is there; for I suppose you have heard of his leaving the ——shire, and of his being gone into the regulars. Thank Heaven! he has *some* friends, though perhaps not so many as he deserves."

Mrs. Bennet could not resist this reproach of Mr. Darcy, but her words drew Elizabeth into the conversation, who asked Mr. Bingley how long he intended to stay at Netherfield. Elizabeth was right, thought Mrs. Bennet. She should not let her resentment of Mr. Darcy lead her to say anything that might cause him to persuade Mr. Bingley to leave the country again.

All was going well. Mrs. Bennet observed Mr. Bingley glancing more and more frequently in Jane's direction, so Mrs. Bennet filled the room with talk until they were sufficiently at ease to converse themselves. She noticed Elizabeth addressing Mr. Darcy – how considerate of Elizabeth, to distract Mr. Bingley's friend, so that Mr. Darcy would not urge Mr. Bingley to depart!

While Mrs. Bennet prattled on, finding additional reasons for Mr. Bingley to call – surely Mr. Bennet would be happy to share his coveys with the gentlemen from Netherfield – she kept reviewing what she had planned for dinner, trying somehow to make it sufficient for a man she hoped would marry her daughter and another who surely had two or three French cooks. However, there was no fish in the house; the dinner ordered for that day would not do. No, she had to wait, which might be for the best – she did not want to appear desperate.

Instead, Mrs. Bennet invited Mr. Bingley – and Mr. Darcy, it could not be helped – to dinner in several days. By then she would be able to acquire ingredients as well as other company to make it an excellent occasion. She resolved even to invite Mrs. Long's nieces; she owed them and besides, such plain young women would only make Jane seem prettier.

Mr. Bingley and Mr. Darcy departed. Mrs. Bennet was pleased; she was convinced that Mr. Bingley was as in love with Jane as ever.

Mrs. Bennet's Advice

I was sorting through the trash, separating items into categories for the recycling center. Mrs. Bennet hovered with interest; she had never examined plastic before.

"You know, your daughters were very embarrassed during that meeting."

"Of course, they were embarrassed!" cried Mrs. Bennet. "Jane had not seen Mr. Bingley for nearly a year, and there was even more tension between Lizzy and Mr. Darcy. Both girls were desperately in love and so particularly sensitive when they saw the objects of their affections."

I rinsed out a wine bottle and put it with the box for glass. "I'm not just speaking of romantic embarrassment, but embarrassment due to you and your behavior."

Mrs. Bennet, like everyone else, did not appreciate criticism. She demanded an explanation.

"You insisted that Mr. Bingley come and shoot with Mr. Bennet. Elizabeth felt that was too much."

"Oh, that! Mr. Bingley was shy; he needed to be encouraged. And given how Mr. Bennet had not called on Mr. Bingley upon his return to Netherfield, I needed to let Mr. Bingley know that Mr. Bennet approved of him."

"There was your rudeness, too, to Mr. Darcy, especially when you implied that he had treated Mr. Wickham poorly."

"I suppose these are Lizzy's opinions. Well, *that* is completely her fault, you know."

I worked at getting a lid completely off an aluminum can. "How are your words your daughter's fault?"

"If Lizzy had informed me of the real relationship between Mr. Darcy and Mr. Wickham – how Mr. Darcy arranged the match between Wickham and Lydia – I would have treated him as an honored guest. If Lizzy had told me about his love for her, or if she had confessed her feelings for him to me, then I would have been as happy to see him as I was to see Bingley. Instead, Lizzy kept that information, as well as many other things she should have told me, secret. Besides, my treatment of him was for the best."

"What?" I asked, as I finally got the lid off the can. "How can you say that?"

"Mr. Darcy clearly did not like me much. By making it plain that I did not like him, he did not need to worry about the prospect of my becoming a fixture at Pemberley."

"Does that bother you, to be disliked by Mr. Darcy?"

"At that time, his dislike did not bother me, because I disliked him so much. And let me remind you, Young Lady, I formed my opinion when he insulted Lizzy. For many months, she disliked him as much as I did – or even more! Yes, afterwards her opinion changed, but she did not confide in me, so how was I to guess?"

I consolidated eggs from two different cartons so one could go into recycling, then washed my hands.

Mrs. Bennet continued. "I will always put my daughters, who I love, before my dignity and my dislikes. I am not the least ashamed by anything I do to fight for their happiness. So, here is my advice, Young Lady, this time given without prompting: do not be embarrassed to do what you need to do, especially for your children, or anyone else you love."

"That's good advice," I told her, as I dried my hands.

"Yes. Let's go on," said Mrs. Bennet.

CHAPTER 35

Mrs. Bennet made quick arrangements for the dinner party, sending out invitations and telling Mrs. Phillips to inquire of Mrs. Nicholls what exactly Mr. Bingley preferred to eat these days.

Everyone arrived in good time. One advantage of a noisy crowd was that Jane and Mr. Bingley could get reacquainted without having every phrase of theirs attended to.

Mrs. Bennet did not interfere, but she occasionally glanced at the pair she hoped would soon be betrothed. Only when they were choosing their seats at the table, was she prepared to speak to Mr. Bingley directly. Mr. Bingley had always sat next to Jane before, but he might not be comfortable taking the position now. Mrs. Bennet was prepared to invite Mr. Bingley to sit next to her, but he sat next to Jane. The observation pleased Mrs. Bennet so much that she asked Mr. Darcy to take the seat she had been reserving for Mr. Bingley.

By inviting Mr. Darcy to sit next to her, Mrs. Bennet believed she was doing everyone a favor. The attention on her part was an effort to make up for rudeness of the past. By keeping the disagreeable Mr. Darcy to herself – and she still thought of him as disagreeable – she kept him from inflicting his ill humor on anyone else, especially Jane and Mr. Bingley. Mrs. Bennet attempted to engage him on subjects such as food, harvests, and hunting, but the friend of Mr. Bingley was as reserved as ever. She thought he had something heavy on his mind. Perhaps, she hoped, he regretted his terrible treatment of Mr. Wickham.

Mrs. Bennet, at that point, was not especially interested in Mr. Darcy. Instead, she watched Jane and Bingley and saw how happy they were in each other's company. Mrs. Bennet was not alone in this conclusion; her dear friend, Mrs. Long, noticed the contentment of the couple as well. "Ah, Mrs. Bennet, we shall have her at Netherfield at last," Mrs. Long whispered to Mrs. Bennet, which Mrs. Bennet took as an excellent omen.

Mr. Bingley started calling at Longbourn House without Mr. Darcy, who returned to London for a while. This was a blessing, indeed. In fact, Mr. Bingley needed only a little encouragement to call often, and Mrs. Bennet made a point of giving it to him. One morning he arrived so early that Jane was not yet dressed! His affection was easy to see, and Mrs. Bennet knew her eldest daughter was in love with Mr. Bingley. Mr. Bingley, however, needed to get around to the business of actually proposing. The challenge was to give him the opportunity.

After dinner, Mrs. Bennet was sitting in the drawing-room with Mr.

Bingley and three of her daughters – Jane, Elizabeth and Kitty. Mrs. Bennet tried winking at Kitty, but Kitty, alas, did not comprehend. Mrs. Bennet, to her annoyance, had to be even more direct; she left the room and made Kitty come with her. Shortly after that she called for Elizabeth, compelling her to depart as well.

"We may as well leave them by themselves, you know," said Mrs. Bennet, when Elizabeth joined them in the hall. "Kitty and I are going upstairs to sit in my dressing-room."

Mrs. Bennet went up the stairs to her dressing-room, accompanied by Kitty, but not, as the mother had expected, by Elizabeth. No, Elizabeth, out of misguided delicacy, went back into the drawing-room to keep company with Bingley and Jane.

Mrs. Bennet, in her apartment with Kitty, quickly realized what had happened. Foolish, foolish Lizzy! Mr. Bingley was in love and wished to make Jane an offer; Jane was in love and desired a proposal. Elizabeth adored Jane, and surely wished every happiness for her favorite sister. Yet Elizabeth prevented the would-be couple from being alone together, a situation that was necessary for him to make an offer. If Elizabeth persisted in this unreasonable behavior, Bingley could grow discouraged again, and Jane would be miserable. Yet Mrs. Bennet also understood Elizabeth could not be reasoned with, and possibly Jane, too, was embarrassed. Mrs. Bennet had to navigate around the sensibilities of her two oldest daughters.

"Shall we play cards, Mamma?" asked Kitty, as they sat in one of Mrs. Bennet's rooms.

"Very well, Kitty, go ahead and deal," said Mrs. Bennet. Then she exclaimed, "Of course! Cards!"

"I do not understand you, Mamma," said Kitty.

"It is not important," said Mrs. Bennet, and although she had just devised an excellent scheme, she did not share it with Kitty or with anyone else.

The very next time Mr. Bingley called, Mrs. Bennet – aware Elizabeth wanted to write to Mrs. Collins – arranged for her, Jane, Kitty and Bingley to sit down to cards. With the four of them at a table, Elizabeth was duped into believing that Jane would not be left alone with Bingley, and she went off to attend to her letter. Shortly after Mrs. Bennet was certain her second daughter was safely away, she told the other card players she had a little headache and wished to lie down.

Jane offered to accompany her, but Mrs. Bennet would not hear of it. "Kitty, come with me," said Mrs. Bennet. Mrs. Bennet would have liked to remain outside in the hall in order to listen through a keyhole, but, aware of Jane's scruples and Bingley's shyness, Mrs. Bennet retired once again to her rooms. In order to be sure they did not alert Elizabeth to the scheme, Mrs. Bennet led Kitty on a different path through the house.

MRS. BENNET'S ADVICE TO YOUNG LADIES

Soon all was as it should be. Mr. Bingley proposed; Jane accepted, and Mr. Bennet gave his blessing. Within the hour, everyone at Longbourn was rejoicing. Mary, the great event pulling her away from her studies, asked if she could peruse the shelves of books at Netherfield, while Kitty – not as vociferously as Lydia – begged Jane to put on a ball. Elizabeth was so happy for Jane she was almost ready to cry. Mrs. Bennet, who had held her tongue for days, even though she had been sorely tempted to urge the young man to make an offer, could not find enough words to express her happiness – although she kept trying.

Soon, after so many years of effort, Mrs. Bennet would have two daughters married!

Mrs. Bennet's Advice

Mrs. Bennet, reliving that happy evening, waxed at length. "I knew Jane could not be so beautiful for nothing. And she caught a husband worth 5000£ per year!"

Squeezing toothpaste on to my toothbrush, I congratulated her. "Well done!"

"Yes, I had plenty to do with it, you know. Mr. Bingley was so modest, he wanted encouragement to visit. Jane was always pleasant, but she was so reserved when he first returned that I had to do all the talking. And of course, Lizzy" – she raised her volume as I began brushing my teeth – "Lizzy, with her ridiculous propriety, would have prevented Mr. Bingley from having any opportunity."

I tried to say something about embarrassment, but because I was brushing my teeth, my diction was terrible. Mrs. Bennet understood, however, and continued. "Yes, Lizzy was embarrassed, but that is because she was young and insecure. As was Jane. As was Mr. Bingley! Their affection for each other was obvious to anyone with eyes, so why should it be embarrassing for them to admit it? I knew they needed to be alone, and who cares if it was obvious? Did I need to create a more elaborate scheme so we could all pretend their being alone together was an accident? Should embarrassment prevent a lifetime of happiness?"

I spat out my toothpaste, rinsed and spat again, then as I washed my hands and my face, I could finally reply to Mrs. Bennet. "Jane Austen said something similar." I grabbed the text and found the passage I wanted. "After Mr. Bingley and Mr. Darcy first visited at Longbourn, this is what she wrote in chapter 53."

The first wish of my heart," said she [Elizabeth] to herself, "is never more to be in company with either of them. Their society can afford no pleasure that will atone for such wretchedness as this! Let me never see either one or the other again!"

Yet the misery, for which years of happiness were to offer no compensation, received soon afterwards material relief, from observing how much the beauty of her sister re-kindled the admiration of her former lover. When first he came in, he had spoken to her but little; but every five minutes seemed to be giving her more of his attention.

"That is correct, and it is so satisfying to see Miss Jane Austen coming around to my way of thinking, understanding that suffering through a little embarrassment may be necessary in order to achieve a lifetime of happiness. Anyway, we have already spoken about embarrassment, and how shyness can keep you from doing what you need to do. But the important lesson from the scene above is that sometimes, for everyone's benefit, you need to do a little scheming."

"You did not tell Elizabeth that you were planning to break up the card game so Jane and Bingley could be alone."

"No, I did not. And you see, even though Lizzy and Miss Jane Austen may believe I can never hold my tongue – and I admit that I do not *like* holding my tongue – on this occasion I managed it. I also showed that despite my second daughter's pride in her intelligence, I can outwit her."

I had to agree with Mrs. Bennet, that she had, in this instance, succeeded in both.

"The story is not yet over," said Mrs. Bennet.

CHAPTER 36

A week after Mr. Bingley finally proposed to Jane, during which Mrs. Bennet enjoyed how all her neighbors were declaring the Bennets the luckiest family in the world, a chaise pulled by four horses could be seen making its way to Longbourn one morning. Kitty knew all the carriages of their neighbors; this one she did not recognize.

"It's very grand," she reported.

"Ring the bell for refreshments, Kitty," said Mrs. Bennet. "I expect someone is coming to see your father, but just in case it is someone else, we should be prepared."

Kitty did as she was told, and Mr. Bingley and Jane, still fresh in their engagement, escaped out a side door so they would not be importuned by a third party.

To Mrs. Bennet's amazement, a servant announced the arrival was not a man of business for Mr. Bennet, but Lady Catherine de Bourgh, Mr. Collins's patroness. Lady Catherine was soon in the breakfast-parlor that contained Mrs. Bennet, Elizabeth and Kitty. Mrs. Bennet remembered Elizabeth had called at Rosings Park, Lady Catherine's estate, while visiting the Collinses in Kent, so she glanced at her second daughter for an explanation. Elizabeth, who appeared puzzled, did not notice her mother's inquiring look and so Mrs. Bennet had to receive their grand visitor without any assistance.

As the daughter of an earl and the widow of a knight, Lady Catherine outranked all the Longbourn ladies; protocol dictated she must speak first. For a while, her ladyship said nothing; Mrs. Bennet wondered if she were fatigued from her journey. Then Lady Catherine addressed Elizabeth, which was not surprising, as Elizabeth was the only person in the room with whom she had any acquaintance.

"I hope you are well, Miss Bennet. That lady, I suppose, is your mother."

Elizabeth replied that Mrs. Bennet was, indeed, her mother.

"And *that* I suppose is one of your sisters."

"Yes, madam," said Mrs. Bennet, who, after the exchange about her, which she counted as an introduction, could speak to Lady Catherine. "She is my youngest girl but one. My youngest of all is lately married, and my eldest is somewhere about the grounds, walking with a young man who, I believe, will soon become a part of the family." Mrs. Bennet was still so euphoric about Jane's engagement to Mr. Bingley that she was ready to share the news with this noble stranger.

Mrs. Bennet inquired about the health of Mr. and Mrs. Collins – since Bingley's engagement with Jane, she could pose the question with tranquility, instead of with the anxious resentment that had haunted her before – and Lady Catherine informed her they were in good health. Mrs. Bennet offered refreshment, but her ladyship refused. Mrs. Bennet searched for another topic of conversation, but her ladyship, after criticizing the room in which they sat, asked Elizabeth to join her for a stroll in the Longbourn shrubbery.

Elizabeth and her ladyship went outside, leaving Mrs. Bennet with Kitty. Kitty kept watch and reported that Elizabeth and her ladyship were having an animated conversation. Mrs. Bennet joined Kitty at the window.

Lady Catherine was wagging her finger at Mrs. Bennet's second daughter. "What can they be speaking about?" wondered Kitty. "Do you think Lady Catherine is complaining about the bench or the house?"

"Or the dirt on the path?" asked Mrs. Bennet. Lady Catherine had objected to the breakfast-parlor having west-facing windows, proclaiming that the room would not be suitable for the evening. But they had met there in the morning, and most houses, unless they were oddly built, had a west-facing wall with windows in it.

Mrs. Bennet and Kitty continued to observe the animated conversation. Clearly Elizabeth was better acquainted with Lady Catherine than she had let on. But what, exactly, was going on? Mrs. Bennet tried to recall what she knew of Lady Catherine. The patroness of Mr. Collins, the widow of Sir Lewis de Bourgh, and a woman with one daughter, the heiress to Rosings Park.

When Elizabeth re-entered the house – without Lady Catherine, who had climbed back into her carriage – Mrs. Bennet made a point of meeting Elizabeth in the vestibule. "She is a very fine-looking woman! and her calling here was prodigiously civil! for she only came, I suppose, to tell us the Collinses were well. She is on her road somewhere, I dare say, and so, passing through Meryton, thought she might as well call on you. I suppose she had nothing particular to say to you, Lizzy?"

This was the question Mrs. Bennet put to her second oldest daughter, but Elizabeth said nothing of import had been discussed, and she hurried away.

Elizabeth was lying to her, Mrs. Bennet realized, but she did not know why.

Mrs. Bennet's Advice

The sun was shining; I did something I rarely did these days. I opened the garage and climbed into my car.

I was driving back to the vaccination center for my second dose.

Mrs. Bennet accompanied me, and I was grateful, because I wanted to think about something besides the shot I was about to receive. I expected to have unpleasant symptoms, mostly because my body always reacts to everything.

Mrs. Bennet was eager to continue our discussion of her story. I told her my doubts about what had just happened. "Am I supposed to believe you knew Elizabeth lied to you about Lady Catherine?"

"How could I not be aware something was going on?"

I pulled into a parking place, took out my insurance card, and put my mask over my nose and mouth. I then entered the vaccination center, took care of the registration, and entered the queue.

When that was done, Mrs. Bennet continued. "Lady Catherine had arranged to be alone with my daughter. I, who have schemed so often, recognize when others are doing it. And I also know when Lizzy – remember, I am her mother! – when she is not telling the truth."

I conceded mothers usually could tell when their children were lying. "If you knew Elizabeth was lying to you, why did you not press her?"

"My first concern, at that moment, was that something might impact Bingley and Jane; keeping that engagement intact was my highest priority. But I could not see how Lady Catherine could have any influence on that alliance. Instead, I assumed Lady Catherine's calling at Longbourn was something to do with Mr. and Mrs. Collins."

"Did you not care that Elizabeth was not telling you the truth?"

"Oh! Yes, of course, I cared! But despite her falsehood, I trusted her. First, Lizzy is good-hearted. Second, Lizzy has enough self-control not to get into trouble herself. So, I was not really worried – not about *her*, although she might know something about a friend. Third, despite being Lizzy's mother, I was not her confidante. If she needed counsel, she would speak with Jane or with Mr. Bennet."

The medical personnel waved me forward. In a moment, the shot was given. I was told to wait – in my car if I liked – for a few minutes to make sure I had no allergic reaction. I climbed back into the driver's seat of my car, and removed my mask.

While I waited for the required amount of time, Mrs. Bennet rejoined me. I asked her what lesson I should take from the previous scene.

Mrs. Bennet answered, "Understand that people – even people you love – may not be ready to confide in you. Sometimes, they need a little time and space."

I agreed with the advice, although I wondered how good Mrs. Bennet was at following it. Then I recalled how willing she was to let Jane and Elizabeth spend time with the Gardiners, and how she held herself back on other occasions, too.

The fifteen minutes was up, and I was fine so far, although I could expect symptoms later as my body learned to combat the virus.

"Very well," I said, and I drove home.

CHAPTER 37

A few days after Lady Catherine's visit, Mr. Bingley brought Mr. Darcy with him to Longbourn House. Mrs. Bennet was not pleased to see Mr. Bingley's friend, but her humor these days was so excellent that treating him with politeness was not a struggle.

It was one of the golden days of autumn, where the leaves were turned but still mostly on the trees and the roads were dry. Mr. Bingley remarked on the fine weather and suggested they all take a walk.

Mrs. Bennet was not a walker, and Mary had tasks planned for the day, but the other Miss Bennets agreed to the excursion. Mrs. Bennet had a rare day of an almost empty house, because Mr. Bennet was needed at the farm as the rest of the harvest was brought in. Mrs. Bennet spent the morning listening to Mary at the pianoforte, discussing accounts with the housekeeper, ordering something fine for dinner, and chatting to Mrs. Phillips, who called for a few hours, about the wedding clothes she was to order for Jane.

The walkers returned, but not all at the same time. First, Mr. Bingley and Jane arrived. They were followed by Kitty, who had not walked long, but had called at Lucas Lodge, to visit Maria. When dinner was ready, they were joined by Mr. Bennet and Mary, but Mr. Darcy and Elizabeth had not yet returned.

"Mr. Darcy and Lizzy?" inquired Mr. Bennet, who smiled, as if he enjoyed the idea of this unlikely pair.

"Should we wait dinner for them?" asked Mrs. Bennet, who was still prejudiced against Mr. Darcy.

"A little while, Mamma," said Jane. "It is not that late."

"If they have walked far, they will be hungry," said Mr. Bingley.

"Very well," said Mrs. Bennet.

"Does Mr. Darcy know his aunt called on us last week?" Mr. Bennet inquired of Mr. Bingley.

Mrs. Bennet had forgotten that Lady Catherine was Mr. Darcy's aunt. What a small world it was!

"He does," said Mr. Bingley.

Jane went upstairs for a moment, and while she was there, Mr. Darcy and Elizabeth finally returned. Elizabeth ran upstairs to comb her hair and to neaten her appearance, and then at last, at last, they could sit down to dinner.

"Lizzy, we are all so hungry," said Mrs. Bennet.

"My apologies, Mamma," said Elizabeth.

"They wandered to a lane Lizzy had never seen," reported Jane, who had spoken with Elizabeth upstairs.

"Lizzy has always been an excellent walker," Mrs. Bennet said, addressing her remark to Mr. Darcy.

"If she lost her way, I do not see how she can still claim that," said Mr. Bennet.

Elizabeth, blushing, did not answer but applied herself to her soup.

"The day was excellent for walking," said Mr. Darcy, but after that he was silent.

The evening was pleasant. Mr. Bingley and Jane led most of the conversation, talking about a dog they had played with during their less ambitious stroll.

The next day, another golden October day, opened like the previous one, with an early arrival of the gentlemen from Netherfield.

"Good gracious!" cried Mrs. Bennet, as she stood at a window, "if that disagreeable Mr. Darcy is not coming here again with our dear Bingley! What can he mean by being so tiresome as to be always coming here? I had no notion, but he would go a-shooting, or something or other, and not disturb us with his company. What shall we do with him? Lizzy, you must walk out with him again, that he may not be in Bingley's way."

When the gentlemen were arrived, the possibility of long walks was actually introduced by Mr. Bingley. "Mrs. Bennet, have you no more lanes hereabouts in which Lizzy may lose her way again to-day?"

"I advise Mr. Darcy, and Lizzy, and Kitty," said Mrs. Bennet, "to walk to Oakham Mount this morning. It is a nice long walk, and Mr. Darcy has never seen the view."

"It may do very well for the others," replied Mr. Bingley, "but I am sure it will be too much for Kitty. Won't it, Kitty?"

"I would rather stay home, Mamma," said Kitty.

Mrs. Bennet frowned, but Mr. Darcy said he would enjoy seeing the view from the Mount, while Elizabeth nodded her acquiescence. "Let me get ready," she said.

As Elizabeth went to her room to change her shoes, Mrs. Bennet, feeling guilty, followed her. "I am quite sorry, Lizzy, that you should be forced to have that disagreeable man all to yourself. But I hope you will not mind it! It is all for Jane's sake, you know; and there is no occasion for talking to him, except just now and then. So, do not put yourself to inconvenience."

Mrs. Bennet had an agreeable day, with Sir William and Lady Lucas dropping by, and congratulating the engaged pair. They spoke, too, of Mrs. Collins's being with child. "I so long to be with her," said Lady Lucas.

"Of course," said Mrs. Bennet, who was too happy to feel any resentment towards Mrs. Collins, even though any son she produced could expect eventually to be the master of Longbourn House.

MRS. BENNET'S ADVICE TO YOUNG LADIES

"You are fortunate, Fanny, that Netherfield is only three miles away," said Lady Lucas. Sir William and Lady Lucas departed shortly before Mr. Darcy and Elizabeth reappeared, flushed from their walk.

After dinner Mr. Bennet, who had endured enough company for the day, retreated to his library, but Mr. Darcy followed him. When Mr. Darcy returned, he spoke briefly to Elizabeth, then she rose and left the room as well.

Elizabeth took a long time to return. When she did, both Kitty and Mary were sewing, and Mr. Bingley, Mr. Darcy and Jane were discussing different horse mishaps they had experienced. Elizabeth, when she reentered the room, joined that group, even though she was no horsewoman. Mrs. Bennet overheard Darcy recommending she learn; it was a skill worth having.

After tea, the sun was low, and the gentlemen departed for the evening.

"That Mr. Darcy keeps coming with Mr. Bingley," complained Mrs. Bennet.

"I do not think, Mrs. Bennet, we can stop him," said Mr. Bennet.

"Why not? Why do I have to continue to host someone I dislike? Someone who dislikes us?"

"Mamma, Mr. Darcy is perfectly agreeable when you get to know him," said Jane.

"I am glad *you* think so, Jane, since Mr. Bingley insists on being his friend. Ah! What a day! I am going upstairs to change into something more comfortable; Mary, perhaps you will find something to read to me." Mrs. Bennet went into her rooms and changed into a dressing-gown and slippers.

Soon afterwards, Elizabeth joined her. "Mamma, I have something important to communicate."

The evenings were growing cooler; Mrs. Bennet rummaged in her wardrobe for a shawl. "I am listening, my dear."

"It is about Mr. Darcy."

"You have been *such* an angel, keeping him away from Jane and Mr. Bingley!" Mrs. Bennet found the shawl she wanted and arranged it around her shoulders. "We cannot thank you enough, but if you are weary of his company, perhaps we can ask Sir William to invite him to Lucas Lodge."

"I am not weary of Mr. Darcy's company," said Elizabeth, and she was smiling.

"Oh?" asked Mrs. Bennet, moving to her favorite chair and sitting down in it.

"In fact, Mr. Darcy has made me an offer of marriage, and I have accepted," announced Elizabeth.

Mrs. Bennet stared at her daughter. She had heard the words, but she was not sure she had understood them. "I beg your pardon?"

"Mr. Darcy has made me an offer of marriage, and I have accepted," Elizabeth repeated. "We have already spoken with Papa, and he has given us permission."

Mr. Darcy! Mr. *Darcy*? Mrs. Bennet could not comprehend. It could not be true; it could not be possible!

No, it had to be a joke; Elizabeth was playing some foolish trick on her. But Elizabeth was not like that, not at all. Lydia might tell a story like this for a laugh, but not Elizabeth. Especially as it might inflict harm on the relationship between Jane and Mr. Bingley – and Elizabeth always protected her dear Jane.

And then Mrs. Bennet, with this new information, realized that Mr. Darcy's frequent visits to Longbourn House had not been just because of his friendship with Mr. Bingley. And it explained, too, Elizabeth's odd moods and her sudden distaste for Wickham – and even the surprise visit from Lady Catherine. Mrs. Bennet was quick enough to understand the very great advantages – still, Mr. *Darcy*?

Mrs. Bennet, shocked into several minutes of uncharacteristic silence, finally found her tongue. "Good gracious! Lord bless me! only think! dear me! Mr. Darcy!" She clapped her hands together. "Who would have thought it! And is it really true?" As her daughter nodded, Mrs. Bennet rose and embraced her. "Oh! my sweetest Lizzy! how rich and how great you will be! What pin-money, what jewels, what carriages you will have! Jane's is nothing to it — nothing at all. I am so pleased — so happy. Such a charming man! — so handsome! so tall! — Oh, my dear Lizzy!" – and Mrs. Bennet thought of her own behavior, even her own remarks, only ten minutes earlier "— dear Lizzy, pray apologize for my having disliked him so much before. I hope he will overlook it. Dear, dear Lizzy. A house in town! Everything that is charming! Three daughters married! Ten thousand a year! Oh, Lord! What will become of me? I shall go distracted."

"Mamma, I am glad you approve," said Elizabeth. "Now that I have told you and Papa, you may tell the others."

Mrs. Bennet, who had been planning a quiet evening in her rooms, could not sit still. Mary arrived with a novel, but Mrs. Bennet pushed past her, with a brief, "Lizzy is engaged to Mr. Darcy!" and then went into the corridor and entered Elizabeth's room. "My dearest child," she cried, "I can think of nothing else! Ten thousand a year, and very likely more! 'Tis as good as a Lord! And a special license. You must and shall be married by a special license. But my dearest love, tell me what dish Mr. Darcy is particularly fond of, that I may have it tomorrow."

Elizabeth mentioned several dishes, and soon the other Miss Bennets – Jane, Mary, and Kitty – joined them.

"Kitty, ring the bell and order us each a glass of wine!" cried Mrs. Bennet. "Dear Lizzy is engaged to Mr. Darcy!"

Mrs. Bennet's Advice

"Did you really have no idea Mr. Darcy and Elizabeth were in love?" I asked. I was back on my sofa, my computer on my lap after an absence of several days. My second vaccination had given me the unpleasant symptoms experienced by so many. Those unpleasant symptoms were finally passing, and they were far better than severe illness or death. I was relieved, because my own husband would be joining me in a few days.

"I did not," admitted Mrs. Bennet. "I am not one to ignore any potential suitor, but when Mr. Darcy called, he did not behave like one. Besides, most of their courtship took place away from Longbourn House."

"True," I said, considering the story. "Netherfield. Rosings and the Hunsford Parsonage. And, of course, Pemberley."

"The day I learned about their engagement was such a great day! With three daughters married, two to wealthy men, I no longer had to worry about their futures. As you can see, Miss Jane Austen's story was really about *my* business."

I agreed her goals had been achieved, but I was not sure *she* had achieved them. "Do you think you should take credit for Mr. Darcy and Elizabeth? As you say, you did not detect their interest in each other!"

"Not directly, perhaps, but my influence was important. I mattered in the match between Jane and Bingley, and their alliance gave Mr. Darcy and Lizzy many opportunities. I also encouraged Lizzy to take advantages of opportunities in other places – traveling to Hunsford, and later, traveling with the Gardiners to Derbyshire. And you know, sometimes when you are working to accomplish something important, you will succeed in an unexpected manner – but only because you are ready."

"Is that your advice to me?"

"Oh! My advice from the scene is that, don't hold grudges. Did you notice how I asked Lizzy to apologize to Darcy for me?"

Indeed, I had noticed.

"When you're feeling better, let's continue," said Mrs. Bennet. Her concern for me reminded me how she had taken care of Jane at Netherfield. "There's just a little more."

"All right," I said.

ENDINGS

Mrs. Bennet was full of joy, spreading the news to anyone who would listen. As Miss Elizabeth Bennet was dear to the people of Meryton, they did their best to adjust their opinion of Mr. Darcy.

Mr. and Mrs. Collins arrived at Lucas Lodge for a visit, and with one daughter married, and two more about to make excellent matches – far superior to marrying Mr. Collins – Mrs. Bennet was no longer distressed by seeing them together, especially as they reported they had chosen to visit in order to escape Lady Catherine's anger. Her ladyship had wanted Mr. Darcy to marry her daughter, and was furious when her nephew selected another.

"Mr. Bennet, her ladyship is so upset," said Mr. Collins, turning to his older cousin for advice and comfort. "She blames us for inviting my cousin Elizabeth to Hunsford."

Mr. Bennet pointed out that Mr. Darcy and Elizabeth were acquainted long before Elizabeth went to Hunsford, and so Lady Catherine could not reasonably hold Mr. Collins responsible. "Even if this logic does not persuade her, I still think she will come around," said Mr. Bennet, "for what clergyman has ever shown so much devotion to his patroness? And if not, well, Mr. Darcy is a useful man to know."

The Miss Bennets held a double wedding, befitting a pair of sisters marrying two best friends. Mrs. Bennet visited Mrs. Bingley and spoke with pride of Mrs. Darcy. Then Mr. Bingley bought an estate in a county neighboring Derbyshire, and Mr. and Mrs. Bingley moved away as well.

Mrs. Bennet had only two unmarried daughters remaining, but Kitty was rarely home. Kitty spent much of her time at Netherfield with Jane, and then at Pemberley and Mr. Bingley's new estate.

That left only Mary, who, now that her two older sisters were married, was the official Miss Bennet.

Mrs. Bennet did not care to sit alone, and so she made Mary spend some of her mornings with her.

After marrying off three daughters, Mrs. Bennet was ready to try again, this time without the desperation she had felt before. Given the fortunes of Mr. Darcy and Mr. Bingley, Mrs. Bennet no longer had to worry about the future, but could enjoy the business of finding a husband for her third daughter.

Matchmaking for Mary might be a challenge, as she had always been the plainest of the Miss Bennets. On the other hand, after her previous successes, Mrs. Bennet was ready for a challenge.

"Mamma, I do not need to marry," said Mary. "I am perfectly fine at home."

"Nonsense!" said Mrs. Bennet. "You do not know what you are missing, my dear!"

Mrs. Bennet enjoyed improving Mary's appearance, by choosing fabrics and styles that brought out her best features. With all this attention – and no comparisons to the beauty of her absent sisters – Mary began to bloom, in both looks and self-confidence.

"Mary, I need you," said Mrs. Bennet to the daughter who had her nose in a book. "Put it down, and let us make some calls. Mr. Bennet says we can take the carriage."

"Mamma, I like what I am doing," she protested.

"You can return to your studies later," said Mrs. Bennet. "Now, come with me. It is time to live life instead of just reading about it."

Mrs. Bennet's Advice

The story was finished, but Mrs. Bennet was still with me. "Have you learned anything from our conversations, Young Lady?"

I had. I was not ready to give Mrs. Bennet credit for every good thing that happened in *Pride & Prejudice*, but I thought her reputation deserved better than was usually given. I had grown fond of Mrs. Bennet. And, some of our conversations had provoked me into thinking about principles I might apply to my own life, in order to increase the happiness of myself and those around me. Nevertheless, I pointed out that some of her advice seemed contradictory.

"Of course it does," said Mrs. Bennet, completely unbothered by my complaint. "Each person and each situation is different. No rule can apply to all situations."

I found myself in agreement with her.

"Good. Now, during our time together, Young Lady, I have been observing you. You are too much like my husband and my third daughter."

"Mr. Bennet?" At first the comparison surprised me, but then I understood her point. I did tend to hide in my modern equivalent of his library.

"Yes. So here is my last piece of advice. You are vaccinated now, and so are many of your friends."

I reminded her my husband was about to arrive.

"Excellent. Now, close the book and go spend time with real people."

I thanked Mrs. Bennet for her visit, and we closed the book.

MRS. BENNET'S ADVICE TO YOUNG LADIES

COLLECTION OF MRS. BENNET'S ADVICE

Beginnings: If you won't complain, how can you expect things to improve?

Chapter 1: Seek out the truth, even when it is not to your liking.

Chapter 2: A good marriage works with the strengths *and* the defects of both partners.

Chapter 3: You cannot take steps to improve your life until you understand what is troubling you.

Chapter 4: If you can do something to avoid getting the red plague, the smallpox, or whatever sickness prevails in your time, then do it!

Chapter 5: When you require others to do something for you, make it as pleasant as possible for them.

Chapter 6: Take care with your appearance. Perhaps looks *should* not matter, but they do.

Chapter 7: Make an effort to understand how anyone dear to you is feeling. Be ready to defend them, especially when they will not defend themselves. *Young Lady's note: Gather enough information to make sure your response is reasonable.*

Chapter 8: Raising children is complicated, but praise yours when you can.

Chapter 9: Sometimes you need to risk rain for love.

Chapter 10: Be ready to act quickly when your children – or your friends – need something.
And if you receive help, give thanks to those assist you!

Chapter 11: Sometimes you have to repeat yourself. We cannot expect others to change overnight, much as we would like them to. ... A lesson is more likely to be learned if it comes from different people.

Chapter 12: Listen to your mother!

Chapter 13: Be willing to change your opinion when offered good enough reason.

Chapter 14: To be a great lady, you must act like a great lady.

Chapter 15: This is one of those times, when you should learn from my failure instead of my success.

Chapter 16: If achieving something is important, do not take *anything* surrounding it for granted.

Chapter 17: It is unwise to provoke your partner while on the dance floor.

Chapter 18: When managing something important, do not loosen your tongue with wine.

Chapter 19: Sometimes those you love will work against you. Sometimes you must give in with good grace. Other times, you must persist in working for those you care about, even when they resist.

Chapter 20: Timing matters, but not just your timing. You must take advantage of opportunities when they appear.

Chapter 21: Sometimes, when you attempt a great project, you will be disappointed. This does not mean you should give up – but you may need to take steps to restore your spirits.
Young Lady's note: Today we know depression often has a physical origin; this should be explored and addressed as well.

Chapter 22: When you are out of options, ask for help from others.

Chapter 23: If your children will not take your advice, find someone trustworthy whose advice they will take.

Chapter 24: Treasure friendships, and put effort into them, especially when it is hardest.

Chapter 25: Better to suffer a few months of unhappiness than to be stuck with a bad partner for life.

Chapter 26: If you are given an unexpected opportunity, do not refuse immediately. Take time to consider – to imagine the possibilities. Ask for advice; consult with someone you trust.

Chapter 27: We should rejoice in the success of those close to us.

Chapter 28: You cannot expect an invitation from your sister if you treat her poorly.

Chapter 29: To get things done, to make others act, often you have to make a big fuss.

Chapter 30: It is useful to plan for the worst, as well as the best – and then, to do all you can to make the best happen.

Chapter 31: Enjoy successes when you can. They may not happen exactly as you wish or even as you expect, but they do happen, and when they do, they should be celebrated.

Chapter 32: If *you* cannot persuade someone to do what you want, get another to argue for you.

Chapter 33: Sometimes, if you want a scandal not to matter, you need to behave as if it does not matter.

Chapter 34: Do not be embarrassed to do what you need to do, especially for your children, or anyone else you love.

Chapter 35: Sometimes, for everyone's benefit, you need to do a little scheming.

Chapter 36: Understand that people – even people you love – may not be ready to confide in you.

Chapter 37: Don't hold grudges.

Endings: Close the book and go spend time with real people.

AUTHOR'S NOTE

Much of what I would usually mention in an author's note has already been covered in the text, but here are a few additional reflections.

I first read *Pride & Prejudice* when I was twelve. The copy I read belonged to my mother, and I read it so often that the volume fell apart. I now use several editions, both in paper and electronic.

My twelve-year-old self approached the novel very differently than I do now. Even though Jane Austen died when she was only forty-two, her insights into human nature apply to all levels of maturity. My viewpoint is different, but what I harvest is just as rich.

It may seem strange to turn to a novel as a source of wisdom, but it has been done before. The ancient Greeks often referred to Homer, even though the characters in *The Iliad* and *The Odyssey* are not always worthy of emulation. As Mrs. Bennet says, we should learn from failures as well as successes; we should not always strive to have our lives imitate art.

Besides Jane Austen – and her wonderful creation, Mrs. Bennet – I wish to thank Patricia Walton for her feedback on this novel and Alice Underwood for her assistance with the artwork. I thank you, as well, for reading.

Victoria Grossack

Printed in Great Britain
by Amazon